First Creatures
A Journey Through Grief

Tami Liberati

ISBN 978-0-692-26618-2

Pewter Press

www.thesilversideoflife.com

Cover design by Create Space

original artwork by Cyndy DeHenzel

To Alec Sellan, who even as a young child understood the meaning of perseverance, and never lost sight of success.

To Tori Lowe, whose excitement for everyday life could never be contained in a gentle sentence.

To Mia Scabis, whose soft spoken demeanor painted a calming atmosphere in the classroom.

And last, but certainly not least, to Danielle Johnson, who always risked being scolded for leaving her seat to hug me. To you, I say, "Hmph."

What first began as a smile had nowhere to go but friendship
...Tami Liberati

Acknowledgement

As with all things in my life, I give thanks to God for all He has blessed me with: For an imagination that just won't stop, for inspiration that fills me with wonder, and for the gift of storytelling.

For my husband, Robert Liberati, and our children, Amelia and Robbie, I thank you a thousand times over for allowing me to sacrifice family time so my story could find a comfortable home in print.

For my parents, Margie and John Price, and for my sister, Keri Price, and my brother, Scott Price, I thank you for being my biggest cheerleaders, and most of all, for asking for more.

PROLOGUE

The mercury rose steadily through dawn on the beginning of the third day as the garden inhabitants were once again preparing for another record setting, sweltering afternoon. Few stirred due to the impending heat, and chose instead, to hunker down in the safety of shade. Many of them had already moved about earlier in the garden, nibbling on night's juicy leaves and roots; anything for water. Most of them had also noticed and pondered the figure that lay curled on its side, covered in dirt and compost. Though it didn't belong in the garden in this manner, it was still and didn't bother them.

As the sun relentlessly climbed into its high noon position, nothing was spared of its damaging effects. Though once cared for regularly, the garden was now suffering from exhaustion, and its leaves curled closed and wilted in neglect.

Perhaps sensing that the end was near, the figure stirred. She was no longer perspiring, and her skin was taking on a reddish, dry hue. Her rapid heartbeat was weakening, and her breaths were now shallow. Her body craved water, needed water, and her core temperature, like that of the mercury, was rising. Through blurred vision in her depleted state, she sensed wildlife peering at her. Without meaning to, she uttered the smallest groan that was perceived as a plea, and in return, one creature moved. Judging that the intruder was in dire need, it pulled down a wide striped leaf toward her open mouth and allowed the smallest trickle of life saving water to transfer to her tongue. Immediately, her moistened

1

breath rose from her mouth and into the animal's face, causing it to pull back quizzically and cock its head to one side.

Fearing another animal would help, she pushed away. The heat had robbed her of any strength or will she had left, and it took all her ability to turn away.

"No," was all that escaped in a raspy whisper. The creature understood her final wish, gently stepped back, but remained close.

Shutting her eyes again, her thoughts spiraled in reverse to a time of long ago, when laughter lived and love began. She felt at peace and longed to stay in this state that knew no pain. The creatures were curious about her so they remained close and watched, and it wasn't until the sound of quickly approaching footsteps and sirens did they scurry into hiding.

CHAPTER ONE

Two steady beeps from the back of the kitchen announced the completion of the coffee cycle, causing the chocolate lab lying close by to open one eye lazily in anticipation of what would follow. As expected, footsteps scuffed their way toward her and brought the start of a new day as lights flickered on and shutter slats opened. "There you are, Martha. I thought I might find you out here," Ruth said to her beloved companion as she did every morning. Like clockwork, she opened the back door for Martha and bent down to get her water bowl. "Another day started and another day running through the motions," she thought to herself as she prepared her coffee. She let Martha in and took her place in a rocking chair; the same chair in which she sat every day. As she cocooned herself deeper in the chair, she kicked off her slippers and allowed her toes to brush over Martha's back, and while doing so, coaxed herself to relax. She breathed in slowly as she sipped her coffee and wondered, as she did every morning, if this would be the day she would remember.

She often began her day in the back room of her house, her favorite room, in her much loved rocking chair. She'd look out to the back yard with its gardens, stone walls, paths and woods beyond, taking in the beauty and peacefulness they once provided. She didn't mind the quiet mornings in her home; they were actually peaceful for her. It was the blatant emptiness upon returning home to an empty house in the afternoon that got to her, so she sat quietly at the moment, daring to think back to happier times.

It had been almost a year since the well established life that Ruth once led abruptly ended. She had lost her beloved husband, Roger, eleven months prior and missed him terribly. She had never known such pain, but had been told repeatedly by well wishers that time would heal her wound. She certainly hoped so because she was reminded every day with stares and whispers that she was not healed. She was aware that her prolonged grief was unusual, and that some thought her to be odd because of it. Others, such as her son, were frustrated with her. She had overheard a private conversation between co-workers who didn't understand how her son could stand it. What 'it' was, she didn't know. Others, she'd heard say, that 'it' was right in front of her face; how could she not know. She had given up trying to figure out what was what anymore.

According to her grief therapist, she should be able to discuss her husband and the events that led to his death, but as of today, she couldn't. So much of her former life remained a mystery to her, and it hurt too much to think back in time. Trying to remember what happened to Roger caused all the symptoms of panic, and Ruth desperately avoided it at all costs. Shaking, hyperventilating, and eventually, shut down, meant hospitalization, and she wouldn't allow it again. So instead, without actually meaning to, she suppressed much of her former life and memories to the point of partial amnesia. Her therapist explained to her that she was suffering from dissociative amnesia as well as experiencing symptoms of a prolonged grief syndrome called, complicated grief. With time and a hands on plan that her therapist had put together, she believed Ruth would recover. Ruth liked her therapist, and certainly hoped she was correct because she had the strangest sensation that life was continuing without her. Little did Ruth know that her days were about to change again, for at that very moment, at that very time, on what appeared to be as normal a day as possible for Ruth, she began to heal. For in her gardens, where she had once traded life for death, it was determined that the time was now.

4

CHAPTER TWO

The morning light was just beginning to provide enough clarity for her to enjoy the view, and the fog was beginning to lift when she first caught sight of movement at the oak tree. This particular tree sits way back in the garden, located in a higher section, but she could see it from the angle in which she was sitting. It wasn't much movement that she noticed, and it was close to the bottom of the tree. She was used to catching glimpses of animals in the early morning so she leaned forward to get a better view. While trying to focus, she thought she saw the tree's trunk expanding a bit. Still thinking that an animal would come into view, she waited, whispering, "Come a little closer." It was then that she saw it. She blinked a few times and opened her eyes wide. It wasn't the tree widening, though, but some sort of creature forming itself out of the trunk.

And so it came to be that the change for which Ruth had been waiting had begun. She had imagined it differently, though. She thought her memories would slowly seep back to her and be cause for celebration within her family. She envisioned making the phone call to her son letting him know the good news, and that life would now be able to continue in a way that most lives do. What she didn't expect was this; fear, bewilderment, and more confusion. She had never given it a thought that she might slip even further backward in the healing process. She never thought that she might start hallucinating. But as she sat mesmerized by what was happening, a whole new realm of mystification entered this picture; her life.

Early that morning while darkness painted its last few moments, fog lightly played with the blackened air. Because of outdoor lighting in the backyard, particles of fog mist could be seen ever so delicately dancing, bouncing, and twitching as they settled toward their journey's end. To say the creature was timid and meek was putting it mildly. It slowly and gently evolved from the trunk of an oak tree and quietly stood guard against the steadfast trunk, unsure of its purpose.

It kept its back to the trunk with its palms also against the tree and its head turned sideways toward Ruth. It resembled a frog standing upright on its hind legs and it stood about four feet tall. Its skin was tan and rough like that of a reptile and Ruth noticed that it had long skinny fingers with knobby knuckles. Its legs were very knock-kneed and its feet stuck out at a ninety-degree angle from its legs. This made its feet appear way too large for its physique. It was dressed in a tattered sheath which appeared to be rather dirty. Ruth stared without blinking while taking in the creature, and when she finally looked at its face, she gasped inwardly at its eyes. They were huge and full of sorrow. She jumped backward in her chair, crying out. She felt such sadness, and yet, she didn't understand. She cried out again and thought she would be sick. It was as if she could see directly through its eyes, yet they were looking at her. She wanted to look away, but simply couldn't. The creature never moved and Ruth held her breath as their eyes remained locked. Just as she thought she could no longer bear it, the oven timer beeped in the kitchen, signaling her to get going. The sudden break in concentration with the creature was all it took for it to shrink back into the tree.

"No!" she yelled, jumping up and pressing into the sliding glass door as the creature disappeared. Gasping for air, she fell to her knees, still searching. She remained on the floor as she steadied her breathing, wondering what had just happened. And as her thoughts cleared, she realized the heaviness in her heart had disappeared.

What just happened? She replayed in her mind what she had seen. She was not dreaming! That much she knew. Was she hallucinating? Was this a panic attack? She squeezed her eyes tightly a couple of times and shook her head. "No, I don't think so," she reassured herself out loud. But, she knew she had seen a creature and she knew it had seen her, too.

CHAPTER THREE

The remainder of that day was nothing more than a blur to Ruth. She ended up being fifteen minutes late for school because she was so uneasy about what had occurred. She burnt her toast, forgot to pack a lunch, and left her school bag by the door. She didn't have duty on the parking lot that morning, so slipping in late was no big deal.

She was able to get through the normal greetings with her grade partners that morning without any suspicion on their part, but she was definitely out of sorts by the time morning recess came around. She couldn't wait for the last student to leave so she could close her eyes for a few minutes. She couldn't make sense of what she had seen and found herself slipping into the restroom a couple of times just to see herself in the mirror. Could anyone tell what had happened? Could she have been dreaming? She didn't think so. In fact, she was confident she had been awake. Should she share this with her grade partners, her true confidants? They already knew everything she'd been through this past year, but would they talk secretly behind her back when she left them, wondering if she were in the beginning stages of another panic attack? Would they believe that she saw a creature? She didn't think so. Something embarrassed her about the whole situation because of a nagging feeling and the fact that she couldn't answer her own questions, so she remained quiet. Instead of discussing it, she decided to wait and see if it happened again.

Now that she had made that decision, she tried putting her concentration back to where it belonged, in the classroom with her students. But try as she might, she found herself stealing glances out her classroom window, wondering if she'd see the creature again.

Ruth was so excited when the last bell rang so she could get home. She was usually happy to stay a couple of hours after her students left to organize her classroom and prepare for the next day, but not today. She was sure she looked out of sorts hustling through the halls, grabbing her mail from the copy room, and keeping her head down. That's not usually the way Ruth functioned.

Since Roger passed away, Ruth tended to spend a lot of time at school, not in any hurry to leave. She enjoyed the closeness she shared with her co-workers and considered them her second family. They often included her in their own family celebrations, knowing that she was now alone.

The school's hallways were the perfect gathering spot for teachers after the students left, and Ruth enjoyed the spontaneity they provided. She couldn't seem to get through the halls without hearing, "Well, hello, Miss Ruth. Don't you look lovely today." Or maybe it would be, "I love that shade of lavender you're wearing. Did you read the article recently that states that wearing lavender really compliments the eyes of those going gray?" An explosion of laughter would erupt as her good friend and co-worker, Mel, held up her matching lilac arm. Mel was the truest friend Ruth had. Similar to her in age, they had experienced some of the same commonalities of growing older. Most importantly, she was with Ruth in her most difficult time last year when she lost Roger. Mel was her rock through and through and was the strength she needed for so many months. It wasn't unusual for Ruth to call Mel right around dinnertime when the sun was going down. That was when she felt most alone. It didn't matter that they had just said their goodbyes an hour earlier. She was the voice on the other end of the line that Ruth needed to hear and she always picked up the phone for her call. Friends didn't get any better than Mel.

So when Ruth dashed through the halls at the close of school, she was sure it didn't go unnoticed, but she was on a mission. She wanted to get home and prove to herself that she had either imagined or dreamed the creature in her garden.

After shutting down her computer and gathering her purse, she marched with deliberate steps out of her classroom while allowing the door to slam shut. She squinted at the bright afternoon sunshine, surprised that she actually made it out the door.

CHAPTER FOUR

Her short drive home gave her a few minutes to think about her life as it did every day. It was right about now that she became agitated and felt the need to call Mel, afraid of going home to a house without Roger. Mel somehow had the right words to say each time Ruth called, and Ruth wondered if the feeling would ever stop.

As she put her car in park, she acknowledged the familiar feeling that gnawed at her stomach. She breathed in deeply and shook her head. "Stop it, Ruth! You can do this. Think happy."

A few more breaths enabled her to calm down and clear her thoughts. Perhaps she'd call Bryce instead of Mel to see if he and the family were free this weekend. She was proud of her son and knew he led a busy life and successful business, but she wished he would call more often. She didn't hear from him lately, and she wondered if he knew how much she missed his visits. She also missed his wife, Bev, and her grandchildren, Hayden and Heather, terribly. Before Roger died, they had spent a lot of time together. Nothing had suited her and Roger better than to have the grandkids stay the night. But that was a long time ago, and come to think of it, she should arrange a sleepover soon because she hadn't done that since Roger died. "I can do this without Roger. Maybe it won't be as exciting without him, but I've got to try."

She relaxed and was able to let some memories of the grandchildren filter in. She remembered Hayden telling his friends that he has a cool grandma with an awesome back yard. He was always fascinated with the stone paths and high garden walls that she and Roger had created so many years ago. He spent hours roaming the paths and playing make believe with his figurines, having them hide in the plants. She and Roger had built the garden into quite a large hill, so the walls were four feet high in some areas. They built stone steps into each section so they could easily be entered in to work. Hayden had created his own little world in the garden and she loved watching him play.

"Be careful not to roll over on the plants, Hayden," she remembered calling out to him. She didn't mind him getting dirty. She actually expected it just like she had expected his dad to get dirty when he was little, but she didn't want the hydrangeas to get ruined.

"I won't, Grammy, I'm careful," he'd answer. "Do you believe me?" Being her first grandchild, they had formed a special bond, and she really didn't think he could do wrong. "Do you, Grammy?" he'd ask again.

"Do I what?"

"Do you believe me?"

"I do, Hayden. I certainly do," Ruth remembered saying to him. She also remembered 'the look' he'd give her sometimes when one side of his lip turned up. He looked just as his dad had when he was younger.

Hayden also enjoyed burying notes and hidden treasure behind some of the stones that had worked themselves loose through the years. He had assured Ruth that he was not disturbing the walls, but actually making them more secure when replacing the stones. Sometimes he'd ask for a rubber mallet to pound them back into place.

His sister, Heather, also loved playing in the back yard as well, but her true fascination lay in actual gardening. She'd drill Ruth with questions about the plants' names and how to take care of them. Ruth remembered now how proud she had been at Heather's curiosity in gardening at her young age, and wondered why she had let so much time slip since Roger died.

She felt better now that she had a tentative plan to call Bryce. She reached for her keys to turn off her ignition when she suddenly realized that she had come home directly after school with a different mission in mind. Glancing at her watch let her know that she had been lost in thought for over an hour. Slightly disgusted that this had happened once again, she gathered her things and headed up the walk. And as she did, she noticed a small silver car pull away from the curb from in front of her house. She'd seen it before, and wondered why it was parked out front.

Martha scooted past Ruth as she entered. It was the same routine every afternoon. Ruth dropped her bag and purse at the kitchen table and retreated back outside to watch for Martha. Like Mel, Martha was another treasured presence in Ruth's life when Roger died. If Ruth was in the kitchen, so was Martha. If Ruth went to gather the laundry, Martha was right on her heels. Somehow she just knew that Ruth didn't want to be alone and she never left her side.

Feeling a bit nervous to test her theory about the creature, Ruth found herself stalling. She fed Martha, reheated some leftovers for herself, and finally situated herself in the back room with her dinner. She had found, since losing Roger, she preferred to eat most of her meals in the back room in her rocking chair. She and Roger hadn't done that, but since she was by herself, that's what she liked. She also had come to realize that she had many conversations with her dog. Martha was the truest sounding board she had at home since Roger died, and she found that Martha was a great listener, especially when she needed to unload.

As Ruth nestled further back into her rocking chair, she noticed Martha staring at her. Something about her eyes made Ruth uncomfortable. Ruth ignored her and looked back toward her salad bowl, but was drawn back again to Martha's eyes. Was Martha trying to tell her something? With a sudden rush of adrenalin, the events from this morning came flooding back to Ruth. She looked out the sliding glass door, and to her relief, there was nothing there. The creature was not there. She looked at Martha again who still holding her stare.

"It's not there, Martha. That...that...that thing is not there!" she said sternly. Martha in turn cocked her head to one side, bewildered at Ruth's frustration, yet fully taking it, and all the while held her gaze. "Stop it, Martha!"

Ruth could feel the effects of an attack beginning. She knew the cycle well and braced for it. It began in her ears with a quickly moving heat, and then followed by erratic breathing. Her thoughts flashed quickly as she grabbed the side of the rocking chair tightly with one hand, bracing for what was still to come. The part she hated more than any other was the sound of screeching so loud that it cut to her brain. But just before the sound this time, she instead began pleading. "Stop! Stop! Stop!" And it did. All went silent except for her panting. "I stopped it, I stopped it," she said, gasping to Martha. "Oh, I'm so sorry Martha. Come here. Did I scare you?" Hugging her dog and continuing, "I stopped that one. Can you believe it? I've been so worked up all day thinking about that...that thing. But it's not possible, Martha. I...I don't know what to think. I don't know what's the matter with me. I've been waiting and hoping all year to make progress, and now this."

She reached for her phone and thought about calling Mel, but put it back down. "Obviously, I was dreaming this morning. It just seemed so real," she said, holding her head. As always, she was forgiven with a nudge of Martha's nose and a wag of her tail to prove that all was okay. Her steadfast companion had once again been her rock.

CHAPTER FIVE

The warm April afternoon sunshine once again casted its enchantment on Annapolitans and their neighbors alike as they strolled throughout the grounds of Stonehenge Gardens in search of just the right selection. Spring was booming and the crowds at Stonehenge were present to prove it. A good day easily brought in thousands of sales, so it took a large and efficient crew to keep the tables stocked full of both annuals and perennials.

Bryce Lily, founder of Stonehenge, put his heart and soul into his business and was said to be both a fair yet stern boss. He was found to be approachable by his employees but knew how to hold his ground when making decisions regarding his business. He attributed his agreeable character to his faith, and gave God credit for his success and peace. He and his family were regulars at St. Francis of Assisi and were known throughout the congregation. His ability to lean on his faith and proclaim its necessity helped bond a friendship with the pastor, Father Joe.

Many presumed the events of the past year would have put an end to Stonehenge Gardens. But Bryce, possessing the same sheer strength of the national mountains for which he was named, repeatedly demonstrated the magnitude of his force with his ability to hold his family together, when every fibrous seam of family glue was ripped apart in a split second.

CHAPTER SIX

Bev Lily, Bryce's wife, was known throughout the Stonehenge Garden community for her sweet and effervescent personality. She enjoyed making social rounds, as she called them, throughout the nursery to visit each department. Her official title, Director of Pond Aquatics at Stonehenge Gardens, was only superfluous to more important ones, she said, such as mother, daughter, friend, and with a laugh, wife of the big guy. Her stature compared to her husband's was striking. She was tall, but as slender as he was bulky. Her shoulder length blond hair was usually pulled into a ponytail, exposing her facial silhouette. Years of sun exposure caused freckles that highlighted her nose and cheeks, and though she faithfully applied sunscreen, her skin displayed a warm caramel tone. Her slim frame was accentuated with broad shoulders and defined muscle tone earned in her teens from years of swim practice. Her sport of choice changed, though, after marrying Bryce and moving to Annapolis. Always drawn to the water, and eager to try something new, she began rowing with a small crew club on the Severn River.

Bev's early morning commitment to rowing was made possible because of Bryce's willingness through the years to get the kids up in the morning, get them fed and take them to where they needed to be. Bryce was accustomed to this early morning routine from the time his children were born.

CHAPTER SEVEN

The rowing club was a year round commitment, though only half the year was spent on the water. Spring in Maryland was fickle and air temperatures swayed heavily back and forth. The cold waters of the Chesapeake took time and constant warmth to bring the frigid fifty degree waters back up to the bearable sixties.

The Severn River with its vast tributaries, as any body of water, could be dangerous. However, smart boaters who practiced caution found magnificent scenery, mingled with rich historic heritage. When the waters allowed, the members of the rowing club found themselves encompassed in the most beautiful water country Maryland had to offer. The Severn River was most famous for housing the United States Naval Academy campus, and midshipmen were often seen rowing as well on the Severn.

The togetherness of the rowing club produced strong friendships that lasted through the years. Two such friendships that Bev embraced within the club provided her with good times, laughter, and the support she so unexpectedly needed the past year.

Annie was a few years younger than Bev. Recently married, she frequently relied on Bev when looking for advice about the give and take of marriage. She worked at George's, one of the waterside restaurants on the dock, and her bubbly personality and ease of talking made her the perfect waitress. She regularly related events from her work while jogging with Bev and described them in such detail that the two of them finished their morning workouts before she was done talking.

Bev's other close friend in the rowing club was one of the older club members. She also stood as Bev's stand-in mother, and was none other than Mel Thompson, Ruth's best friend at school. Age was not a factor when it came to physical fitness, as Mel could run laps around most of her club members. She had always lived on the water and was involved in water activities since she was a young girl.

She began each week day with the rowing club, and after a full day of school, ended each day on the water with her husband, Pat. Together they enjoyed a scull, a rowing vessel made for two. She and Pat headed for the water any chance they got. They had an appreciation for rowing and believed the same synchronization needed to row the vessel worked wonders for a marriage by practicing the essential movements of give and take.

One such consideration that Pat practiced was accepting the fact that his wife was a talker. She talked the moment she woke up, even though Pat was still under the covers. She greeted him with a happy good morning and began quietly confirming, though out loud, the tasks which lay ahead of her. It was an amusing habit they shared for many years. Her job as school counselor was fulfilling, and she greeted it head on each day, never allowing an inkling of suspicion to pass by her. When approached by a teacher with an uncomfortable suspicion about a student, not much had to be said. Mel made it her duty to know all the students in the school by name and frequently lunched with them. Mel, known as Mrs. Thompson to the students, was also a regular in the classrooms, stopping by to chat with the teachers, just as she would stop by to chat with neighbors. She was friendly, vivacious, and had the unique ability to draw details out of people, especially those harboring secrets.

A good counselor had to be a good listener. Mel knew to stop talking when a troubled soul was about to open up. Her twenty years of social work greatly contributed to the cases she saw at school.

This same listening skill had never been more necessary than this past year for her dear friend Ruth, whose world turned upside down in a single second. She received a phone call almost daily from Ruth shortly after saying goodbye to her each day. Mel's training with those who experienced death and grief taught her to be available when Ruth called. She had only somewhat encouraged Ruth to speak about the tragic day, but had not been successful in helping her remember. Mel allowed Ruth enough time to mourn her own way, and knew and respected the therapist Ruth was seeing.

Mel and Pat enjoyed rowing daily together after work, but Pat was all too aware that Mel's phone would ring, so he came prepared. He carried a book in a small backpack while rowing so when she needed to take a phone call, he could occupy his time. They lived further in on Weems Creek where the waters were quieter than the powerful Severn's. It was not unusual to see rowers stop on this piece of water, a tranquil cove that offered serene surroundings.

CHAPTER EIGHT

Saturday morning had all the signs of forming into a perfect April day. Even at seven-thirty in the morning the temperature had reached an already pleasant sixty-five degrees. Today looked like a winner, and the forecast was calling for a high of seventy-nine with light clouds and soft, variable winds.

Ruth found herself already sitting in her rocking chair on the back patio with a shawl wrapped around her shoulders. "As nice as it is going to be today, I'm just a little chilly right now," she said aloud for the birds to hear. "But it's nothing this cup of coffee and another hour of sunshine can't solve." It had been a few days since she had seen the creature, so she came to the conclusion that she had been dreaming. She had brought a clipboard outside with her and some scratch paper to sketch an area in the garden that she was planning to redesign. "I really don't mind the way you look," she spoke to the plants left of her, "but redesigning you is supposed to help me in making decisions. At least that's what my therapist said. You see, Roger made most of the decisions for me for a long time. I was his assistant. I liked it that way. Life was easy then, and fun," she sighed. She sat quietly for a few moments. The morning birds that had been answering her in song slowly brought their music to a softer volume. Barely able to get the words out above a whisper, she softly said, "I miss you, Roger. Why did you have to go? I'm all alone and we used to have so much fun together." With that, Ruth gently leaned forward and wept, quietly. "I don't want to work in the garden without you…please come back." A cold and wet nose softly nudged her right arm, forcing it to move up a bit and slide around the warm and furry body of a faithful friend.

CHAPTER NINE

"This was definitely a good idea," Bryce said appreciatively to Bev as he finished his last bite of omelet. "We'll have to do more of this now that it's warming up." The two of them had just spent a rare breakfast-time together, alone.

"Well, thankfully we have plenty of dinners together, just not breakfasts," Bev replied serenely. "And thank you for helping me continue to get out the door every morning. I might have quit last year, you know."

"I know, Babe. When the world came crumbling, the doctor said to help you get out the door every day. Hey, and anyway, it's all I've ever known since the kids came along."

Bev leaned over and gave him a playful swat. "Whoever thought that the word, sleepover, would lead to this," she smiled, remembering Annie's offer to host a sleepover so Bev and Bryce could have some alone time.

"Hey, when she said sleepover, this *was* my first thought," laughed Bryce. "Ah, you're not saying you didn't enjoy having a sleepover, are you, Mrs. Lily?" he asked, somewhat shyly.

Bev loved it when he called her Mrs. Lily. She loved *being* Mrs. Lily and everything that went along with being Mrs. Lily. "Are you kidding? I just never imagined dragging a mattress onto the porch and sleeping out here. It was an incredible night, in more ways than one." She stopped to give him a quick kiss and smiled at him. "We haven't held each other all night long in forever, but it looks like we're gonna make it, Mr. Lily, you and I. I can't wait to do this again. I only hope we haven't scared Annie and Jim off from having kids," she laughed. "And if they're not scared yet, then maybe they'll volunteer for another sleepover.

"I'm game. I don't know why we didn't do this earlier, but next time I'll make you breakfast in bed," he said contentedly. They sat in silence for some time listening to the morning birds chirp amongst themselves.

"About what we were saying last night," she led in. "Do... do you think your mom is still seeing her grief counselor? I mean...sometimes she seems so normal, but I get the feeling she's covering up something; like she wants us to think she's getting better. She'll say things to Mel at school that make it appear she's beginning to remember. But Mel gets the feeling that she's kind of just biding her time; still lost. I think she needs us, Honey. Mel says she still calls her almost every afternoon right after they leave school. But the other day she said your mom was so distracted that she buzzed out the door without saying goodbye to anyone. You know your mom. That's not like her; it takes hours for her to leave her classroom."

Bryce sat quietly for a couple of minutes, taking in what Bev had just told him. "I should have been stopping in more often...or at least calling," he said, shaking his head, frustrated with himself. "I...ahhh...I get so uncomfortable around her. I mean, I don't want to say. I...I...I want to tell her the truth; tell her to stop sticking her head in the sand. We've accepted it! Why can't she? I just want to tell her again, but she's my mother."

"I know, Sweetie. I don't know the answers, either."

"I'll call Dr. Brooke again to see what she thinks," he said. "And...I'll stop by to see my mom later. You know, I even went so far as to ask her a couple of weeks ago if she'd like for me to take her to the cemetery, you know, to get the ball rolling on her therapy.

That's what Father Joe suggested. She just mumbled something about not being ready and she'd go by herself."

"I'm sorry," Bev said soothingly. "What else did Father Joe say?"

"Ahh," Bryce grunted. "That's just it. He asked that we encourage her to come back to church. So I did. I asked her if she wanted to go with us and she cut me off pretty quickly. She went on about people staring at her and making her uncomfortable; I don't know. She used to love going. I don't know if she still believes. Father Joe said he understood her and that she needed more time. Whoa, he's a brave man, because he also said that he'd be happy to talk with her."

"You're a good man, Bryce Lily," Bev said giving him a long steady hug. "We're doing what we can and we know it will be slow going, so don't get discouraged. You've been *my* strength this past year, so please lean on me if you need to. See your mom when you can...and call her. But as for now," she said with a light slap on his backside, "let's get this mattress back where it belongs."

CHAPTER TEN

Some hours later Ruth awoke, still sitting in the rocking chair. She didn't know how long she'd been asleep, but she looked around and saw Martha sleeping under the patio table near her. "You are just beautiful, you know?" she said lovingly toward her.

Martha opened one eye and flopped her tail on the patio pavers one time as if to say, "Oh, good, you're finally awake."

"Okay, now that I've wasted another couple of hours sleeping, I had better get out of this chair and accomplish something; doctor's orders," she chastised herself.

She picked up a shovel and began making her way toward a section of garden near the back of her property. Life was buzzing throughout the garden with flying insects at the moment. She reached up to swat a gnat hovering about her face. As she made her way around a bend between some high garden walls, she bumped into a rock. "Oooh, yikes! That hurt," she called out. When she looked down she saw one of the rocks in the wall protruding out a bit. "What on earth is happening? Why are these rocks loosening after all these years?" She tried pushing in the rock with the side of her leg, but it wouldn't budge. Next she tried backing up against the wall, using her foot to push it backward, but that didn't work either. Finally, she knelt down to get a better look. "Of course it comes out, now that I'm on the ground," she said a bit disgusted. Kneeling, she took the rock all the way out and looked in its hole. She saw something, kind of beige, reached in and pulled out a piece of paper.

"Hayden," she said out loud, smiling. "This must be one of your notes to the old country." She sat down to get a bit more comfortable to read. The paper didn't make any noise when she opened it due to dampness, and it was very thick. She wondered where he had gotten it. Did she have any like that in her house? Expecting to read a note written to some soldiers from a far away land, she was a bit surprised. "Do you believe?" was all it said. She smiled as she remembered her conversation with Hayden when she had asked him to be careful of her plants. He told her that he was always careful in her gardens and asked if she believed him. "I do, Hayden," she smiled. "I do believe."

At the precise moment the words were uttered she sensed movement above her. She looked up above the rock wall to the raised garden section, once again expecting something different than what was about to happen. The oak tree was widening; the same oak tree from a couple of days earlier. She sat entranced, unable to move and afraid to breathe. Identical to the first time, as the tree widened, a shape was forming at the bottom. She knew exactly what she would see and it terrified her. Her breathing became erratic, moving in and out with a chopping motion, almost as if she were trying to cry. And then it was there. The same creature she had seen earlier, stood above her, connected to the oak tree once again.

It looked exactly as she had remembered. It was plastered against the tree as if it were trying to hold on, and it really did look like some sort of an amphibian wearing clothes. Once again, she took it all in and when her eyes finally made it to the top of its body to meet its gaze, she gasped. "Oh! Why? What do you want?" she said in a small voice not sounding like her own. With that, its eyes filled with tears and she felt her own heart cramping. She began to weep out loud, sure that danger was imminent, either physically or psychologically. She quickly figured the latter when she noticed a bright star forming in the Frances Williams Hosta next to her. "Oh, please, God, help me. I think I'm hallucinating. Am I going crazy since Roger died? Please, God!" she cried out.

With that the bright star rose out of the Frances Williams Hosta and popped, much like that of a soap bubble. There in front of her stood another creature, but this one was only one foot tall. She wasn't at all sure what it was, but it resembled some kind of a rabbit, also standing on its hind legs; very skinny legs, also knock-kneed like the amphibian creature. This little creature wore shoes; little brown leather ballet slippers that were rather tattered. It wore a little tutu and leotard, the same shade of green as the Frances Williams, which was olive and lime striped. A little dingy linen jacket the color of butter covered a very skinny body and arms, and a barely pale peach fur covered its hands, neck and head, but not its face. It had floppy ears at the top of its head that fell forward like a lop-eared rabbit and there was a bit of straight brown hair surrounding a somewhat human face. Then, at last she met its eyes.

"Ahh," Ruth exhaled, barely able to breathe.

This little creature was definitely a girl and she had hazel colored eyes. The creature cocked her head to one side, held her paw-like hands together at her chest, turned her lips inward, yet puffing out and made a little sound, "Hmph hmph."

Not feeling so scared at the moment, but still in utter disbelief, Ruth said aloud, "Oh, this must be a dream of some kind. I was asleep on the patio. I remember that. Maybe I'm still dreaming."

"No, you're not dreaming," said the petite creature in a squeaky little voice.

"Whoa, you said something!" Ruth said, feeling the urge to crawl backward, but choosing instead to hold onto her own cheeks. Maybe if she pulled her hair and caused some pain she would snap out of this.

The little creature came toward her, but it didn't hop like she thought it might since it looked like a rabbit. She walked on her toes instead, keeping her paw-like hands at her chest. As the creature came closer, Ruth gasped again and tried backing away, but she was somewhat wedged against the stone.

"My name's Velo," squeaked the creature, oblivious to the fact that Ruth was afraid. "Um, why did you make Mr. Gabriello cry?"

By this time Ruth was wringing her hands near her mouth. "I....I...him?" she asked timidly looking toward the amphibian. "I didn't know I did that," she whispered. "What...wait...you know it...him?" Ruth asked, rather startled and confused.

"Mm hmm, we all do," Velo replied while tip toeing back to the Frances Williams and looking under a fallen curled stalk.

"Uh...what...what are you looking for?" Ruth asked timidly.

"Hayden's paper," she replied. "Mr. Gabriello uses them as a hanky to dry his eyes because you made him cry."

"I...I.... have his paper here," Ruth responded, realizing it was in her hand, but rather crumpled. "I'm sorry he's crying. Who are you, anyway? And why are you here?"

"Um, you wanted us here," Velo squeaked as she tippy toed closer to Ruth and took the paper. Ruth continued to watch in disbelief as Velo climbed the rock wall toward Mr. Gabriello. The wall was four feet high at this section, so it took a bit of maneuvering on Velo's part. She stretched up high on her tip toes and put the paper in Mr. Gabriello's hand. Ruth realized that she hadn't looked at him since being surprised by Velo, and she saw a slow trickle of tears running down his cheek. He gently lifted the paper to his cheek, and it immediately absorbed his tears.

"Who are you?" was all Ruth could whisper. She was feeling a little woozy and was relieved to be sitting.

"We're First Creatures," Velo said matter of factly. She then climbed down the wall, tippy toed with her paws at her chest back to Ruth, cocked her head to one side with her lips curled inward, yet puffing out a bit, smiled, and sat down on Ruth's leg. At that, Ruth's head slumped forward and she was out.

CHAPTER ELEVEN

"May I help make the cookies this time?" a young excitable Hailey asked her mother.

"You sure can. What kind shall we make this time? Peanut butter, chocolate chip…"

"No," responded Hailey. "I think Miss Ruth likes the ones with the big Hershey Kiss in the center!"

"Oh, you mean Peanut Blossoms," her mom, Mary, said. "Good choice. There's both peanut butter and chocolate. And you're right, she does like them. All right, let's first get the ingredients together. Come on over here to the pantry and help me carry them back to the counter, will you?"

Mary and Hailey Davis were next door neighbors to Ruth Lily. Their friendship began seven years ago when a pregnant Mary and her husband, Bill, moved in to the vacant ranch style house situated to the right of Ruth and Roger's home.

Ruth and Roger had already become grandparents one year earlier with the birth of Hayden, but they played the role of honorary grandparents to Hailey as well, whose own grandparents lived in Florida. They did a fabulous job as stand-ins and celebrated with Hailey and her parents when she achieved all the usual milestones that came along in a child's first few years.

They celebrated birthday parties together and even some holidays as well. When Hayden's little sister, Heather, was born, it seemed more like a third grandchild to Ruth and Roger, when in reality, it was only their second. Hailey often came over to play at Ruth and Roger's when their grandchildren were visiting.

The change in Ruth was painful to more than just her family. Little Hailey and her parents missed Roger terribly, but longed to spend time with Ruth once again. Ruth used to initiate dinners with the Davis family, but no longer did, and where she used to stand at the fence and share stories back and forth with Mary, a simple glance was all Ruth now offered. Mary understood that Ruth was working through her grief, yet she wanted her to know that she was still available. She missed their closeness and yearned to get it back. She and Hailey often brought cookies to Ruth because they knew how much she loved sweets and they hoped to break down the barrier that obstructed their friendship.

Together, Mary and Hailey worked until they had a batter that was quite firm, but perfect for rolling into small balls.

Hailey's little hands were skilled at cookie making, and Mary found that Hailey was more open to conversation when transfixed in the art of rolling cookie dough. "Maybe this will be the magic plate of cookies to make Miss Ruth like us again," she hoped out loud.

"Oh, Hailey," exclaimed Mary. "Miss Ruth still loves us, she's just hurting and finds it hard to be happy right now. I have a feeling she'll heal with a little more time. I just want her to know that we still love her, no matter what."

"I see her at school a lot," Hailey volunteered. "She seems different there. I see her talking with some of the other kids. She seems to like them more than me because she smiles at them and gives them hugs. She won't even look at me," Hailey paused for a minute, trying to explain what she felt, but found it hard to speak. "Mommy, I'm not sure she likes me anymore," she said with tears beginning.

Mary was quick to wrap her arms around Hailey and hold her. "I'm so sorry you feel that way," she said. "Miss Ruth's world came crashing down last year, Hailey. We were a big part of her life and I think it hurts her too much to be with us right now. I don't see Mr. Bryce and his family too much either, and I'm sure they miss her, too. There are too many memories associated with us that she can't handle right now. She needs a little more time, or at least that's what Miss Bev said. How about I call Miss Ruth soon and invite her over?"

"Okay," Hailey agreed, with some sniffling. "I hope she wants to play with me again soon because she was just playing with someone else this morning in her garden."

"Oh, really?" Mary exclaimed. "Who was with her?"

"It was some other little girl, but I couldn't see. I could just hear Miss Ruth talking to her. That's what I mean, Mommy. Why won't she invite me over anymore?"

"Now, Hailey," it was probably Heather, and you can't blame her for spending time with her. Just keep Miss Ruth in your prayers and I'll give her a call," Mary reassured her.

CHAPTER TWELVE

"Hey, Martha," exclaimed Bryce as he came out of the house through the sliding glass door and into the backyard. "Somehow I knew I'd find you two out here." He squatted down to give Martha a genuine pat and rubbed behind her ears. "How are you, Ole' Girl? Are you taking good care of Mom? I bet you are." Martha gave Bryce a lick, but seemed impatient with him. Looking around, he asked, "Where is she, Martha?" Martha whined and walked over toward a path which led toward the back of the property. She stood, waiting for Bryce to follow. "Mom!" he yelled up the hill, "are you back there?" He began walking as Martha ran ahead of him.

Ruth stirred and blinked groggily as she lifted her head. It took her a moment to regain her bearings and remember what transpired between the First Creatures and herself. Quickly looking around to see if she were alone, she let out a sigh of relief. Just then Martha bounded around the corner and Ruth let out a startled scream, not knowing it was her dog. "Mom!" yelled Bryce. "Oh, jeez, what's wrong? Are you okay? Did you fall?" he asked, reaching out to help her.

"Oh, Bryce!" she cried as she fell into his arms. She held on tightly and tried to subdue some sobs.

"Mom, what's wrong? Are you hurt?" he asked hurriedly.

"No," she answered, still trying to stifle her sobs.

"What were you doing on the ground?" he asked her again.

33

Ruth was afraid to tell him the truth, which was one of two things. Either she had some kind of a psychological problem or there were creatures living in her yard who could talk. She had her senses enough to know that creatures don't exist so she believed the first choice to be true. Just the thought of a disorder alarmed her, and if this were the case, she was going to have a long road ahead of her.

"Mom! Can you hear me?" Bryce was shaking his hand in front of her. "Here, take this," as he handed her his handkerchief. "Wipe your eyes."

Ruth gasped at the remembrance of Mr. Gabriello needing to wipe his eyes. She backed away from the handkerchief, eyeing it cautiously; all the while Bryce observing her suspiciously.

Trying to cover her actions, she mumbled, "I...I... remember what I was doing on the ground. I bumped my leg on a stone which was protruding. I...I... couldn't get it to go back in line so I sat down to fix it. I found a note behind the stone that Hayden left me so I was just reading it when you showed up."

Bryce paused and looked at her intently. "Okay, Mom. Let's go sit down and get a drink." They walked back to the patio table and Bryce told her to sit while he got them some drinks. Once inside, he stood at the refrigerator, wiped his eyes and let out a long sigh. "Bev was right," he said to himself quietly.

"Here you go, Mom," he said as he handed her a glass of iced tea. He sat down across from her at the patio table, the same table which housed many family gatherings. Unsure of how to start a conversation that he knew would end uncomfortably, he slowly leaned back in the rocker and looked quietly at the gardens that were created years ago out of dedication and love.

Reading her son's mind, Ruth volunteered, "I'm fine, Bryce, really. I saw Dr. Brooke last week and she gave me some homework," she smiled. "Actually, she calls it 'grief work.' She'd like me to take a more active approach to push me through the mourning process. She hoped I'd be further along by now," she circled the glass with her finger, thinking how else to convince Bryce that she was sane. "My current assignment is to create a project in which I make all the decisions by myself. I have chosen to re-design part of the back garden.

"You see, in the past, your dad made most of the big decisions regarding the gardens because it was his passion. I was his assistant and I loved it. I ended up learning quite a bit from him. Anyway," she patted her thighs, "the thought process here is for me to consciously transfer the control of the gardens from Dad to me; to help me acknowledge that he's not here. So…here I am," she said nodding. "That's what I was doing on the ground."

CHAPTER THIRTEEN

The remainder of Saturday afternoon was quiet. Ruth dug up a couple of Nandina Fire bushes and re-arranged the layout moving them to a sunnier spot. She felt good making the decision to do that. It took a while and some envisioning, but she did it. She felt a sense of completion when she was done and gave herself a pat on the back. "Look, Roger, I did it all by myself," she said out loud. Her grief therapist, Dr. Brooke, had warned her against talking to her deceased husband, but it felt as natural to talk with Roger now as it did last year. But on second thought, she also said out loud, "Good job, Ruth."

Ruth turned down Bryce's invitation that night for dinner. As much as she wanted to see them, she wanted some quiet time to sort through what had happened to her in the last couple of days. Was she hallucinating? She didn't think so. She could picture Mr. Gabriello and Velo as if they were sitting in the kitchen with her right now. "One came out of a tree and the other popped out of a plant," she mused.

"It has something to do with Hayden's note, I bet. I've got to remember to ask him if he left that note for me," she continued out loud. "However, I don't want to scare him or have him tell his parents. He and Heather love the gardens too much. But what if I'm experiencing some psychological problems? Oh, I...I don't know what to do. Perhaps I'll mention it to Dr. Brooke next time I see her."

"Dr. Brooke, how nice to see you," she practiced. "Oh, yes, and by the way, I talk to creatures in my garden." After rehearsing a few different practice conversations out loud, Ruth realized that this was going to be even more difficult than she imagined.

CHAPTER FOURTEEN

"Oh, I'm so glad you're here already," Lydia sang as she whizzed into Ruth's classroom. "Oooh, I love that sweater. Is that from the outdoor store in the mall? Oh, what's that place called anyway?" She was flipping through a stack of papers in her hand while she talked.

Lydia was one of Ruth's beloved grade partners. The youngest on the team, she was finishing her third year working with Ruth and Julie. She was well liked throughout the school and had a reputation for spunk. All of her mannerisms were exaggerated and peppy and she had an uncanny way of making people smile. It was difficult to get angry with her because she'd cuddle up to someone if she thought they were annoyed with her. Her fiancé, Paul, called it her most important survival skill. He often said if she weren't so cute and cuddly, like a puppy, she'd have no friends at all because she would have annoyed them too much.

"Do you have the homework sheet to run off?" she kept going. "I can't find my copy anywhere this morning. I thought I had it with me. Oh my gosh, have you seen the weekly schedule yet? Look at this. We have an assembly this afternoon. I completely forgot about it. What's it about anyway? I'll have to ask Mel. Has that been on the schedule for long? Oh, wait a minute; I think it has. It's about bullying, right. I hope it's the same crew who taught it last year. They did a good job. Hmm, well, I'll manage. Oh, look at this. We have to give the spelling tests today.

Remember, we weren't able to issue them on Friday because of the fire drill? Drat; I guess I will squeeze it in this morning after recess. Here are your spelling templates, Ruthie. Ruthie?...Ruthie?...are you okay?"

"Oh, Lydia," Ruth replied rather distractedly. "Yes, I'm fine. Just put the templates on my desk. Yes, I'll give the test later."

"Oh, Ruthie," Lydia scowled, "I'm talking too much again. I promise to slow down." She ran up to Ruth, gave her a hug and a kiss on the cheek, and dramatically, but playfully, begged, "Ruthie, do you still love me?" And with that, she was out the door.

Ruth was just picking up the spelling templates when Lydia popped her head around the corner. "Oh, I almost forgot. Paul and I would like you to sit at the head table with my mother. I hope you'll like that. Oops, gotta go." And she was gone again.

"I'm blessed, no doubt about it," Ruth said aloud as she got her lesson plans out for the day and gathered the correct oral reading cards. She planned to double check her email before heading outside to get her students, but when she turned toward her computer, she let out a scream! "What is going on! What are you doing here?" she half yelled, half whispered. There, in Ruth's comfortable swivel desk chair, attired in her olive and lime striped tutu and leotard set, sat Velo, who looked very much like a stuffed animal, and quite at home.

"Do you?" asked Velo, in her little voice, once again oblivious to Ruth's agitated state.

"Do I what? What in the world? What if someone walks in here and sees me talking to a rabbit; a talking rabbit? This is absurd!" she hissed.

"Um, Lydia wants to know if you still love her because you didn't say anything," Velo nonchalantly continued. At this, she stood and climbed on to the chair's arm and then on to the desk. She tippy toed to the back of Ruth's desk and slid down against her quart sized water bottle. "Would you like to sit down?" she squeaked, cocking her head to one side, turning her lips inward, yet puffing, and smiled. She faced Ruth with her little legs sticking straight out in front of her.

"Yes, I still love Lydia. Of course I do," replied Ruth softly, hoping that if she answered Velo, then she would disappear.

The toothy grin which met Ruth's stare caught her by surprise. She wasn't sure if this little Velo really listened to her, but this time she could tell that she had her full attention. And at that, she softened toward her. "I don't always answer everyone's questions," she started softly; "it's kind of an understood thing."

"Mr. Gabriello wants you to," Velo squeaked in return.

"He wants me to do what?" Ruth asked.

"He wants you to love Lydia...and the others. He says you forgot," she squeaked softly again.

"Okay, I can't believe I'm having this conversation, but, what have I forgotten?" Ruth responded, getting a little harried.

Velo tip toed toward Ruth, sat down, inched her way toward the edge of the desk using the bottoms of her little brown leather ballet slippers and slipped down onto her lap. "Come to the garden. He wants to show you."

A loud chime broke the stillness of the moment, signaling the beginning of the school day. Ruth jumped up and quickly looked to the floor, expecting to see Velo in a heap, but there was nothing; she was gone. Ruth felt apprehensive about her last comment, *Mr. Gabriello wants to see me in the garden and show me something I've forgotten.* As Ruth walked outside to greet her students, she thought she heard a small "hmph, hmph" coming from the bushes outside of her classroom door.

CHAPTER FIFTEEN

As Ruth continued to the parking lot to gather and greet her students, she noticed Lydia had Julie, the third component of their teaching trio, pinned to an imaginary interrogation wall. Ruth smiled at the sight. If only Lydia would pause for a breath, she'd receive some answers. She was laying questions on Julie a mile a minute. "Did you have any problems with the caterer, Julie? I've tried calling him a few times, well, maybe a little more than that. I want to make a teensy weensy change to the menu. It's no big deal, really. But I get the feeling he's ignoring my calls. I know I'm a little bit demanding, but I should think that every bride is."

"Breathe, Lydia!" smiled Julie. "I really liked your menu selections, so stop doubting yourself. I wouldn't call you back either if you kept calling me with changes. Leave the poor man alone," she smiled at Lydia. Lydia was the baby in their trio and both Ruth and Julie acted on their maternal instincts toward her.

"Oooo, what's the matter with me?" Lydia pouted back to Julie. "Truly, I wouldn't call myself back, either. Poor man. Do you think I should call him back and apologize?"

"No!" Julie and Ruth piped back together. "Your plans are wonderful, so relax a bit."

"Ah," Lydia wanted to come back with just one more thought, but Julie stopped her.

"Face the flag, Lydia…Pledge!"

CHAPTER SIXTEEN

Ruth's morning was flowing smoothly. Her students seemed a little tired, which was the norm for a Monday morning. Their pace usually picked up a bit by mid-morning once they re-adjusted to the school routine.

Following Lydia's reminder to issue the spelling test today, she passed out the templates before lunch and had the students get their pencils ready. "Okay, boys and girls, I hope you remembered to practice this weekend since we couldn't take this on Friday," she prompted them. Coaxing them along, she reached the last spelling word and read aloud, "Believe."

In a flash, her mind began racing to recent events. "Oh, my....of course," she said quietly in utter astonishment. "It's 'believe'. Every time I say 'believe' I meet with the First Creatures." With that comment, she spun around to look at her desk chair. "Velo?" she called out loud. Would she be there again? Her chair was empty and Ruth actually felt a slight disappointment at her absence. "I can't believe that I'm actually growing attached to that little rabbit girl," she smiled.

The sound of giggling spun Ruth around again in time for her to meet her class' bewildered stares. "What's happening to me?" she thought silently. Not knowing what to say to her first graders, she paused.

"Who are you talking to, Mrs. Lily?" some of the students asked together.

"Oh, um…I'm sorry," she stammered. "I was thinking about something and I…I got confused. Okay, please pass your papers forward."

CHAPTER SEVENTEEN

After finishing the inventory of the stone pallets, Bryce slipped into his office for a moment of privacy. He loved Stonehenge Gardens and was proud of its success, but owning a garden nursery in the springtime was downright overwhelming. Summer and fall were almost as busy, with his only reprieve in winter. He was incredibly thankful that he had good, if not fabulous, people working under him, and because of that, he still had a decent family life.

He was glad he had agreed to stay home in the early morning with the kids so Bev could get in her rowing workout. He wanted to be a 'hands on dad' and early morning was a practical time. There were conflicts in the past with early morning meetings that couldn't be rescheduled, but he took it in stride. Hayden and Heather had learned early on that breakfast might be at the kitchen table, on the road with Dad, or maybe in his office at Stonehenge. They knew from the time they were born that flexibility worked best.

He leaned forward, resting his head in his hands and massaged his temples. He felt strong on most days, but every now and then the memories of the past year slipped in and caused him to catch his breath. He pulled out his cell phone, sighed out loud and shook his head. He had put off making this call long enough and needed to get it done.

CHAPTER EIGHTEEN

Once again Ruth found herself rushing to leave school in order to get home. "If anyone asks, I'll just tell them that I have a date with an amphibian," she chuckled. "Can you only imagine? I'm spending time with a frog. Alright, so Velo said Mr. Gabriello wants to show me something and I think I know how to make him appear. I just want to get home to find out."

As she rounded the corner of her street, she saw Mary waving to her from her front yard. "Hi, Ruth," she yelled. "I was hoping to see you today," she continued as she hurriedly walked toward Ruth. "Here, let me help you carry your school bags."

"Oh, I've got them, Mary. I'm balanced with one in each hand," she smiled.

"Hailey and I would like you to come for dinner," she blurted out. "She's been asking repeatedly. Are you free on Friday night?"

"Oh, oh, I...I...don't know," she stammered. "You don't have to go to the tr..."

"Please!" Mary interrupted. "It would mean so much to both of us. Bill is away on a business trip and it's just us girls."

"Really, Mary. It's very kind of you. I...I...I don't...haven't felt ready to socialize since...well...you know...th..."

"I do. I do know that you don't feel ready. I just wonder if it's time you tried." Mary pleaded.

Shaking her head and looking for the right words she tried to speak. "Thank you, but no."

Mary reached out and grabbed Ruth's elbow to stop her from walking away. "Have we done something wrong, Ruth? Hailey said you hardly acknowledge her at school."

"I...I...I think I just need more time at home," she responded, pulling away and getting upset.

"She's heard you playing with someone and I assume it's Heather. She'd love to come over and play as well. Have Hailey or I offended you, Ruth?" she asked again.

"She's heard me talking to her? Hailey can hear her?" Ruth whispered softly. "If Hailey can hear Velo, then maybe I'm not crazy."

"Ruth....Ruth...are you Okay?" Mary reached out again. "Ruth, have you seen Bryce lately?"

"Oh, Mary. I have seen Bryce. He was here on the weekend. It's just that sometimes I get a little confused. I...I...just need a little more time. Please tell Hailey for me. I've got to go." Ruth replied as she turned and hurriedly walked toward her front door.

CHAPTER NINETEEN

Mel was just finishing up a follow-up report on the school assembly held earlier about bullying when Julie knocked on her office door. "Hey, Mel, do you have a second?" she asked, somewhat timidly.

"Sure do. I'm all finished for the day. What's up?"

"Well, this is a little different," started Julie, a little uncomfortably. "I'm not here to talk about a student this time."

"How about you close the door, Julie, and then come on in and have a seat," Mel responded professionally.

Julie did as she was directed and sat on the sofa in Mel's office. At first glance she almost looked like one of the students. She had a small frame accentuated by silky strands of blond hair and vivid blue eyes. She had such a young look that it was hard to believe she was a teacher, let alone a mother of two elementary school aged boys, both of whom attended this school. She had such a sweet voice to match her young face, but the content of her language let it be known that she was tougher than she looked. Her thirty-five years included thirteen years as a teacher, and ten years as a mother. She was accustomed to directing children with ease and handled her authority well.

A look of passionate concern was written across her face and Mel could sense her discomfort. "What brings you in here today, Julie?" she asked in a tone professionally directed.

Julie hesitated, sighed, and hung her head momentarily before speaking. "I think I'm about to rat out a friend," she spoke directly to Mel. "I'm concerned about Ruth. I've had this growing feeling, just lately, that something is amiss with her. I wish I could tell you exactly what it is, but it all seems mysterious."

"You know," Mel began, "sometimes it's the vaguest of symptoms that speak the loudest. Take your time."

"We're very close, as you know. We know her...I..I know her. Something's wrong. She won't look me in the eye, she...she....she rushes out of school without stopping by to talk, and there was this weird thing today. It scares me, Mel. I was about to walk into her classroom and I think she was giving a spelling test. As I walked in, she was spinning around looking for someone around her desk, while talking gibberish. I wasn't the only one who thought it was strange because her students asked her right in front of me who she was talking to. She mumbled some sort of incoherent answer. But the worst is, she didn't even know I was standing there! She was so upset that her students questioned her, that she couldn't see me. When she turned around toward her desk, I walked out. I didn't know what to do and I didn't want to embarrass her anymore. I listened outside of her door and she was fine. Whatever it was, she recovered from it and began teaching again. I wanted to talk to her after school, but she disappeared again," Julie spilled it all out. "I'm afraid we're losing her again, Mel. I think she's in the beginning of another nervous breakdown. You know it's coming up close to one year next month," Julie sighed heavily and looked at Mel pleadingly. "I know that you've been best friends with her for a long time and that you were able to help her so much last year. I'm not speaking to you as a counselor at this minute, but as her friend. Have you noticed any changes in her? What should we do?"

After thanking Julie for her concern and assuring her that she would keep a special watch on Ruth, she began to review her own thoughts. She was going to let an earlier conversation she had with Ruth go, but after talking with Julie, she knew she couldn't.

Ruth had agreed to dinner at Mel and Pat's the previous evening. When she was thirty minutes late, Mel began calling, but was never able to reach her. When she asked Ruth about it early Monday morning, Ruth couldn't remember what she had done the day before. Mel could tell that she was trying to remember, but simply couldn't. Mel figured she probably spent some time with Bryce and the family. She made a mental note to call Bryce later and ask him about his mother's progress with her grief counselor. She was thankful that Ruth allowed Bryce to be included on her patient confidentiality privileges.

CHAPTER TWENTY

The office of Bayside Counseling had a serene atmosphere about it. With mixed shades of ocean blues and greens in the carpeting, it brought out a calming nautical environment. The receptionist's lounge was painted with multiple shades the color of sand, and the walls held pictures of coastline cottages and sailboats. The soft honey colored leather couches offered a strong supportive console as if to say, "Give me your cares, and I will hold you."

Ruth's therapist, Dr. Grace Brooke, was one of three psychologists who worked at Bayside Counseling. Her many years of experience and a deep rooted compassion for those who suffered, provided her with the unique skills necessary to help those who were grieving. The same calming water theme in the waiting room was carried through into Dr. Brooke's office. Though not a native of water country, she eagerly adopted its lifestyle many years ago after following her husband from grad school to his hometown of Annapolis.

Dr. Brooke was the third counselor to join the practice twelve years ago when it called for expansion. Her partners agree with her that she transferred into the role of "grief counselor" naturally. Though she had more than enough field experience during her schooling, her own persona seemed to supplement her experience from the beginning. While some counselors took years to lose their timid behavior and lack of authority with patients, Dr. Brooke was a natural. Her unusual ease to confer with patients comfortably, she stated, came from years of living with her grandmother, the small town do-it-yourself psychotherapist. Her grandmother had a wealth of common sense that she was able to apply to much of people's troubles. She also had a firm belief in the motto, 'time heals all wounds.' What time wouldn't heal, Dr. Brooke's Grandma Bailey said, could be helped along with a creative outlet. Dr. Brooke spent many-a-days listening to her grandmother give advice, and after years of living this, she joined in. In other words, all the common sense needed in dealing with patients and people in general, was mastered by the time she graduated from high school. To Grandma Bailey's delight and prediction, her granddaughter was the first in her generation to attend college and make her mark on the world.

As Dr. Brooke was finishing her notes from a previous patient, the receptionist buzzed in, "Dr. Brooke, your ten o'clock is here."

CHAPTER TWENTY-ONE

With her spirits dampened, Ruth walked into her house and greeted Martha, who in turn gave her a wag, but passed her, intent on getting outside. "Right, go on out," she said, still feeling perturbed. She dumped her bags and headed outside with a plastic bag in tow to pick up after Martha. Ruth sat in her rocking chair on the front porch and waited while Martha found the perfect spot. When Martha finished her business, she joined Ruth on the front porch and held up her nose to smell all of what nature had to offer today. Watching Martha perform slight sniffing motions made her think of Velo and her delicate maneuvering abilities. Ruth surprised herself by wanting to see Velo again. There was something so appealing about her nature.

The rocking motion began to soothe her and she opened up to Martha. "I don't understand why Mary wants me to join her for dinner," she began. "and…and her little girl. Why can't I just come home and find some peace after a busy day? It just makes me angry when she keeps asking. Why? Why? I don't want to be disrespectful, but why can't she leave me alone!" she vented. Martha stood and looked at her, wagged her tail, and rested her head on Ruth's thigh. "You don't get it, do you? Maybe you'd like to go to their house and play with them!" she got out with some sobs starting. "Maybe I'm no fun for you either!"

CHAPTER TWENTY-TWO

"Thank you for seeing me, Dr. Brooke," Bryce said as he sat down. He sighed as he leaned over with his hands on his knees. Not knowing exactly how to start, but feeling Dr. Brooke's welcoming presence, he started, "There's been a change in Mom's behavior and I want to talk with you to see if it's normal. I'm not going to say I see her memory coming back, but…she's acting a little squirrely, if you will. We've all been waiting for some time now...f...f...for...her to remember, but…I…I just wanted to touch base with you to see what you think."

"Okay, Bryce. Thank you for keeping me in the loop. I know that you've been waiting for some signs of recognition, and it may not look to you how you picture it to start. Why don't you explain to me what you've noticed," Dr. Brooke responded.

"Alright, I…um…I went to go see her the other day," Bryce started, "and she was out in the gardens. I guess I really startled her because she nearly jumped out of her skin when I came around the corner, and then she started crying. I really don't know what else to say to describe it, but it wasn't her normal behavior. I got the feeling she wasn't telling me the truth. I know you've said not to push her too fast, but how much longer are we talking? I…I…I'm having a hard time moving forward because of her. How will I know when she starts remembering?"

"Oh, Bryce," Dr. Brooke responded, "You'll know, without a doubt in your mind."

They sat in silence for a moment. She was intuitive about knowing when patients and their family members needed a moment to gather their thoughts.

"Did you give her some homework to do, in the means of a project?" Bryce inquired.

"Grief work, yes," she answered. "Did she tell you about it?"

"She did. She's working on re-designing a part of the garden. It's...something she said my dad would normally have done."

"I'd say we're on course, Bryce," Dr. Brooke said, standing slowly, signifying that the session was closing. "And, you'll know when she remembers. Feel free to contact me with more questions or concerns. And Bryce...she does stay in contact with me. Just thought you'd want to know."

CHAPTER TWENTY-THREE

Pat held the screen door for Mel as she made her way toward him. "Thanks, Hon," she sighed. Together they walked toward the shed and in synchronized silence, reached up, lifted the shell off the shed's outer wall and walked toward the water's edge. After placing the vessel on the ground, Mel headed back to get the oars while Pat gave the vessel a "once over," always checking for defects. Like clockwork, they positioned the oars and entered the water. No words were necessary when starting their route. They preferred it this way. After so many years of the same routine, they found solace in knowing what to expect. The repetitive motion of rowing in the quiet waters of Weems Creek created peace and tranquility. Occasional rowers passed them and exchanged friendly nods, keeping their hands on the oars.

On this day, though, Pat broke the silence. "So...missed dinner...no phone call? Come to think of it, she hasn't called lately," he said, speaking of Ruth. Mel sighed in response, but remained quiet. "If this were a good thing, I think you would have been filling my ears with details," he read into her sigh. "So, do you want to talk about it?"

Mel sighed again, not knowing exactly how to explain. "She's slipping," she cried out softly. "She's slipping into silence and distance and I'm not sure yet what to do. I'm not her therapist for this, Pat, I'm her friend and I'm scared. She's pulling away from me and I don't think she's ready."

"Don't slight yourself for being just her friend," he interjected. "You're the friend who has given her every moment she's required to listen to her fears, to dry her tears, and to read her silence." They stopped rowing as they both pondered the situation.

"I've spoken with Bryce," she said, "and he told me that she's following some directions from her therapist. We both like the therapist she's seeing, and I agree with the projects she's given Ruth, but come on! She should be able to remember more details than she's alluding to by this time."

"Do you still agree with her doctor in not giving any details to Ruth to help her remember?" Pat asked.

"I do, Hon," she responded. "No one can paint the picture in Ruth's memory of that day. It's there," she paused for a moment, "but she's got it tucked so deeply inside herself to protect her from the pain," she said slowly, then pausing again. "In cases like these, the memories come…in time…and in pieces, much like trying to put a jigsaw puzzle together without knowing the final picture."

"So what do we do now?" Pat asked.

"We wait…but I don't want her to move in the opposite direction, and that's what it looks like," Mel shared. "I would think she would be showing some signs of recognition of her past, but I'm not picking up on it."

CHAPTER TWENTY-FOUR

Ruth stepped outside into her backyard, once a sanctuary shared with Roger, a place where peace and tranquility thrived, a home to the wildlife, and where life was lived to the fullest. "Apparently, our backyard is now a home to more than the wildlife, Roger," she spoke aloud. "It's also a home to creatures…First Creatures, they're called. And by the way, I'm hoping to meet them here tonight and I'm a little nervous, I must admit." she continued softly. "One of them, Mr. Gabriello, wants to tell me something I've forgotten. I…I…I can't imagine what I've forgotten, Roger. "But, I think I know the magic word to meet with them, Dear, it's… "believe," she said. "Hayden has left some cute little notes in the stone walls asking if I believe…and…I..I.. think that's all I have to do is say it. I'm ready to try it," she said somewhat timidly. She positioned herself facing the entire backyard, breathed in deeply, let it out and said, "Okay…..believe." She stood perfectly still. "What do I do now?" she asked. She looked around, but didn't notice any movement or any other noise for that matter. "Velo…where are you?" she called out. "Will you help me find Mr. Gabriello?"

Ruth sat down in the rocking chair at the patio table to see if either of them would appear. She closed her eyes and slowly rocked, trying to soothe her nerves. "I want to talk with you…and I…I really want to see you again, Velo," she said in a humble request. With that she stood and began walking on the path up the hill. It made for a silent walk due to the trodden down soil and Ruth realized how very quiet and private it was here. "I hope I know what I'm doing," she breathed. And when she reached the same area of garden where she first met Velo, she stopped and listened again. She saw the same Frances Williams Hosta from which Velo appeared and bent down to have a closer look. It was completely undisturbed as if a miniature creature had never floated out of it. It saddened Ruth to think that she might not be seeing Velo today, and then realized how much she was looking forward to spending time with her. She slid down, confused, against the rocks to rest a while and to think about her tiny friend. What was it about Velo that drew Ruth to her? Ruth liked the way she felt when she thought about her and admitted to herself that she liked the fact that she wanted to see her.

She opened her eyes when she heard a soft grinding noise and noticed one of the stones directly in front of her sticking out a bit. "Did that stone just move?" she wondered out loud. She reached forward and tugged on the stone a bit. At first it seemed as if it wouldn't move so she wiggled it back and forth while pulling on it, and it slowly released. It didn't take much maneuvering on her part to see a note deep inside the hole, and with hurried anticipation, she reached inside and pulled it out. Once again she noticed the texture of the note to be quite thick. "Where did Hayden get this paper?" she whispered. Like last time, it was dampened and therefore made no noise as she unfolded it.

"Do you believe?" was once again written on the note.

"Yes, I do," she said out loud, hoping for the same scenario as the last time. To her relief, yet bewilderment, that she was somehow controlling this moment, she could sense that the tree above her was widening. In expectation of what she thought she'd see, the world became perfectly still and silent. She could hear herself breathing and wondered if she was doing it too loudly for him. She knew he was above her, waiting for her to acknowledge him, and she had an unstated acceptance about this situation, knowing that when she looked up she was going to enable an element of her life to move forward; an element that she would not be able to stop.

She slowly lifted her face toward the oak tree above her and breathed in deeply, yet not too harshly so as not to offend him like last time. His presence paralyzed her movement and thoughts. Why did it hurt to look at him? Why did she want to scream out loud when looking at his eyes? The sorrow in them was practically ear-piercing, yet there was no noise. She wanted to scream and turn away, but she held his gaze out of respect.

"Who are you?" she whispered. "I don't understand what you want. Please say something," she whimpered.

"Um, he's Mr. Gabriello. You already know that," a familiar voice squeaked dispassionately directly to her right.

"Oh, Velo!" Ruth sobbed out loud. "I don't understand and I'm frightened. What does he want? Please help me," she cried while crawling fast toward her to get away from the tree.

"Don't be afraid of him, Miss Ruth, he's not going to hurt you," she responded while tip toeing toward Ruth. Her tiny body squatted down and she patted Ruth's hand that was covered in dirt from crawling.

"He doesn't speak. What does he want?" Ruth said, still trying to hold back sobs.

"He takes things," Velo responded without excitement. "He's The Keeper. He took what you didn't want."

"Is this what I forgot? Something I didn't want?" Ruth asked her.

"Um hum, you didn't want it so Mr. Gabriello took it and he will keep it for you," Velo said while climbing over Ruth's legs and looking into her other hand.

"What are you doing?" Ruth asked her, calming down a bit.

"You know, Hayden's note. Mr. Gabriello keeps them. He has to get all of them back," she squeaked, dutifully taking the note from Ruth's other hand.

"How many notes does he want? Sh...sh...should I be looking for them?" Ruth responded still trying to calm down.

"No," Velo said softly, but nonchalantly. "The notes aren't ready yet."

"How many, Velo?" Ruth asked.

"Um, they're not ready, but there's eleven." she said.

"Eleven notes? I don't know how they'll get here," she began to cry again. "My grandchildren don't like to play here anymore since Roger died. They don't want to come see me anymore. I don't know if there are any m...m...more notes for Mr. Gabriello," she got out between sobs. "I...I...I don't think I'm any f...f...fun anymore," she cried falling over and curling up like a child.

Velo tippy toed closer to Ruth and squatted near her face. She noticed Ruth's sobs were subsiding and that she was falling asleep. She gently dabbed Ruth's eyes and cheeks with Hayden's note and then curled up next to her.

CHAPTER TWENTY-FIVE

On the other side of the fence, from a distance and through the trees, peered Hailey, wide-eyed and confused. "Whoa...Who is Miss Ruth talking to again?" she whispered to herself. "I don't see anybody, and I wonder why she's crying."

Hailey could remember being invited over to play in the gardens with Miss Ruth and Mr. Roger along with Hayden and Heather a long time ago. They used to have so much fun playing Hide and Seek, Treasure Hunt and I Spy. Miss Ruth gave them cookies and lemonade and let them play in the sprinklers when it was hot. Ruth loved having them at her house, Hailey could tell. That's the way Hailey remembered it until all of a sudden it stopped. It just ended one day and it was all over. Suddenly all the fun was gone. She didn't know why and no one would tell her. "Miss Ruth is no fun anymore; I heard her say it!"

CHAPTER TWENTY-SIX

"Are you ready? Are you ready, Miss Ruth," she could just make out in a peeped voice. She could feel the slightest patting on her hand as she started to open her eyes. The prettiest colors of the garden were swirling in her sight as she tried to focus. She saw pretty shades of green and soft yellow swaying back and forth before her and she had the most serene feeling about her. It was one of warmth, that melted right into her bones. She was safe and felt accepted. She didn't feel the invisible wall blocking her from this feeling as she usually did. She liked it and she wanted it to last longer. What was it? She used to know.

As her eyes adjusted to being awake, she first focused on a little toothy grin. Ruth smiled in response and uttered, "I like you, you know...whoever you are. You make me feel good on the inside." With that, the little toothy grin became a fully fledged smile, causing her nose to wrinkle.

"Are you ready now? You slept," Velo said. "Mr. Gabriello wants to show you now," she squeaked as she pulled on Ruth's hand to get her moving. Ruth instantly snapped into remembrance of why she was outside and became nervous.

"Whoa...w...w...wait. Where am I going?" she asked nervously.

"Mr. Gabriello will show you," Velo replied. "Here," she said as she tugged on Ruth's pant leg. Ruth bent over toward her and Velo stuffed Hayden's note back into her hand. "Give this to him. He wants you to give it to him and then he'll show you," Velo explained softly.

Ruth turned around cautiously to face Mr. Gabriello. She was very unsure of this moment, but she knew she had inwardly agreed earlier, by looking at him, to have this part of her life move on. She walked forward slowly to get to the steps to the raised section of the garden where he was standing against the oak tree. She could never walk on the stone steps in this garden without remembering how difficult it was to build them with Roger. It took many summers of planning, first on paper and then on land to get the stone work correct. They were both fanatics about stone and their years of hard work had paid off. The Lily gardens were legendary throughout the garden clubs in Annapolis. Colonial Field Stone was both of their favorites and it was used endlessly throughout the back yard. Each piece was large, strong, and somewhat flat. It made for good stacking as well as side by side placement for making steps. They both loved the grayish tan color, which provided neutrality in planning plant life.

As she reached Mr. Gabriello, she noticed that he only stood as high as her chest. She thought he was bigger since he was on higher ground during her previous sightings. She already knew the feelings she would experience when looking at him so she was more prepared than an hour earlier. Looking at his skin close up reinforced in her how aged and rough it was. His sheath was indeed tattered, but then again, did creatures wear clothes?

She tightened her stomach as she looked down to reach his eyes. She knew she wasn't going to like it, but somehow she also knew it was part of the plan. There was a very small part of her that was telling her to go backward in time and wake up from a probable bad dream. These creatures weren't real, were they? But, the other part of her was ready. Ready to move forward and fix whatever was wrong with her, or find whatever it was she had lost.

She was ready. She very slowly looked down to meet his gaze. She didn't tense, though, this time. When she looked at him, she was able to look through his pain and find familiarity. What was it though? She didn't know.

"Hello, Mr. Gabriello," she said softly to him. He didn't move any part of his body to acknowledge her except a very slight nod of his chin. She moved her hand forward toward him as she said, "I have one of Hayden's notes for you." He very slowly reached his hand toward her to take it. The exchange took place quietly, without any earth shattering event, much like Ruth imagined might happen. They both stood very still while looking at each other. Ruth steadied her breathing while waiting for something to happen.

Mr. Gabriello raised his left hand above his head toward her exposing his palm. Instinctively, Ruth's right hand rose to meet his so their hands could join. Immediately upon uniting, Ruth felt herself being jerked forward into the tree along with Mr. Gabriello. A deafening shrill followed them and caused her to squeeze her eyes shut while trying to block out sight and sound.

"I...I...I can't see anything! Where am I?" she shouted, panicking. "No! What have I done?" she cried. All at once a light started to form and her vision began returning, but it was so blurry. She reached out her hands to feel around her, but touched nothing. "Oh! Help me!" she screamed. She was so angry at getting herself into this situation. "Darn you, Ruth! What are you doing? Why did you let this happen?" She slowly sank down to the ground and felt her back scrape along something really rough, like a tree. She sat on the ground and began to sob.

After a few moments of despair, she felt a little movement on her legs and then a little tugging on her shirt sleeve. "Um, why are you crying?" a familiar squeak met her ears between jagged breaths. "Mr. Gabriello wants to show you now, but you won't be able to see it until you open your eyes."

"Ahhhh!" Ruth jumped. "Velo, please don't leave me again!"

64

"Hmph, hmph, hmph, I didn't, you just closed your eyes," she said nonchalantly as she reached up to push on Ruth's eyes. "Look, Miss Ruth, look what Mr. Gabriello wants to show you." Ruth began to see figures as her sight cleared and then she heard laughing.

As the picture cleared, Ruth could tell she was standing behind a food buffet in a cafeteria. She saw young adults standing next to her with serving utensils in their hands and then she noticed that she held one, too. She and the others were sharing stories and laughing together as more young adults came toward them waiting to be served. "Whoa!" Ruth exhaled as she realized where she was. "I'm in college again in the cafeteria," she whispered. It took her a minute to realize that while she was seeing out of her own eyes, she was also seeing out of her younger eyes, as she had been years ago. She couldn't control what she was saying out loud in the dream, but she could still think her current thoughts in her head. "I'm reliving my past...whoa...oh my gosh...how is this happening?" she spurted silently.

"Ruthie, Ruthie, Ruthie!" a girl named Sarah whispered hurriedly. "Here he comes. Look at me. Is there anything in my teeth?"

"You're good," Ruthie answered. "How about me?" she smiled at Sarah before spinning toward the people in line, still smiling.

"Hey, Ruthie," he said. "You look so pretty when you smile. Is that smile for me?"

"Huh," she gasped. "Oh, hi, Roger. How's it going?"

"Oh, it's goin' just fine...now," Roger replied with a wink. "But you never answered me. Is that smile for me?"

"I...I...I guess so," Ruthie hardly got out. She thought she was going to faint if she didn't take a breath pretty soon.

"May I have some eggs?" he smiled. She obliged and even put a second scoop on his plate.

"Would you like some grits, too, Roger?" Sarah gushed loudly.

"Nah," he replied, looking directly at Ruthie. "Just eggs today."

Sarah slowly stepped on Ruthie's foot under the serving counter while Roger continued to smile at Ruthie, who in turn kept blushing. "I'm glad I met you yesterday," he said again with a wink. "I've got to eat quickly and then meet over in Wicomico Hall. My professor is taking us out on a field trip. We're collecting water samples from the Chesapeake. Should be great, and warmer today. So..., I'll see you around, I hope."

With no response from Ruthie, Sarah pressed harder on her foot. "Oh, sure, I...I...I hope so, too," Ruthie smiled. And with that, he took his serving tray and walked toward a group of young male students, who were already finished with their breakfast and waiting for him.

"Hey, Rog, over here. You'd better hurry, we have to go."

"Oh....my.....gosh!" Sarah got out. "You are so lucky, Ruthie! How did this just happen? You didn't tell me you've met him. Talk...talk...talk...tell me everything," she begged.

Ruth listened to herself explaining to Sarah that they had met the day before in the hall after class. Ruth remembered it now as if it were yesterday. She slipped in a puddle of water in the hallway near a water fountain and her books went flying one direction and she fell backward, literally right into Roger's arms.

"Whoa, Baby!" was what he had said when she fell. After he helped collect her books, he asked for her name. He got the biggest kick out of the fact that her name was Ruth.

"Hey, do you think it's okay if I call you 'Baby Ruth'?" he asked jovially, trying to make light conversation with her. When she turned down that request, he promised not to call her that in public. Ruth smiled now, sweetly, remembering how much he loved to call her "Baby Ruth" when they were alone together.

The picture in Ruth's vision became blurry and white and she thought she could hear birds chirping. She relaxed for a moment, basking in the memories of long ago. She knew that moment when being greeted by Roger in the cafeteria that she loved him. He was a true gentleman and she trusted him implicitly from the very beginning. He was a 'looker' for sure, and many a girl swooned for him, but he made it known that his eyes were only for Ruthie. They became an item that fall of their senior year of college, and were inseparable from then on.

They were a handsome couple, both blessed with fine features. His six feet, two inches towered above her five feet, four, and he loved scooping her up piggy back for fun. They both had black hair, but hers was bone straight and his was coarse and wavy. He combed his hair to the side, and when it got too long, he had a habit of swinging his head to get it out of his eyes. Ruthie loved his hair and didn't mind when it was long. It was never long enough for a ponytail, but definitely long enough for Ruth to enjoy running her hands through it.

Another moment of quiet remembrance passed, when all of a sudden life was fast forwarding. Ruth relaxed as she waited to see where in her life she'd be next. As the picture began to clear, she heard a crunching sound. It grew louder, but only a grayish white color remained for her to see. As she exhaled, the picture came in to focus and she realized why she couldn't see it too well.

It was a moonlit night and she and Roger were walking up a snow crusted hill. Actually, Ruthie was pulling Roger along jokingly as she said, "Just a little bit further, just wait til you see it."

"It's so pretty right here, come on, let's set up here," he laughed. She continued to pull him along as their boots crunched in unison.

"Okay, okay, here we are. Look, Roger, look at this view!" she exclaimed happily.

"Oh, Ruthie, whoa!" he suddenly exclaimed upon looking. As they reached the top of the snowy hill, they could look down on the snow-covered lake below them. The moon was so bright and it reflected off the snow-covered ground, providing enough light to see clearly. The view off the mountains in Hagerstown, Maryland, was spectacular, to say the least, but with some of Mother Nature's frozen gifts added to the picture, it was incredible!

The two stood in silence trying to take it all in. Some of the water wasn't completely frozen and it sparkled and gleamed in the moonlight like small twinkling lights. "I'm so glad you brought me up here," Roger said with his arm wrapped around her. "This is unbelievable."

"And I'm so glad you like it," Ruthie smiled at him, reaching up to give him a kiss. "Come on, let's set up the tarp."

One of their back packs held a waterproof tarp which they laid out on the snow. The other held a large thermos of hot chocolate and snacks packed by Ruthie and her mom. They had packed cheddar cheese slices, green grapes and chocolate chip cookies, all of Roger's favorites. Ruthie and her mom, Charlotte, had just baked the cookies that afternoon while waiting for Roger to arrive.

Charlotte had met Roger a few weeks earlier during their Thanksgiving break and thought highly of him. Ruthie had told her mom how respectful he was and that her mom should be thankful that she could trust the two of them alone. Charlotte picked up on that characteristic about Roger and she did trust him. So when Ruthie asked her mom if she minded if she and Roger went for a hike up the mountain in the dark after dinner, Charlotte consented. "Dress warmly and bring flashlights," was all she told them. "And don't stay out too long. You know how the temperature drops."

Roger offered to pour the hot chocolate so Ruthie could get the snacks. "Let's just eat the cheese and grapes for now and we'll save the cookies," she said as she put them on a paper plate and laid it in front of them. They sat side by side on the tarp eating, talking, laughing and admiring the view around them.

"You know, Baby Ruth, I never want you to get hurt, but…I sure am glad you slipped in the puddle of water the way you did," he said sincerely. "What if you hadn't slipped? I wouldn't know you and I wouldn't be the happiest guy in the world. I wouldn't be sitting here on a hilltop overlooking the most incredible view I've ever seen, and I wouldn't be sitting next to the prettiest candy bar girl in the world. I love you, Ruthie," he said sincerely.

"Hmmm, I'm glad I slipped, too," she said, snuggling up to him. "Right into your life. I love you, too, Roger." She looked up to him and their lips met; neither of them aware of how cold it was in the middle of December.

"Um, speaking of candy bars, can I have a cookie?" he asked sweetly.

"Of course you can. I'll get them out," she replied. She pulled the back pack closer to her and reached in. While feeling around for the plastic container full of cookies, she felt another box, much smaller and made of velvet.

"Huh," she gasped looking at him. He was looking directly at her, his eyes brimming with tears.

"Take it out," he smiled as he got up onto his knees. She took the little box out and opened it.

"Huh," she gasped again, looking up to him. The brilliant reflection which shone out of the box glimmered in the bright moonlight above them. Roger reached for her hand to pull her to her knees and face him. He took the box from her, took out the ring and held it before her.

"Ruthie Baylor…I love you…I've loved you since the moment you fell into my arms. Will you marry me and make me the happiest man alive?" he asked adoringly.

"Oh, Roger!" she squealed. "Yes! Yes! Yes!" she said as he was already reaching for her left ring finger. She threw her arms around his neck and hugged him tightly. "Oh, Roger, I'm so happy." They continued to embrace each other, both overwhelmed with their happiness.

The scene became quiet and distant and the picture began to fade. Ruth sat silently for a few minutes, basking in her very special memory. Oh, how she loved his proposal. She remembered sitting for a while longer with Roger that night, just engulfed in their happiness, and already making plans, before heading back to share their good news. Together, she and her mother cried for joy, and they, too, talked of plans. It turned out, though, that Roger had asked permission to marry Ruthie when meeting Charlotte a few weeks earlier.

After a few quiet moments, Ruth realized she was fully coherent and not in any type of dream state anymore. She noticed that she was sitting on the ground leaning against the same oak tree out of which Mr. Gabriello appeared. She turned around and felt the tree. Nothing. She turned back around again and gasped, "Hah!" There sat Velo half under the Frances Williams Hosta with her head cocked to one side, her lips turned in, yet puffing out, and her paw-like hands at her chest. Her little legs were sticking out in front of her, but she pulled them toward her as she began to get up. For a moment, she was camouflaged in the Hosta, but she used her arms to swat away the leaves gently, kind of like walking through a thick forest.

"Um, did you like what Mr. Gabriello showed you?" she squeaked as she got up and tippy toed toward Ruth.

"Who are you?" Ruth asked shaking her head.

"I told you, we're First Creatures," she replied.

"But, why? Why are you called First Creatures?" Ruth asked.

"Because we were here first," Velo said softly as she hopped up on Ruth's leg and sat down.

"Ah, Velo," Ruth started. "When will Hayden's notes be ready so I can see more?"

"When you are," she piped, snuggling up against Ruth.

CHAPTER TWENTY-SEVEN

Five-thirty came awfully early, but Bev never minded, as this was her normal morning routine to which she adhered almost always during the week. Hopping into her rowing spandex and a quick five minute drive barely took any time to get her to the boat house by five-fifty. As the majority of her boat members arrived, they made their way to their boat that was kept on a rack inside the boat house. Carefully they lifted it off and heard, "Shoulders, ready, up," from their coxswain, Sharon. At this command, they began their trek down to the water's edge.

With careful skill and balance, learned over many years of practice, the ladies entered the shell without much commotion after the command, "Sit in." With another order from Sharon, they heard, "Hands out," as they prepared to shove off from the dock. Once they cleared the dock, they heard, "Ready all, row," and began their morning journey as they headed toward the mighty Severn. The job of the coxswain was crucial to the easy flow of the boat and its rowers, and was responsible for every command, from how high to pick up the boat when walking, to how to set it down, when to shove off and how to row. It was helpful for the coxswain to be small framed because she was positioned in the stern of the shell and was tucked in tightly, out of the way of the rowers.

"It's a beauty, all right," someone called out from the boat, referring to the glorious day. "Would you look at that sky?"

"And how about the water? Hardly a ripple in it, well, not yet anyway," someone added. They all knew that College Creek was often times smooth, but not the Severn. Like all rivers, the Severn gained strength as it grew closer to a larger body of water, and in this case, the Chesapeake Bay. The Chesapeake, in turn, became even more powerful as it neared the Atlantic Ocean. The boaters respected the unknowing power that the water possessed and always proceeded on the side of caution. They didn't take chances by rowing when it was deemed too choppy, especially in a fragile crew shell. Some roughness was to be expected, due to the nature of water, but caution was necessary, for safety's sake.

"Good morning, ladies," Sharon's voice echoed through the cox box, the portable voice amplifier. "And good morning, Severn, you're looking a little choppy today. Keep your heads in the game, ladies. It's a bit rough out here, but nothing we can't handle if we keep our smarts on."

As Sharon maneuvered the lines to alter the rudder, the powerful sweeps of all eight rowers aimed the shell toward its new direction to turn northwest into the Severn. "OK, even it out, ladies, and...hit it," she commanded, knowing they would row until she instructed them differently. To an onlooker from shore or a passing motorist on the Naval Academy Bridge, the shell appeared to move effortlessly and gracefully through the water. Only the rowers knew, though, that unity and extreme strength were needed to present such a depiction, and years of practice to perfect such an image.

Bev, Mel and Annie were part of the Engine Room; that is, they were positioned in the middle seats within the shell--seats four, five, and six. Those who sit in the Engine Room are, by and large, the biggest and strongest rowers, who supply most of the power to the boat. Bev was in seat five with Annie in front of her and Mel behind her.

"So, Bev, (stroke) have you seen your (stroke) mother-in-law lately? (stroke) I haven't heard you mention her (stroke) and I was wondering how (stroke) she's been progressing," Annie called backward to Bev.

"Yea, actually (stroke), we did. (stroke) (stroke) She came out to us (stroke) (stroke) for dinner (stroke) and…

"Wait, what?" Mel called forward to them. "I can't hear (stroke) what you're saying. Talk louder!"

"Yea, it's been so (stroke) phew, (stroke) long, but (stroke) (stroke) it was good (stroke), I mean (stroke) (stroke), better," Bev responded, getting quite winded.

"You know, Bev, I thought the (stroke) same…

"Cut the chatter, ladies!" Sharon chastised. "Get your heads in the game! It's too rough for socializing."

"Yikes, sorry, girls," Mel responded.

"Hey, I don't feel so," Bev started, but right at that moment, she didn't release her oar blade from the water properly and it dipped back in while she was reaching forward. The tremendous power of the vessel moving through the water caused her oar to shoot backward and strike her in the chest with such force she somersaulted backward out of the boat.

"Hold Water! Hold Water!" Sharon yelled into the cox box. "Man overboard!"

Immediately, the remaining seven rowers squared their blades in the water for an emergency stopping.

"Bev! Bev!" they yelled. The sun caused glares and the choppy water slapped against the shell, creating confusion among the ladies. The club's motorized launch boat that mandatorily follows the rowers, immediately picked up speed and circled around the ladies' shell.

Meanwhile, Bev, who had been struck so hard in the chest, reeled backward across the water's top, somersaulting a couple of times. She felt like a baseball having been hit by a bat and she thought her lungs were going to explode if she weren't able to get a breath. When she did, she got a mouthful of water instead and began coughing and gasping. She needed help. She could smell the launch coming before she saw it and never thought gasoline smelled so inviting. "We gotcha, Bev, you're okay," was all she heard as she felt herself being pulled up and out of the water, like a limp rag doll. She continued to cough up water and catch her breath when she heard one of the coaches say, "You caught quite a crab, there, Bev. Are you okay?"

"Yea, (cough, cough), I got hit pretty hard in my chest, though. I need to sit the remainder out," she said. She waved to her boat members to let them know she was okay. As she closed her eyes to rest, she heard Sharon ordering the shell to turn around, "Ports check. Ports back. Starboards, row. Weigh enough. Watch your blades. Ready all, row."

CHAPTER TWENTY-EIGHT

Ruth was in her classroom enjoying the quiet time before the students came in. She arrived at school an hour before she worked with any students so she was able to get most of her loose ends tied up before the fast track of six and seven year old activities began. It was quiet in her classroom and her thoughts had a way of wandering during this time. Once the children arrived, she was all theirs, with no chance of slowing down for the next six and one-half hours. Her intent was to check yesterday's written stories so she could place them out in the hallway. Her students loved to see their work displayed and she really tried to not let them down.

As she looked at a story in front of her about flowers, her mind drifted to her own gardens. She sighed peacefully and thought how scared she was at first to meet Mr. Gabriello, and how amazing it actually turned out. She couldn't stop thinking about the dream, or the memory she experienced last week. She was still not sure how it happened, but she really didn't care. She was able to relive a very special time in her life when she met Roger, and she'd been thinking about it all week.

She must have been reminiscing deeply because she never heard Lydia's quick and perky footsteps coming through her doorway until she was already talking.

"It's May, it's May. Can you believe it, Ruthie? It's May! Oh, my gosh, I love May, don't you, Sweetie? Oh, I wonder why I love May so much. Oh, yea, I know. I'm getting married," she half sang, half yelled for the entire hallway to hear. "Ruthie! I'm getting married in three weeks! Ah! I'm so excited. Were you this excited when you got married? Oh," she paused. "I'm sorry, Sweetie, I'm not thinking clearly and I'm being insensitive. Please don't take offense, because I didn't think before I said that. Yikes, I wonder if I'm supposed to be this excited. Do I appear normal? Ah, what a silly question. Could I be any more normal, Ruthie?" she said as she twirled in a circle.

"Are you finished?" Ruth smiled sweetly at her.

"Ruthie! I love you!" she sang out as she ran up to Ruth and gave her a squeeze.

"Do you know, Lydia, that you and Roger are the only people in the world who call me "Ruthie?"

"Oh, Ruthie," Lydia actually said quietly. "I'm so sorry, Honey. Is it okay that I do?"

"Of course it is. I was just thinking about him when you walked in."

"Well, I'm sure I would be thinking about my husband all of the time as well," she responded. "Even if…I…I…I mean, I already do think about Paul…all day long actually. Is that normal? I think it is. Oh, by the way, we'd like you to come to our rehearsal dinner. We've booked George's on the dock. I think Mel has a friend who waitresses there. Anyway, we've been there before and we like it. They have a sectioned off area for private parties and they seem very accommodating. I thought it would be nice if we had the option of walking downtown by the water after dinner. We could all stop for ice cream or gelato at that cute little shop past George's. I thought that would be fun if our entire party just got up and kept changing locations. Wouldn't that be fun?"

"That sounds lovely. Thank you for inviting me. It will be nice seeing your m…"

"Oh, really. I'm so glad you want to come. And my mother can't wait to see you again. She had a nice time meeting you at the shower. Oh, and you know what? I'm not the only person who calls you "Ruthie." When my mother asks about you, she calls you "Ruthie" as well. I hope that's okay. Oh my, is that the bell already? Ah, I came in here to ask you about some menu selections at George's," she squeezed in as Ruth stood up and gently guided her to the outside door to greet the students for the Pledge.

"Yes," Ruth responded simply.

"Yes to what?"

"Yes to all of your ideas on the menu selection."

"Oh, Ruthie, you're so sweet to me. And...you seem....happy...I mean happier."

"Shhh. Pledge," she smiled.

CHAPTER TWENTY-NINE

Bev sat in the waiting room of her doctor's office with her head slightly down and her eyes closed. It felt better to keep out the light and the noise. She thought the only repercussion she would have from the oar hitting her yesterday was going to be tenderness in her ribs, but as the day wore on, she got a headache and felt her entire body stiffening.

"I guess I took more of a beating than I thought," she had said to Bryce when she woke up. "You would think I had done a belly flop from way up high by the way I feel. My entire body aches, including my head. I wonder if I hit my head on the side of the boat."

"Whether you hit it on the boat or on the water," Bryce started, "it doesn't matter. I think you should see the doctor. You might have a concussion. But regardless of what she says, you should rest for a day or two. You also said that you didn't feel so good before you caught a crab, so... take it easy. I'll tell Jan to cover for you at work."

"I think you're right," Bev had agreed, so thankful that she didn't have to get up, which was very unusual for her. She hurt all over and hoped a day off from a hectic spring schedule would help her.

"He is always so good," she thought as she snuggled back under the covers. "Man, I really lucked out with you, didn't I, Mr. Lily?"

"You certainly did," he said with a wink. "Do you want me to call Mel and let her know you're not coming to practice?"

"Um hmm, thanks," she said as she started to drift off. She really did count her blessings and thanked God every day for her solid marriage. She and Bryce had just lived through a nightmare of a year, and survived it, still together, which said a tremendous amount. She felt a wisp of hair being gently pushed away from her face. She opened her eyes a bit and saw him looking at her, smiling. Hayden had the same smile with one side of his lip rising higher than the other. "Yea, lucked out," she smiled back.

As he walked away, she marveled at his sight. "First thing in the morning and look at him," she thought. With his almost black, dark brown hair, tousled and respectfully shaggy, she would never grow tired of looking at him. His broad shoulders, from years of hard labor in his outdoor business, appeared too large for the crumpled t-shirt in which he slept. "He looks more like his father every year," she thought, "and that's a good thing." She had always thought that Roger was incredibly handsome, as well. Yes, her mother and father-in-law had been a beautiful couple. Bev really missed Roger this past year and could only imagine how Ruth felt.

She opened her eyes, feeling bittersweet, only to remember that she was sitting in her doctor's office. After being called back to the examination room, Bev explained the accident and her concerns to her doctor. Bev didn't think she had any broken bones and told her doctor so, but she did have a bruise forming on the side of her rib cage, which was very tender upon examination. Her doctor concurred with her self-diagnosis of no broken bones, and wasn't too eager to send Bev for a CT scan after examining her. She, too, thought a couple of days' rest would benefit her aches and pains. She did order lab work, though, when Bev mentioned that she had been winded while rowing, which Bev thought contributed toward the accident. Perhaps she was slightly anemic, which would account for that condition.

CHAPTER THIRTY

"I thought this might be you calling," Mel said when she picked up the phone. "Oh, Bryce, hello, I thought it was Bev calling. How's our girl feeling now?"

"She's back home and napping right now," he whispered into the phone. "Her doctor doesn't think there are any broken bones or a concussion, thank God, but I want to ask you something," he paused. "Bev said that she was out of breath before she caught a crab. She thinks it caused her to drop the oar too soon so the doctor ordered lab work. She said that maybe she was slightly anemic," he paused again. "Um, did you notice that, about her? It's not normal for her, and, well, you know. I...I...I just get a little nervous, you know?" he stammered.

"I do know, Bryce, so you don't have to explain yourself. Yes, she was a bit tired, now that you mention it. We were talking, which we shouldn't have been. We all saw that the water was getting choppy, but in hind sight, we didn't know...I...I didn't know she was struggling. It all happened so fast," she tried to explain, getting a little upset.

CHAPTER THIRTY-ONE

Ruth had just finished frying a few pieces of bacon and set them aside in order to finish making her BLT. It was one of her favorite sandwiches and she made it often during the spring and summer, mainly because the tomatoes were fresh and plentiful at that time. She had also made some potato salad yesterday and put that on her plate as well. After pouring herself a glass of iced tea, she headed out the back sliding glass door to have her dinner on the patio. As long as the weather was nice, this is where she wanted to be. She'd sit in a rocking chair, along with her meal, and Martha, of course, and enjoy the view of her gardens. The plants and flowers seemed to grow and change a little bit every day during late spring. Because she was so accustomed to looking at them, she seemed to notice even the smallest change. Her gardens were almost always full of chatter from the flocks of birds that took refuge in the trees and birdhouses that she and Roger had added over many years' time. The only times her gardens became quiet were the few opportunities she'd had to see Mr. Gabriello, including the last meeting with him, when he showed her what she had forgotten. The memories of when Ruth met Roger in college and then when he proposed to her were now held close to her heart. It was a time in her life of which she hadn't thought for so long, and she now treasured it as a gift to be able to remember, and to envision it as scenes replayed in her mind.

"Thank you, Mr. Gabriello, for showing me a part of my past," she said out loud. "You're right, you know, wherever you are. I had forgotten that lovely time in my life, and it was wonderful to see it again. I'm ready to see more, if it's okay with you," she said, softly. "I can't remember things from the past, but I'd like to."

She sat quietly for a while, listening to the birds chirp about her, busy finding their meals and feeding their young. She finished her own meal and set the plate on the patio table next to her, and then rested her head on the back of the rocking chair while closing her eyes.

She thought she heard a little giggle so she sat up and looked around. Not seeing anything, she sat back again and rested. A little tugging on her pant leg brought her just who she was thinking about, complete with a toothy grin.

"There you are," she smiled. "I've been wondering where y...," she stopped and looked up into the garden because she thought she heard giggling again.

"Somebody wants to meet you tonight," Velo squeaked, very matter of factly.

"Oh, Mr. Gabriello again?"

"No," she replied as she tippy toed away from Ruth toward the garden. "Okay, she's ready," she called out.

Ruth was really curious and sat wide-eyed, but she didn't have long to wait because directly in front of her, in the closest garden, the Temari Verbena began to shake. Ruth opened her eyes even further, not even trying to guess what was happening. It looked like the beautiful bright pink verbena was growing at warp speed. Then as magically as the other First Creatures appeared, a little figurine the size of Velo broke away from the flower.

"Whoa, there's...more...of...you?" Ruth asked slowly, almost speechless. The little creature, who was most definitely a girl, shook with excitement, especially in her arms and hands. She sashayed quickly toward Ruth, which startled her, causing her to sit back further in her patio chair.

"Ahh, haa, ahh, haa," said the creature, who sounded like she was hyperventilating. "Hi, I'm so happy that I'm finally here. I was waiting for my turn."

"Ahhh, are you…a…flower?" Ruth asked cautiously.

"Yea," she responded, giggling and kind of rolling her eyes.

Why Ruth would be surprised at seeing a talking flower after cozying up with a talking rabbit and a creature made from a tree, she didn't know. Maybe she was more amused, or maybe just in disbelief. She looked at this new little creature in amazement. She had pulled apart from the Temari Verbena, and she looked exactly like an extension of it, except for her face, which, like Velo's, seemed human. Her body was a mass of brightly colored tiny pink flowers, and her limbs, both arms and legs, were dark green stems, and leafy.

"Well…do you have a name?" Ruth asked, wondering to herself if it were time to make an appointment with Dr. Brooke. She should start rehearsing again on how to tell Dr. Brooke that she talks to creatures in her gardens.

"Ahh, haa, ahh, haa…hee, hee, hee," the little creature laughed. "My name is Ojy. Isn't that funny? Do you like it? Mr. Gabriello named me," she kept on talking while sashaying around Ruth with large steps. Well, as large as a one foot creature could manage. It appeared she was dramatically dancing while trying to look down and admire herself. "Ahh, haa, ahh, haa…I just love my flowers, don't you?"

"Wait a minute. What did you say," Ruth questioned her. "Mr. Gabriello named you?"

"Yea, ha ha ha…he did. He named Velo, too."

Ruth didn't know why this surprised her; maybe she just hadn't thought of that much detail. She looked over at Velo, who had climbed up the patio table legs and was now sitting on top of the table, against Ruth's glass of iced tea. Her little legs were sticking out in front of her again and she was tapping her tattered brown ballet slippers together. She turned her lips inward, puffed them out, cocked her head to the side and made a little noise, "hmph, hmph, hmph."

"You didn't tell me there was another one of you," she said, sweetly chastising Velo. "Do you two know each other?"

"You didn't ask me, and...um, yes," she squeaked, as she got up and jumped off the table, landing in Ruth's lap.

This startled Ruth, and she let out a little yelp, which in turn caused Velo to pat Ruth's arm.

"It's okay , Miss Ruth, it's only me." With that, Velo hugged Ruth's arm and then slid down to snuggle in her lap for a few minutes while Ojy continued theatrical dance movements on the ground around Ruth's feet, all the while enjoying her intense pink blooms.

Ojy broke the silence when she said, "OK, Miss Ruth, ahh, haa, are...are...you ready?"

"Oh! I think I was just about to doze off. Alright, I think I'm ready," she answered. She had been in pure bliss throughout the past week just by remembering not only the scenes which Mr. Gabriello had shown her, but recalling much of her college days spent with Roger. "I guess that's what is called 'young love,' what Roger and I experienced," she said out loud as she stood up, smoothing out the wrinkles in her shirt. "It didn't go away, Roger- that feeling of young love. It's...n...ot....g...one," she cried out.

A little tiny paw-like hand reached up and wiped away a tear which had fallen for the thousandth time. "Hmph, hmph, hmph," she heard and noticed that Velo was clinging to her shirt, almost weightless.

"Ahh, haa, ahh, it's my turn, come on, follow me," sang out a light and cheery, yet small, voice, as Ojy danced ahead of Ruth in a splash of swaying pink.

As they walked on the paths toward the back of the property, Ruth knew where Ojy was leading her.

"Mr. Gabriello apparently only appears out of one particular oak tree," she said aloud. All at once, though, Ojy jumped up high and grabbed hold of a stone which was sticking out from the rest of its neighbors in the wall. She began swinging back and forth, squealing in delight.

"I found it, ha ha ha, here it is, Miss Ruth, I found the spot."

"And I know what I have to do," Ruth said in response, starting to squat a bit to get eye level with the stone. She rocked it back and forth and slowly it came loose. She reached in without first looking and couldn't feel anything. Backing her head away, she focused into the hole. She could see the note much further back inside; she just couldn't reach it. "Hayden has much smaller hands than I do, so he got it further in." Using a stick she found close by, she dragged it forward until she was able to wedge it between her longest fingers. Feeling a bit like a game show participant, she slowly opened the noiseless note and read the familiar question, "Do you believe?"

"Yes, I believe."

She knew he would appear above her in the raised garden. Maybe it was out of respect for him, she didn't quite know, but she waited a minute before looking up to give him time to adjust to being outside of the tree. He didn't disappoint her when she looked for him, so she stood to begin her approach toward her expectations. She felt both excited and nervous about following Mr. Gabriello's abilities to take her back in time, but she boldly raised her hand to meet his.

The same rushed and jerked movements of being pulled into the oak tree occurred again, but she calmed herself to feel less afraid. It reminded her a little of ignoring the uncomfortable sound and feeling she experienced when sitting in the dentist's chair.

"Just wait for the sound and rushing to stop," she told herself with her eyes squeezed tightly shut.

When all became quiet, she slowly opened her eyes and began to focus. She could see two figures inside an oval shape, but couldn't quite make out who they were.

"Oh, Sarah, these are so pretty," Ruth heard her own voice saying. "Where did you get these?

"My mom and I know of a field near our house that is full of wild flowers, so we stopped to pick them on the way here. Mom used to string these through my hair and then I'd string them through my doll's hair. I think they're called 'Hot-Rocks,' which sounds a little unworthy, but I like them, though, for weddings because they look like long white bells."

"They do look like bells and I love them. Thank you, Sarah, for doing my hair," Ruthie replied.

Ruth realized, now, that she was watching Sarah and herself on the morning of her wedding day in her childhood bedroom's vanity mirror. Sarah had come early that morning and helped her get dressed and do her hair for her wedding. She breathed very gently so as not to stop the moving reel of her memory.

When she looked in the mirror, she saw herself at twenty-one, sitting at her vanity, smiling into the mirror. Her best friend from college, Sarah, was standing behind her, fixing her hair.

"Oh, maybe I should have gotten lilies to put in your hair...Mrs. Lily," Sarah swooned.

"Ummm...no, these are perfect," Ruthie smiled back.

As the picture began to fade, Ruth closed her eyes tightly again and begged softly, "No, no, no...please, a little more, Mr. Gabriello."

She slowly opened her eyes and found herself looking directly into Roger's hand holding her hands.

"I, Roger, take you, Ruthie," he began, "to be my wife, my friend, and my love. To build our life together as one, as we face both sunshine and storms. To gain strength from each other, as we walk through life hand in hand, and heart in heart."

"I, Ruthie, take you, Roger," she responded, "to be my husband, my friend, and my soul mate. To follow together, where God will lead us, through joyful times and sorrow. To learn together and to build our lives as one."

As Ruthie continued to look deeply into Roger's eyes, she was anxious to start their life together; one which would include a future of laughing, loving and learning together. She saw him as her source of vitality and guidance. She saw children, and hope, and time. She saw a man full of wisdom and strength who loved her and was pleased with her. She saw someone smiling back at her, deeply into her own eyes, and she knew he saw the same dreams as she did.

As Ruth began to hear the birds singing their own song mixed in with a bit of giggling, she knew her time in the past was finished for now. She kept her eyes closed and held both the picture of that wedding moment and the feeling she experienced at the altar as long as she could before reality sort of sprinkled itself over the memory.

"Ahh, haa, ahh, haa," she heard from Ojy as she opened her eyes. There was her new friend, a bundle of bright pink blooms, sashaying in front of her, as if walking down the aisle. "I picked that for you, hee hee hee. Did you like it, Miss Ruth? I hope so because I got to pick it just for you."

Not that Ruth really minded her new friend's excitement, she just preferred to close her eyes again, remain calm, and cherish her wedding memories. She could look into Roger's eyes forever.

CHAPTER THIRTY-TWO

It was nine-thirty in the morning and Bev had just walked into the kitchen. "I'd better be careful," she thought out loud, "I kind of like this sleeping-in thing." She was even sorer this morning than she was yesterday and still felt rather blah. The bruise on her rib cage was getting darker and still quite tender, but her head didn't hurt anymore. "I guess that's a good sign." She smiled when she saw the coffee pot light still on and thought of Bryce. She had heard them making noise earlier, but was able to tune them out and snuggle under her covers.

"Shhh, Mom's still sleeping," she'd heard Bryce say.

"Why isn't she rowing?"

"Remember? She 'caught a crab' and took a tumble. She's still sore so she's sleeping in."

"Hey, Daddy, can I try strawberry jam today?" accepting his explanation of Bev's presence at home during their morning routine.

Bev poured herself a cup of coffee and padded out to the screened in porch to continue her recuperation. From where she sat she could look into the backyard and into the kitchen. She loved their backyard of beautiful landscaping, hard scaped patios and walkways, and her pond. Her pond, which she dubbed, "The Chesapeake," was a work in progress for her. She continued to add to it each spring and summer and it thrilled her that her family also got so much enjoyment from it. Where it once began as a single medium-sized body of water, she had been adding "rivers and tributaries" to it and had a complete working waterway in her backyard. She had let Bryce and the kids have some input as to where to add rivers, and in which direction they should run so they could share in the satisfaction of this masterpiece. She had built, with the help of the Stonehenge crew, high walls on certain sides of the rivers to mimic the Severn and its high cliffs. She had even concocted some miniature bridges which imitated those found throughout the Chesapeake water system. She had bought miniature houses and placed them sporadically along the cliffs and low lands to contribute to the atmosphere of the river. Stonehenge and other garden shops and catalogs offered miniature decorations which adorned Bev's river system, making it appear to be a real live city. Instead of miniature dolls, though, she used wildlife miniatures, such as frogs, snails and birds.

Her father-in-law, Roger, had enjoyed "The Chesapeake" in their backyard as well. The love of water was something that she had in common with him. Roger had accepted a job after college, working with the Chesapeake Preservation Foundation, and had continued dividing his time between working there and his job teaching at the local college. His expertise in marine biology had helped spur Bev's fascination with pond building and it contributed to her designing the pond aquatics department at Stonehenge. Rog, as she called him, was known as Professor Lily to his students. She, too, had once called him Professor Lily when he taught her a class in aquaculture genetics as an undergraduate many years ago, but her reference to him easily transferred to "Rog" when she married Bryce. She had actually met Bryce on a few occasions when he'd stopped by his father's classroom or office, and she later admitted to him that she had made excuses to see his father with hopes of bringing up the subject of his son. Her clever planning was worth the effort when she walked into Professor Lily's office one day to find him not there, but his office wasn't empty; and the rest was history.

"Hmm," she found herself saying out loud when she remembered really getting to know Bryce for the first time that afternoon. She had just poked her head into Professor Lily's office to ask him a question about an upcoming field trip that was open to all environmental science majors. He was leading a research trip to a learning center near the Florida Keys, that would allow the students hands on research of the coral reef. She wanted to "double check" the dates of the trip to see if she could attend. She knew of the dates very well, but it was just another opportunity for her to touch base with Professor Lily and hopefully bring up the subject of his son. Imagine her surprise when she looked in the office and Bryce was sitting in his father's seat. They ended up talking for an hour and really enjoyed each other's company. Before she left, not only did Bev find out that Bryce was acting as his father's teaching assistant on the upcoming research trip, but they had agreed to meet for lunch the next day on campus.

"Yea, lucked out," she thought out loud, remembering a conversation with him from yesterday. Just as she closed her eyes to nap, the phone rang. The caller I.D. revealed her doctor's office and she tensed a little upon seeing the number, but figured she had to get the news, no matter what it showed. It was amazing how her mind, and Bryce's, too, were prepared for more devastation and she was immediately conscious of her aching body.

"Hello," she tried to sound steady.

"Hello, Bev, this is Dr. Tyler's office calling. The doctor would like to speak with you about your lab results. Do you have a minute?"

"I wish Bryce were here," was all she could think to herself. "Sure," was all she said out loud.

"Hello, Bev, how are you feeling?" Dr. Tyler said as more of a greeting than a question. I have your lab results and...we...uh....need to send you to a specialist.

Bev immediately stood up and grabbed some tissue. "Go ahead," she said stoically. After listening for a few moments, she fell back in her chair, weeping.

CHAPTER THIRTY-THREE

Ruth tapped her feet together nervously, as she waited to be called in to see Dr. Brooke. Most times when she came here, she couldn't understand why she was nervous. Dr. Brooke and her associates and staff were nothing but kind and pleasant. When she left her appointments, she felt positive that she was making progress in her recovery. She didn't think Dr. Brooke was candy coating any of her responses when Ruth shared her thoughts and feelings.

She knew she had started seeing Dr. Brooke after Roger died, under the insistence of Bryce and Mel. She remembered very little else of last summer except for a terrible heaviness and bleakness. She remembered sitting outside in the back yard for many days in the hot sun without eating or drinking. When Bryce found her, he took her to the hospital where it was determined she was suffering from malnutrition and dehydration due to severe depression. When Dr. Brooke visited her for the first time in the hospital, she was able to break through Ruth's invisible wall of pain, enough to make her understand that she was still alive and needed to care for herself. When she asked Ruth about the events of the tragic day, Ruth had no recollection. The only bit of information Ruth could acknowledge was the fact that Roger was dead. When Dr. Brooke approached the sequence of events that led to it, Ruth's eyes became distant, and she became almost comatose. After being pushed to remember, she began exhibiting symptoms of panic, which led Dr. Brooke to change her course of action.

When Ruth slipped further back in her ability to remember and spoke of things in her current situation that couldn't be possible, it was determined that she was suffering from a deeper and more extensive grief. Most people in Ruth's life wanted to force the truth on her, but under the guidance of Dr. Brooke, and with a firm insistence, the truth was withheld from her. Dr. Brooke believed that with time and a grieving plan, Ruth would be healed. It was difficult for some to adhere to the plan, but eventually, all agreed.

Ruth was eventually discharged from the hospital with an understanding that she would meet with Dr. Brooke twice a week until it was deemed to be unnecessary. Bryce was rather sure that Ruth would have to retire, so he told her principal. When he took her to her classroom to organize her belongings, he later told Bev and Mel that he witnessed a miracle. He said that Ruth literally snapped out of a part of her depression upon entering her room, so much so that both he and her principal agreed to see how the summer continued with her progress. Dr. Brooke explained to Bryce that Ruth found it easier to function in the regimented routine of a school day than she did at home where Roger had once existed. Her progress continued as she came to her classroom during the remainder of the summer to organize lessons. Bryce used to stop by daily to check on her and drop her off at her classroom, but no longer found it necessary. He arrived at her house one day to find her car missing from the driveway, only to race down the street and find his mother at school. She told him that she was feeling better and that he no longer needed to fetch her.

Unbeknownst to Ruth, Mel was in constant contact with Bryce for some time, reporting on her behavior and well being. To all of Ruth's friends and co-workers at school, she appeared to function normally. They had been advised of her situation and were asked explicitly not to speak of her husband's death. They were to contact Mel if they had any concerns. And only Mel knew the side of Ruth that broke down daily upon going home. She called Mel almost always just for reassurance when arriving at home. Once the transition occurred and she was safely into a dinner routine, life would continue rather ordinarily. Ruth had relayed this routine to Dr. Brooke, who in turn, reassured her that this type of behavior was called progress.

Now that Ruth was regaining some of her memories from long ago with the help of her new friends, The First Creatures, the breakdowns she experienced upon arriving home were less frequent, and so were her phone calls to Mel. Ruth still couldn't understand who or what, the First Creatures were, and she knew she should tell Dr. Brooke about them, but she had been resisting. What if there were something else wrong with her and Dr. Brooke wanted to admit her to the hospital for re-evaluation. Ruth was actually enjoying her time in the gardens and looked forward to spending minutes or even hours with her new friends, especially if it meant traveling back in time with Mr. Gabriello.

"Hello, Ruth," the receptionist said, as she opened the door into the waiting room. "You can come on back now."

CHAPTER THIRTY-FOUR

Bryce arrived home mid-morning to check on Bev. When he opened the kitchen door he found her sobbing on the phone. He ran to her, falling on his knees and began comforting her. "It's alright, Bev, we'll get through this. I knew it was something when you felt weak, but don't worry, I'm right here with you. We're tough people. We've faced the worst already; we know how to handle this. God wouldn't do this to us again unless He thought we could get through it," he blubbered.

"Bryce, Bryce, Bryce, no…no…stop. It's okay, I'm fine. Bryce…we're going to have a baby! That's why I was feeling weak and out of sorts; it just never occurred to me that I was pregnant, but it all makes sense to me now, of course. You remember, don't you?"

Bev wasn't sure she had ever seen Bryce so utterly speechless. He knelt before her, dazed, still trying to take it all in.

"You're okay?" he asked, crying.

"Yes!" she hugged him hard.

CHAPTER THIRTY-FIVE

As Bryce pulled into the parking lot of Stonehenge the following day, he still couldn't stop smiling. It made perfect sense to him that Bev was pregnant. She had all the same symptoms of pregnancy that she'd had last time, it's just that his view had been altered because of the past year. Where he and Bev ordinarily might have thought her accident on the water as just a risk of rowing, they had blown it out of proportion because of their perspective. They both admitted to each other after finding out about the pregnancy that they had feared the worst in her lab results. They wished now that they had remained calm and relied more on God, instead of on their own instincts, and they agreed to be more careful about their outlook in the future.

As Bryce reached behind the passenger seat to grab some paperwork, he smiled again. There would be a car seat in the back of this F250 four door pickup truck in eight months' time and he could hardly wait. His morning duties would pick up, of course, when the baby was a bit older, but they'd manage. "Bring it on!" he exclaimed loudly. "How's that for perspective?" he asked out loud, smiling.

He was situated in his office, reviewing the daily reports when he heard a knock on the open door.

"Howdy, friend," a familiar voice appeared around the corner.

"Hey, Father," Bryce said as he stood. "What brings you to these parts?"

"C…c…can you tell?" Father Joe asked, motioning to his attire. He wasn't dressed in his usual collar. Today, he was dressed in gardening clothes. "It's my day off an…an…and I've got the gardening bug," he added. "I'd like to plant an…other hydrangea s…s…since the other one is doing so well."

"Well, you've come to the right place," Bryce replied. "In fact, I happen to know the owner and perhaps he can manage a discount for you," he added, laughing. "Come on, let's go see what looks good to you." As they walked through the gardens toward the back of Stonehenge to locate the hydrangea section, Bryce shared his exciting news with Father Joe. He also told Father Joe about Bev's rowing accident and how he and Bev, both, had forgotten to rely on their faith.

"This is w…onderful, my friend, not the accident, of course, b…b…but new life; a time of cel…ebration. I…I…I was just thinking about you and Bev. You know, Bryce, as I've always said, God works in mys…terious ways. Um…hmm…now if you don't mind my asking, h…ow is your mother taking this news?"

Father Joe Douglass knew how to ask a question. He didn't waste time beating around the bush nor did he step on any toes. Maybe it was because he was a priest and people just assumed he could do that, but he surely got to the bottom of a subject without much ado. Bev and Bryce really enjoyed his company and his soft spoken, yet insightful ways. His slight stammering gave him a more genuine appeal and they found it very easy to talk with him.

"She's been working in her gardens for the last few weeks as some sort of therapy. It's…um… an assignment from her grief counselor to help her make decisions and come to grips with reality, I guess. She still says some strange things to us. Um, what I mean is she's still in denial. Her therapist doesn't want us to confront her. I'm not sure if you remember this, but, apparently if we tell her what happened, then she shuts down and we have to start all over. Her therapist strongly believes that my mother is able to remember on her own accord. So....we try working around her 'amnesia,' if you will, until she remembers."

"I...I...It's not amnesia, though, is it?"

"Well... yes ...and no...I mean she has memory loss as well as other symptoms like frequent sleeping, anger and forgetfulness. Her memory isn't gone, though, it's just tucked way down deep inside of her so she won't have to think about it. Her therapist calls it dissociative amnesia. She says the trauma my mother experienced is causing it, and it's mixed in with complicated grief. The grief and sadness have taken over her ability to process the events of that day, if you will. So...it's easier for her to pretend that day just didn't occur."

"That's got to be tough."

"Yea, it's hard listening to her go back and forth between whatever concoction is in her mind and a touch of reality. We're anxious for the day when the reality will begin to outweigh her dream state."

"So...y...ou didn't tell her about your j...j...oyous news? Bec...cause I think everybody c...could use some n...news l...l...ike yours."

"Wise words, Father, as always," Bryce said, smiling and patting Father Joe on the back. "We're actually planning to stop by her house this weekend and see her changes to the garden.

"Now, what kind of hydrangea interests you today?"

"I..I...I believe I...I'm looking for an Endless Summer."

CHAPTER THIRTY-SIX

Mel couldn't wait to share the big news with Pat. She had rushed home from school a little faster than usual and got changed into her rowing clothes. She found she had a bit more time recently than in the past year, now that Ruth wasn't calling so often. She had become so accustomed to the phone calls that she discovered she actually missed them. "Hmm…now who needs help?" she wondered out loud.

She hurried to the front door when she saw Pat pull up. "Hey, Hon, guess what? Guess who's pregnant?" she greeted him.

"Wow! Wait until the guys hear this one," he replied, laughing.

"Don't be silly," she scowled, while giving him a light smack. "Come on, guess."

"Annie?"

"No, but that's good."

"Julie?"

"No, but that…that…that's good, too. Come on," she pleaded as he began walking away.

"Bev?"

"What! How did you guess?" she asked, amazed that he'd guessed correctly. "Can you believe it? Isn't this wonderful, Hon?

I'm so happy for them. And here I was expecting something entirely different. It's funny how the mind works, isn't it?

"Well, that's great, really. Maybe they'll have a little guy and name him Roger."

"Oh, wouldn't that be something? They haven't told Ruth yet. They're going to see her this weekend to share their news and to see her gardens. It sounds like she's spending a lot of time outside."

"And it sounds like you're feeling a little better about her, yourself," Pat replied.

"Well...she's definitely a bit more relaxed and ...happier, I think. Time is a wonderful healer."

CHAPTER THIRTY-SEVEN

Ruth set her alarm clock for six-thirty on Saturday morning so she could have an early start. She was hoping for two things to happen today. She wanted to get the daisies planted, which Bryce had dropped off for her, in another sunny spot she had open, and she hoped to visit with The First Creatures. She thought about them all the time, but didn't seem to be able to control when their visits occurred. It usually happened in her back yard, but there was that one time when Velo appeared in her classroom.

She did end up sharing her encounters with the First Creatures with Dr. Brooke yesterday during her appointment. She was undecided about whether to tell her or not, but the words just tumbled out of her before she knew it.

"Have you made progress in your gardens, Ruth?" was all she had asked. Ruth eagerly told her that she had moved some plants around to help with the amount of sunshine they needed and then told her that she liked spending more and more time outside.

"Whose garden do you see it belonging to now that you're making these decisions?" Dr. Brooke asked in quick response.

"Well, Bryce brings some flowers to me that I request, and I put them where I think they should go."

"And was that the way it always was? When you gardened with Roger?"

"No, not exactly. I knew the colors that I wanted, but he knew the types of flowers and what conditions they needed."

"Are you remembering some conversations with Roger?"

"Well... that's... kind of tricky, you see. Well...uh...I...umm...well I...I...I didn't know how to bring this up, but since you asked..."

Ruth ended up telling Dr. Brooke everything. She told her about the notes from Hayden and how Mr. Gabriello appears and takes her into the oak tree with him so she can remember the most beautiful times spent with Roger. She told her about Velo and Ojy and how they both help her to get to Mr. Gabriello.

Ruth was wringing her hands while telling Dr. Brooke because she was so excited about them, yet terrified Dr. Brooke would be checking her into the hospital. She had to give the woman a lot of credit, though, because she sat perfectly content and pleased while her patient spilled out a seemingly delusional story.

When Ruth questioned her if she thought she was crazy, Dr. Brooke asked, "Do you still want to go to school on Monday? Are you eager to remember more of your past?"

"Yes! I want to see more. I had forgotten this beautiful part of my past and I want more. Is it okay for me to want that?"

"Well done, Ruth. Well done. I look forward to hearing more next week." She responded, smiling.

Ruth believed Dr. Brooke had almost opened the door for more interaction with her new friends, but she wasn't too eager to share this with her family because she couldn't yet define what The First Creatures were to herself. She had agreed to show Bev and Bryce her progress in the gardens and thought it was a big step to invite someone to her house. She was also eager to see the grandkids because it had been way too long, and she wanted to ask Hayden how many notes he had written.

Ruth had almost gotten all the tools she needed for digging when she remembered that she didn't have her gardening gloves. As she pulled open the garden shed door, the handle came off in her hands. As she looked at it, she realized that she hadn't thought of it for so long. It was her and Roger's initials, beautifully welded by a friend from Colorado. He had presented it to them as a wedding gift. It looked like the same metal used to make horse shoes and it read, R&R, all connected with a post in the back to use as an outside door handle.

"Oh! How did that happen?" she said out loud. "Maybe Bryce can take a look at it when he comes." She managed to get the shed door open and found her favorite gloves, a teal colored, waterproof pair that had seen their better days. She made her way back to a section of garden and began digging. Bryce had dropped off seven Ox-eye Daisies and offered to plant them, knowing full well this was part of his mother's grief work. She turned him down, thanking him anyway. She had asked for daisies and wanted this particular kind. She was proud that she could actually name them. She figured that Dr. Brooke knew what she was doing so Ruth had better follow her instructions. She told Bryce she was interested in daisies that would grow to be quite tall and have a ragged and wild look to them. Now that she thought about that description, she wondered if she were describing Roger in his earlier days when his hair was rather long.

Digging was tough work, but she continued to think of her beautiful memories that Mr. Gabriello had showed her last week, and it made the time pass quickly. When she was finished, she tossed her gloves onto the rock wall, sat down on the ground and let out a sigh, "I hope you think I'm doing a good job, Roger. And I'm sorry, but our initials came off the shed door."

"It'ths okay, that thometimeths happenths," said a small, but confident boyish voice. Ruth quickly scrambled backward like a crab away from the voice, but she couldn't see anything.

"Who are you?" she called out. "Velo! Are you here?...Velo!"

"Yes," she heard her squeak, but not before she felt a tugging on her shirt sleeve.

Ruth crawled quickly back a little more before noticing the little lime and olive striped figure tippy toeing quickly after her. She breathed a sigh of relief when she realized who it was. "Oh, Velo, you scared me. That didn't sound like you."

"Um, that's because it wasn't," she squeaked, as she cocked her head to the side while turning her lips in, yet puffing them. "It's Pheo, but I think you scared him."

"More? There's more?" Ruth asked incredulously. "Who is Pheo?"

"He's by your gloves, but he's scared," she answered.

It was time again for Ruth to stare wide-eyed as her gloves began to move. She had tossed them on the wall and it appeared now that an entire stone was beginning to move. Right before her eyes, a stone, about one foot long, began forming into a figure. As it sat up, the teal gloves became a jacket, and the black ribbed cuffs of the glove became a pair of shorts.

"I thaid, it'ths okay. That thometimeths happenths to things...they bweak," Pheo said, apparently no longer scared as he stood and walked to pick up a stick. Even though he was formed from stone, he appeared weightless and made no sound while moving. His skin was the exact color of the Colonial Field Stone, a grayish tan, and it looked like stone. Ruth wondered if he felt hard like stone. He had on black boots, which appeared to be too big for his feet, and his legs were very skinny, also knock kneed like that of his friends. He, too, had a human face and it was beautiful. It was chiseled out of stone and his features were finely cut. He had jet black eyes and short, almost-black hair. He continued to play with a stick and it made Ruth wonder why he appeared to her because he didn't seem very interested in talking with her. She looked down to

105

find Velo and noticed that she was tippy toeing after Pheo. She, too, picked up a twig with her paw-like hands and they began tapping their sticks in unison on the wall. She watched this in amazement, mystified that Dr. Brooke wasn't concerned, well…not yet anyway. All at once they got on the ground and started lowering their tiny little bodies down the wall; rock climbing at its best.

"We have it," they called out. "Can you help uth?"

Ruth hopped off the wall, onto the path, and neared them with just a few steps. They appeared to both be pulling on a stone which wasn't even sticking out.

"But how…" she began.

"We jutht know," Pheo answered her assuredly.

And sure enough. With little effort, Ruth pulled out the stone, reached in, and easily felt the note this time. She was excited to get another note and she quickly walked to the back of the garden to get closer to Mr. Gabriello's oak tree. "I believe," she stated out loud, answering the familiar question. Maybe she felt a little bolder and maybe she just really anticipated his arrival, but she watched this time as Mr. Gabriello developed from the tree. "Ahh…incredible," she breathed, as she reached out to join hands with him.

She tolerated the noise and the rushing as he pulled her from reality into the world of yesterday. She began to hear talking after a moment and quickly realized that it was she and Roger. They were looking for something. As the picture cleared, she held onto Mr. Gabriello because she noticed that they were moving. "Oh, I'm in a car," she thought, as the pictures were moving past her side. She slid down against the tree into a sitting position to enjoy the ride.

"I think it's just a little bit further, Honey," she said to Roger. "Can you read the number? Oh, wait a minute, stop. It's this corner house."

"No way, Ruthie. This advertisement said it was a dream house."

"No, I'm reading it now. It says to make this your own dream house. Come on, I think it's cute, Roger. Let's go around back and look in the windows. I don't think anyone lives here."

"Well, with the money we've saved, this would be a steal. It's gonna take a while to fix this old house, though," he said as they rounded the corner. They walked hand in hand, but both stopped in their tracks when seeing the back yard.

"Ohhhh, Roger!" Ruthie let out.

"Would you look at that!" he whistled. A back yard with loosely plotted gardens, wild flowers and birds showered the grounds in front of them. Somebody before them, possibly a long time before them, loved this back yard. In the overgrown grasses and perennials, lay years of dedication and love. It didn't take more than that split second for Ruthie and Roger to fall in love with the property that would one day, very soon after that, become their dream house.

"Wait here, Baby Ruth," he said. "I'll be right back." He ran to the car and was gone for just a moment when he returned holding a heavy iron object. "Remember this?" he asked as he held out the beautifully welded wedding gift from his buddy, Kyle. "Wouldn't this look great somewhere on this beautiful property? Maybe a shed door?"

"Ahh, Roger, I forgot about this. You're right, it would look great and I love it…and I love you, too."

"Welcome home, Baby Ruth."

CHAPTER THIRTY-EIGHT

It was some time before Ruth chose to move after that particular trip down memory lane. She preferred instead to stay sitting against the oak tree that harbored Mr. Gabriello and, apparently, her life's story. It felt so good for her to remember. She was finding throughout the past two weeks that certain memories would present themselves to her in short flashes. She'd stop whatever she was doing and try to seize them, but she wasn't always successful; most of the time they would disappear as fast as they flashed.

After a few more minutes of serenity, she heard Bryce calling out for her. "I'm back here," she yelled out. Martha came bounding toward her, leading the way. Behind her were Bev and Bryce.

"Hey, Mom," he said, as he reached down to pull her up. "Wow, it looks really nice back here. The daisies look good...and the fire bushes, too. You've been pretty busy, huh?"

"Oh, thank you, Honey. Well, I am trying to follow my orders...and, you know, I really love it out here," she responded as she brushed herself off. "Oh, hi, Bev. How are you, Honey? Did you bring the kids?"

"Uh...I....uh...Hailey was outside when we pulled up and begged for a little visit," Bev said feeling a little squeamish.

"Oh, I see."

"But…uh…let's just give Hailey a minute…oh…you have done a marvelous job back here," she recovered quickly. It's very peaceful…well, actually," she said, laughing, "it's rather noisy with the birds."

"And it always is," Bryce added.

"Truly," Ruth responded. "They are rather chatty. You know, I think I've got repeat generations of birds living here. I remember when your dad and I first bought this house. The birds were already here making this much noise."

Her comment was met with incredulous looks from both Bev and Bryce. "You remember that, Mom?" Bryce asked. "This is the first time you've said anything like that."

"I do…I actually remember. And…you'll be happy to know that Dr. Brooke seems pleased that I'm making progress, as well."

"Then…do you…?"

"Bryce, no," Bev started.

"I…suppose…that…that…is…my….goal," Ruth responded quietly.

"It's okay, Mom. I'm sorry. How about we go get some drinks?"

As they made their way back down the paths toward the house, Ruth noticed Bev and Bryce looking behind them.

"What's the matter?" Ruth asked.

"Oh, nothing," Bev responded. "I thought I heard someone giggling and it sounded like Heather, but I guess not, since she's next door."

Ruth's eyes opened wide and she tried to nonchalantly look around the garden. She was pretty sure she saw a flash of olive and lime green stripes move in the Frances Williams Hostas and she was also positive that the Temari Verbena was moving more than the slight breeze should have caused.

"Honestly," Bev began, "Your gardens move so beautifully in the breeze, they almost appear to be alive."

"Truly," Ruth replied, nervously. "How about you sit here and I'll bring out some iced tea."

As Ruth closed the sliding glass door, she heard the giggling as well. "Alright, come on out."

"Ahh, haa, ahh, haa...they're very nice. I like them," Ojy excitedly said, as she sashayed in front of Ruth. "They're happy to be here, aren't they? I can tell. I think you're happy, too," she sang out as she twirled in a couple of circles.

"Well, I never thought about it like you are right now," she replied. "I mean, it's been a long time since I've thought that."

"She loved Roger," a little voice squeaked from the kitchen table.

"Oh, you, too?" Ruth smiled at Velo, who was sitting in a kitchen chair adjusting her own little tattered pale yellow jacket. "I don't suppose the new guy is here, too?"

"Herewi am," Pheo was quick to respond.

Ruth spun around toward the stone fireplace which was on the far side of the kitchen. She continued scanning the area until she saw a little bit of movement. He blended in so well on the hearth that she hadn't seen him when walking in.

"Well, it's nice to see you again."

"Yea, well, I hope they come here a wot cause I wike them," Pheo said, jumping off the hearth, which was about two feet off the ground. Ruth stared at him intently, noticing the grain and color changes in the stone of which he was made, while listening to The First Creatures discuss her family.

110

"Family! Oh, my goodness. My family is here!"

She quickly gathered what she needed and headed back outside.

"I'd like to propose a toast" Bryce said, as he lifted his glass of tea toward Bev smiling.   "Here's to new life...new beginnings...and new hope."

"Huh?" Ruth exclaimed. "Are you...?"

"Yes," Bev and Bryce both answered.

"Oh! Congratulations! I don't know why, but this is just perfect." Ruth replied, smiling intently at them.

"So, you're okay?" they questioned her.

"Absolutely. I think I really do feel happy."

CHAPTER THIRTY-NINE

Ruth had finished the final touches of her makeup and considered herself ready for the rehearsal dinner. She still had a half hour before Lydia and Paul were to pick her up so she headed out back with Martha and a glass of lemonade. She sat in her rocking chair to admire the beginning of a beautiful evening and wondered if her friends were going to visit her. It was so peaceful and the birds were actually chirping softly among themselves.

As Ruth rested her head backwards, she thought she was having a flash of memory. It was something to do with Bryce and what he had said last weekend when he was visiting. "Oh, I know…it's the new baby…that's what I'm thinking about," she said out loud, smiling. She really did feel happy and excited about another baby joining the family. Another baby…wait a minute…what was she trying to remember? Baby…baby…baby. "Oh, I wish I could remember this," she said out loud.

"If somebody would help me find another note from Hayden, then I could visit with Mr. Gabriello," she called out to anyone who was listening in the gardens.

Just as soon as she finished saying those words, a little bright star rose out of the Frances Williams Hosta from further back in the gardens and floated toward her. It hovered directly in front of her, and Ruth held her breath, hoping it would pop. It hung in front of her for a minute longer, almost as if it were teasing her. When it did finally pop, Velo fell directly into her lap, causing Ruth to laugh out loud.

Velo looked up at Ruth and gave her the toothiest grin yet. Ruth laughed even harder at this as they looked at each other. "You're never too far away from me, are you?" she continued to laugh.

With that, Velo stood in her lap and reached up with both paw-like hands and felt Ruth's cheeks while she laughed.

"Um...where are you going? You look nice," she squeaked.

"I'm going to the rehearsal dinner with Lydia and Paul, and Lydia's mom...actually, any minute now. So...up you go, I've got to go inside."

Velo hopped off of Ruth's lap and tippy toed away from her, back into the garden. As Ruth watched her disappear into the plants, she reached up and felt her cheeks, relishing the fact that she had been laughing.

"Come on, Martha, let's go inside," Ruth called to her side kick. After one final canvass of the back yard, Martha followed her best friend back inside.

"Oh, it's a good thing we came in when we did, Martha," she said, hurrying toward the door, eager to answer its chime.

"Oh, I'm so glad you're okay, Sweetie, I rang the bell three times and I didn't hear Martha bark. This is wonderful that you've agreed to come to the rehearsal and dinner, and you know my mother is excited as well," Lydia said all in one breath.

Ruth knew her better than to wait for an invitation to speak, so she grabbed her purse while directing Lydia back outside, nodding her head in agreement. Paul stood outside of the car waiting to get the door for Ruth.

"Hi Ruth, it's good to see you," he greeted her warmly.

"Hello, Paul, it's good to see you as well. Thank you for inviting me tonight," she responded.

"Oh, hello Ruth, it's so good to see you again and so good of you to accompany me tonight," Lydia's mother, Lorraine, said, as Ruth got into the car. Ruth instinctively paused, assuming there was no need for her to speak, before realizing that Lorraine wasn't like Lydia, and actually participated in a standard two-way conversation.

As Ruth and Lorraine made small talk on the way to the church, Lydia and Paul carried on their own unique form of communicating.

"Oh, Honey, did you ever finalize the arrangements with George's? They wanted a definite answer about desserts. I held my ground, though, and was insistent that our group was not going to be participating in the dessert stations. I thought I might as well be honest with them, so I told them that we would be strolling through downtown Annapolis after dinner and be stopping for gelato and ice cream on the docks. I don't think they were too happy with me, which was when I told them that you just might call them as well and let them know that our group might prefer to grab a piece of pizza somewhere else instead."

"Lydia…," was all he said.

"Now, Paul. You know I tend to exaggerate a little bit. Don't worry. I actually had a very nice chat with the gentleman at George's…but I did hold my ground," she cooed at him.

"Okay, ladies. That concludes our entertaining ride to the church," Paul chimed out. I do hope you enjoyed our commentator tonight," he added with a smile.

"Oh, my goodness! We're at St. Francis?" Ruth asked, a bit alarmed.

"Why, of course, Ruthie. Where else would we be rehearsing?" Lydia said excitedly. "Oh, Ruthie, look at this landscaping; it's beautiful! Is this Bryce's work?"

"I...I...I don't know...I...I didn't know we were coming here!"

"Is something wrong, Ruth? Are you okay?" Paul asked, as he held her arm gently.

"Paul, Honey, let me talk with her for a minute. You and mom go on in," Lydia said, as she guided Ruth away from them. "Ruthie, look at me," she said, softly. "Are you afraid to go in there because this is where...um...Roger...? Because if you are, then you can wait right here."

"No! I've got to do this," Ruth answered quickly. "This...this...this is ridiculous; I'm a grown woman and I can handle myself. And...and yes...to answer your question," she said very softly, "I haven't been back to church since Roger died. I...I...I don't want anyone looking at me."

"Oh, Ruthie! You are the bravest woman I know. Look at you. I meant to tell you and I should have earlier...I think you look happier than usual."

CHAPTER FORTY

Ruth was sitting by herself on a bench along side of Ego Alley where boats dock directly in the heart of Annapolis. Stepping out of a docked boat puts one in the center of the city within several minutes' walking distance to a dozen waterside restaurants, taverns and shopping. The evening was busy with its usual Friday night hustle and bustle and the sounds of voices from the very young to the very old filling the air. But there might as well have been no one around Ruth, because she couldn't hear them, see them or feel their presence; she was shutting down.

She had tried her hardest to hold it together inside the church while the bridal party practiced their places and lines. She didn't exactly have a duty to perform, other than to accompany the bride's mother, so she went relatively unnoticed; except for one set of eyes that she never saw looking her way.

Dinner followed in the same manner as the church rehearsal. She smiled on command when someone called her name, but the night felt increasingly distant and insignificant. She wanted to walk out of the restaurant. She didn't think anyone would notice, not even Lorraine. And why would she? She was caught up in the excitement of her daughter's wedding festivities, as she should be. She was the mother of the bride and was enjoying all of the busy, last minute details involved with that title. Once outside, Ruth was finally able to breathe deeply. The party had left the restaurant in search of gelato and ice cream. She made her way to the closest bench and sat down, making an excuse of being too full to have dessert, when in reality she didn't remember eating anything. She just needed some space…and some air…and she wanted the pounding to stop within her head. It felt good to sit here…alone. She closed her eyes, lowered her chin and thought she'd just disappear for a while. Every now and then she opened her eyes a little just to get her bearings. After some time had passed, she saw a figure walking toward her.

"No…no….no!" she thought to herself. "No!...not him. What does he want?"

Father Joe Douglass was making his way toward Ruth while holding a cup of dessert in his hand. "W…w…why, hello. May I s…s…it down?" he asked while doing so. He sat quietly for a minute or two while taking small bites of gelato and wondering how to begin. "I…I….find b….blueberry gelato to be quite refreshing in the s…s…summer." He waited another minute before trying again. "It reminds m…m…me of cold lakes and s…s…summertime and of a b…b…book, a childhood book about p…p…icking b…blueberries." Hearing nothing in response, yet again, he decided to just sit for a few more moments, not knowing what else to do. Then, without even thinking of a plan, he started to talk again, knowing later that the idea had to have been divine intervention.

"I…I…I grew up in M…M…Maine, near the water" he began. "I had a pretty good childhood. I was….the younger of t….two boys. M…M…Michael was my older brother…th…three years older. He was my best friend. He let m…me pal around with him and his friends and always made me feel w…welcome. He didn't let anyone s…s…say anything about m…m..my stammering." He paused, while remembering times spent with his brother.

Ruth was aware that he paused and was surprised that she wanted to hear more of his life. She had never viewed Father Joe as anything more than a priest, a priest without a past, that is. She never took the time to think that he was human like her, with feelings. Just then she felt something poking her in her left side. Not imagining what it could be, she looked to her left and gasped! She tried to stifle the gasp by clearing her throat. Velo was standing on the bench, pushing Ruth backward to sit up straighter. In a panic, Ruth moved her left arm to cover Velo from the public, and in doing so, felt her snuggle up against her side, camouflaged by her sleeve and purse. When she straightened, she heard a little, 'Hmph, hmph," and Fr. Joe began to speak again.

"H…He walked me to school every day and m….met me after as well. I…I…I felt important to him. He loved me," he said, while shaking his head in recollection. He sat quietly, wondering whether to continue. "His n…umber was called f…f…for Viet…Vietnam, right after h…his eighteenth birthday, and j…just b…before college. H…He wanted to be a h…history teacher. He didn't have to s…stay long in Vietnam. He d…died j..ust b…before Christmas," he spoke, softly.

"Father Joe, I am so very …," Ruth began.

"We d…didn't go to M…Mass th…that Christmas. In f…fact, m…my m…m…mother and f..father never went b…ack to church. M…My life b…became very d..ifferent for the remainder of m…my high school. I followed m..my parents' b…behavior…lots of anger…b…bitterness toward God." He paused and the two of them sat silently for a minute.

"So you know…?" Ruth asked, quietly.

"Yes, I…I've been w…w…where you are."

Ruth tried to hold it in, but the more she tried, the tighter her stomach became. Her shoulders began to shake and the sobs came once more, only this time, for the first time, she shared them with her priest. In between sobs, she poured out her heart to him.

"I'm sorry…I don't know… (sob)…I don't know how to stop crying. I want to stop…(sob)…I want to stop so badly, but I can't! I want to understand, but something is wrong…(sob)…something is missing…(sob)…there's a big black

118

hole in my life from last year and I don't know why. Nobody will tell me anything! I'm sorry I don't go to church, but it hurts…(sob)…and I have to be mad at someone. I'm mad at my little neighbor…(sob)…and I don't even know why! Please, Father Joe…(sob)…please tell me how to stop hurting…(sob)," she begged. At some point during her rant, Father Joe had pushed his handkerchief into her hand. She continued gasping a little as her sobs subsided, while wiping her eyes and nose. When she opened her eyes and looked down, she realized she was also holding Velo tightly in her left hand, but she didn't even care if anyone saw; let people wonder.

"If you d…on't mind m…my asking," Father Joe began, "What do you remember?"

"I can remember things from way back when I was younger with Roger…like when we got married and when we bought our house…really nice memories."

"Do you c…consider that a start…remembering that much?" he asked. "Because if y…you do, th..then it sounds like y…you're on track."

Ruth nodded her head in agreement. "Thank you…for listening…it must have been difficult to come over here."

"Oh, he chuckled, "I…I've had t…tougher," he said, encouragingly, patting her back. "H..How a..bout I w…walk with you t..to get some gelato?"

CHAPTER FORTY-ONE

Ruth couldn't believe she was back in the same place where her melt down began yesterday. But today was different. She felt decidedly better and more light-hearted than she had in a long time. Talking with Father Joe was surprisingly uplifting, and it was something she hadn't planned on doing. She even thought that she'd like to talk again when the situation presented itself, but probably not today, because today belonged to Lydia and Paul.

Mel and Pat had picked her up and arrived at the church with plenty of time to spare. Unlike yesterday, Ruth felt such a sense of peace when they pulled into the parking lot. If someone would have told her yesterday that she was going to be excited to arrive at St. Francis the following day, she wouldn't have believed it. "It's funny how time changes things," she thought to herself. "No, not changes, but heals," she smiled. "Father Joe healed from a tragic loss and so will I…in time."

She was escorted to the front pew where she would be sitting with Lorraine, once the mothers were seated. She was able to look around a little since she was more relaxed and noticed many co-workers arriving. "How nice it is that we have such an occasion for which to dress up," she thought, as she smoothed out some wrinkles in her dress. She herself had worn a dress made of raw silk in a soft shade of lavender. She smiled at the thought of the article she read which gave helpful tips as to what colors to wear when going gray. She had added many pieces of blue and lavender clothing to her wardrobe over the past few years since she began turning gray...or silver, as she liked to say. She also switched to a peach colored lip gloss because of what the article had said.

Ruth moved further down the pew to make sure that there was enough room for Lorraine. In doing so, she slid her purse and shoulder wrap further down the pew as well. She really liked her new wrap, which had been a Mother's Day gift a couple of weeks ago. The soft white fabric had silver threads running through it, and she, of course, hoped it matched the silver on her head. While sliding the wrap, though, it seemed to be bulkier than it should. But when she tried to flatten it, she felt a definite wiggle from underneath. She jumped a little and a small gasp escaped her, which she quickly concealed with a cough. She lifted the edge of the wrap just enough to get proof of her suspicion...a toothy grin. "Uh, oh," she thought, and with that, Ruth held down her left hand to keep the intruder undiscovered.

A few minutes later, with everyone in their correct seating, the wedding party procession began. It had been some time since Ruth had been to a wedding, and she found it to be exhilarating. She forgot that she was guarding Velo under her wrap, and when she looked over, there she sat, decked out in her usual attire of an olive and lime colored striped tutu with a butter colored jacket. She could have been a hosta sitting next to Ruth, except for the fact that her little legs were sticking out in front of her with tattered brown leather ballet slippers tapping to the beat of the organist's music. When Ruth tried to arrange her wrap back over her, Velo gave her a pleading look as if to say, "I promise to behave."

"How can I say no to that?" she thought. "There are so many bright and beautifully colored outfits in the church, I'm sure Velo will look like just another jacket or piece of clothing."

While watching Lydia and Paul look into each others' eyes, she had no trouble daydreaming about her recent trips into her past. In some ways it seemed as close as yesterday when she and Roger exchanged their vows.

Mindful of her somewhat secret stowaway to her left, she was careful that her hand remain somewhere around Velo to keep her camouflaged. She heard occasional "hmphs" and saw an expression in Velo's face that she couldn't quite place. She liked it, and it brought her back in time, but she just couldn't remember what point in time it was. But what Ruth wasn't expecting was the not too softly hummed tune, "do..do..dodo," put to the tune of "Here Comes the Bride." With another fake cough, she slid Velo against her hips and motioned with her hand to stop making noise.

"Um, you're squashing me…and, um, I'm not singing," Velo managed to squeak out. At this, Ruth began clearing her throat trying to silence her.

"Are you okay, Ruth?" Lorraine whispered to her. "Would you like a piece of hard candy?"

"It's just a tickle, but thank you," she quickly retorted.

"Do..do..dodo" Ruth heard again, and at the same time noticed a flash of bright pink around her ankles.

"Oh, no!" Ruth thought. She kicked around her ankles a bit to try to relay her displeasure at Ojy's timing. Here she was back in church for the first time in a year, happy about it, happy to be witnessing Lydia and Paul's special day, and The First Creatures chose now to present themselves to the public. Really? She didn't know what to do. She thought she should be paying better attention to the wedding Mass, but she was having great difficulty, fearful her little friends were about to expose themselves and Ruth's knowledge of them.

After declaring Paul and Lydia as husband and wife, Father Joe made light of Lydia's winded vows. "I…I'm sure y…your b…beautifully s…stated vows are indicative of m…many years of g…good conversations." With that, the congregation laughed out loud. At the same time, down below the pew, Ojy escaped from being trapped between Ruth's feet, and she began sashaying as a bride would, away from Ruth. Ruth laughed out loud as well as she noticed Ojy disappearing under the pew. When she looked up again, she noticed Father Joe smiling toward her. She sighed and smiled back at him, feeling happier than she had in a long time.

CHAPTER FORTY-TWO

Ruth was enjoying her morning coffee on the back patio along with Martha. It was overcast with a prediction for rain later in the day. It hadn't rained in over a week so Ruth was glad to have it. She didn't mind the rain, because it fulfilled some of her watering duties, and a well watered lawn enabled it to hold on to its color of spring green for as long as possible.

"Oh, Martha, Ole' Girl, I had a nice time at Lydia's wedding. I was happy there, in the walls of St. Francis, and I think I'll go back," she smiled, looking down at her trusted friend. "I was afraid to go back, but now I'm not so sure why I was afraid." Martha stood and laid her snout in Ruth's lap, wagging her tail. "Life goes on, my friend, life goes on." They rested together in silence while enjoying the serene atmosphere.

A cool spring breeze gently lifted each blade of grass that wafted in the first light's song. It was peaceful in the Lily gardens and Ruth soaked in this sensation that had been missing for a year. Somewhere in the gardens, a mourning dove cooed as if looking for its mate. Ruth sometimes thought that it, too, was grieving for its lost love, but other times, like this morning, she thought it signified tranquility and hope. As the dove continued to coo its song, Ruth thought it sounded rather close, so she opened her eyes to find it.

It didn't take long for her to follow the cooing sound that was coming from a clump of beautiful Russian Sage that stood about three feet tall. The plants had hundreds of light green pencil-thin foliage completely covered in lavender blossoms. They gently swayed with no effort at all in a soothing motion with the slightest breeze. Sage was one of Ruth's favorites, not only because it comes back each year, but because it spreads and blossoms all spring, summer and fall. "Oh, my goodness," she exclaimed. "I wonder if that dove is caught in the sage?"

"Oo-wah-hooo, hoo-hoo," it called. Ruth walked slowly as she got closer, expecting the bird to startle and fly away, but it didn't. It looked perfectly content, sitting in the sage, and continued to coo at her. It was definitely a mourning dove, that she could tell. Its feathers were a combination of colors of soft brown and ruddy tan, with touches of black on its wing tips. It sat gracefully perched on the sage's foliage, just patiently looking at Ruth...waiting.

Feeling a bit giddy at being so close to a wild bird, she spoke nonsensically to it, knowing it wouldn't understand. "Now you know," she scolded, "I don't speak your language, so if we're going to communicate, you'll have to give English a try," she chuckled. Immediately upon saying that, Ruth fell backwards into a sitting position because the dove began to transform and stretch right before her eyes. It was a graceful transformation, if that's possible, and within twenty seconds or so, Ruth was looking face to face with another First Creature, another girl. Maybe Ruth had been through too much lately, or maybe she was just getting used to witnessing creatures form in her gardens, but whatever the case may be, she wasn't afraid.

"Hi," the First Creature said, sweetly. "It's nice to meet you."

Although not afraid, Ruth was still speechless. She sat closely to the creature and marveled once more at this phenomenon. This little girl was the size of the others, about one foot tall. She was wearing tannish brown cargo shorts, and like the others, had very skinny, knock kneed legs. She had sleek dark colored shoes, which resembled something to be worn in the water, and she was wearing a multi-colored brown and tan long sleeved jacket with tails, much like that of a tuxedo. Her soft brown, almost dirty blond hair had a wild appearance with feathers scattered throughout her strands.

After Ruth found her voice, she stated, "And it's nice to meet you, as well."

"I wasn't allowed to talk with you until you invited me," the little bird creature said, softly.

"Well, I'm certainly glad that I invited you, then. And...what is your name?" Ruth inquired.

"Ceepa," she smiled.

"How pretty, and...do you know the other...First Creatures, Ceepa?"

Ceepa smiled and nodded her head, yes, and then motioned for Ruth to follow.

"Oh, I think I know what's happening here. Are you leading me to one of Hayden's notes?"

Ceepa just smiled in response as Ruth followed. Once again Ruth was being led to the section of garden in the rear of her property where the oak tree grew. Ceepa walked calmly and was not in a hurry. She stopped at one point and felt the stone wall with both hands, kind of rubbing her palms along its surface. Shaking her head no, she continued to walk quietly. She stopped again, further along, and rubbed her hands again on the front surface of the stone. Nodding her head yes this time, she began to pull on the stone with both hands, trying to rock it loose.

Ruth moved forward to help her, but Ceepa smiled sweetly and shook her head no. She faced toward the back of the gardens and cooed, "Oo-wah-hooo, hoo-hoo." It wasn't a second later when a hosta leaf was pushed up by two little paw-like hands. The little familiar creature that tippy toed towards them made Ruth's heart beat faster.

"You're always here," Ruth marveled.

"Hmph, hmph," Velo replied, while cocking her head to the side with her lips turned in, yet puffed out.

Together the two First Creatures worked on the stone to loosen it from the wall. They worked in unison to push, pull, and rock it. When they had it sufficiently loosened, they stopped and looked up to Ruth, who was watching them in amazement.

"Shall I?" she asked.

They nodded in agreement so she reached in. When she once again couldn't feel the note, Ceepa motioned that she would retrieve it. She fit easily into the hole and all that could be seen of her after crawling in was her little black shoes. She wiggled out backwards holding Hayden's question and held it up to Ruth, who gently took it and began walking toward the oak tree.

She stood before the tree that protected her memories, wanting to reclaim her past. "I believe," was all she had to say. It seemed respectful to look down as Mr. Gabriello formed from the tree above her. When she sensed he was present, she looked up to meet his gaze. Though no longer appalled by his appearance, her heart ached when she looked into his eyes. She wanted to speak with him and ask him questions, but she didn't have that type of communication with him. He showed her things that he was holding for her, things she had given him. She didn't understand how a creature inside of a tree was keeping things for her that she didn't want. She wanted them now, but he only offered them to her in small segments. Velo had once referred to him as "The Keeper," and Ruth understood now why she called him that. So far Mr. Gabriello had only showed her memories which were joyful and pleasing to her, but she somehow knew that she would see more than that, perhaps even the tragic day that was totally gone from her memory. Sometimes when she was alone and it was very quiet, she tried remembering what she could of last spring. She had found a stack of graded papers at school that were tucked in a filing drawer. They were dated late May of last year. Why had she never returned those papers, and why would she have put them away in a drawer? Wasn't she there? That's where her thoughts stopped. She had also found a calendar shoved in the back of a bookshelf. The last entry was on Memorial Day of last year. She and Roger were going to Bryce's for a BBQ. Although she doesn't remember it. "I'm pretty sure I lost Roger right about then," she figured, "But I do know that it's been a year, a very sad and confusing year." She was making progress, though. Dr. Brooke listened to Ruth relay her memories as she received them, and she assured her that she was moving in the right direction. "You're moving at your own pace, Ruth," Dr. Brooke had told her. "Your psyche knows when and what you can handle, and this is how you are processing it. No two people recall in exactly the same way. You're writing your own story, Ruth. It's nobody else's to tell. And those, my friend, are my Grandma Bailey's own wise words," Dr. Brooke had told her with great satisfaction. Ruth could tell that Dr. Brooke enjoyed including her grandmother's rock solid advice on occasion, and Ruth was happy to receive some of it.

Ruth raised her right hand to join with Mr. Gabriello's, ready to accept more from her past. She ignored the screeching sound, once again, as Mr. Gabriello pulled her from today and into a life she once knew.

When she heard the birds chattering to one another again, she slowly opened her eyes. Wait a minute. She was still in the garden, but it looked different and someone was moving toward her. The figure was blurry, but very tall. She couldn't tell if this was the past or the present, but as the figure drew closer, she sighed and smiled. Roger came into view; young, tall, and beautiful.

"Hey, Baby, how you doin?" he asked. "Come on, sit down for a while. You've been working all morning."

"I'm okay, Hon, I've been taking breaks, and the little guy loves it out here in the gardens we're building," she answered lovingly, while motioning to the life kicking within her.

"Hey, Little Baby," Roger said while pulling Ruth close to him. He had sat down behind her and pulled her up close to him so he could wrap his arms around her and the life she contained. "One more month, Baby, and I'll be able to show you around the gardens, and you can help me make some decisions."

Ruthie loved the way he loved her and the baby they were expecting. He talked to it every day, and was convinced that it could hear him. At night, when they went to bed, he put his face close to her abdomen, and told stories to the baby of when he was a little boy. They couldn't wait for the baby's arrival, and counted down the days.

Ruth began to fidget and pull out of her memory. "No, no, please, Mr. Gabriello, please let me see Bryce," she begged. Just before she closed her eyes to continue, she felt someone holding her hand. She looked down and realized that she was holding Ceepa against her, who was looking up to her with gentle, forlorn eyes.

Ruth was instantly back in the past again and felt an incredible amount of pain. It didn't take her long to realize that she was in hard labor in the delivery room. She was exhausted, but wanted to see Roger. When she opened her eyes, she saw him talking with the doctor. She knew instantly that something was very wrong by the way he looked at her.

"Roger," she said, weakly. "How long has it been?"

"It's okay, Baby," he said, wearily. "Just a little bit longer. The doctor thinks maybe just a few more pushes."

She thought she was going in and out of consciousness and heard a lot of commotion. "She's co…"

Peace…quiet…tranquility…she was comfortable here. She could stay here.

"Got her!" someone yelled. "Let's go!"

When Ruth awoke, she was not in the delivery room. She felt warmth near her hand and noticed Roger's head. He was asleep in a chair leaning over on to her bed.

"Roger!" she said, excitedly. "Where's our baby? Roger!"

When he lifted his head, she saw his tear streaked cheeks as he shook his head. "I'm so sorry, Ruthie, she didn't make it. Our little girl didn't make it," he sobbed.

"No!...No!," Ruth cried out loud, as she fell forward into today. She fell onto her knees, remembering the pain as if it were today. "Roger! No! Where's our baby?" she cried. She remained there, on the garden floor, raining her grief in remembrance of losing their baby girl. As she lay in recollection, she was able to keep remembering more of that time period before Bryce was born, without the help of Mr. Gabriello. She and Roger had clung to each other through their mourning, and received healing and grace. She watched them hunger for their faith instead of pushing it away as she had done this past year. They were afraid to have another child, but they tried anyway, never losing hope. They took some time and traveled out west, exploring the beautiful mountains and canyons, and took in all the beauty that was there for them to see.

Life grew within Ruthie again, and one and a half years after losing their first baby, Bryce was born to them, filling their lives with more joy than they thought possible. Ruth didn't care to remember the birth of him, but somewhat fast forwarded to the time when she was holding him, rejoicing in his life and remembering him as an infant and toddler.

After a very long time lying in the garden, remembering events by herself, Ruth finally sat up and regained her current bearings. Her new friend, Ceepa, had remained very close to her during this period. Ruth remembered the look that Ceepa had in her eyes just before she relived her baby dying. She had a different look now, though. She saw a wholesome gentleness about her, a look of truth and tranquility, and an all knowing, "it happened and I survived it" presence about her. Perhaps Ruth was relating to this look.

"Thank you for being with me. You knew, didn't you? What I was about to see?" Ruth asked.

Ceepa didn't react how most might have when asked that question. She nodded in agreement to it, but without emotion. Meanwhile, a soft pitter-pattering of footsteps in the dirt, followed by a pause, and then more pitter-pattering, brought the little creature which Ruth so yearned to see, into view.

With her paw-like hands at her chest, she squeaked the only thought she could think to say, "Hmph hmph."

"It's okay, I'm alright," Ruth responded, tenderly, while patting her lap for Velo to come sit.

CHAPTER FORTY-THREE

Mel was deep in discussion with another in her office as Ruth approached. Not necessarily eavesdropping, but just trying to figure out if she could join in the conversation or simply interrupt, she paused at the door.

"I want so badly to say something," she heard a voice, demanding. "I need to put my grief to rest as well. Are you sure enough time hasn't passed?"

"Huh!" Ruth gasped, frozen and shell shocked in disbelief as to what she was hearing. "Who's in there with Mel? Are they talking about me?" her thoughts rushed. She wanted to turn and walk away, but her feet wouldn't move.

"Excuse me one minute," she heard Mel say softly.

Ruth turned abruptly at that point, but it was too late.

"Ruth, stop! Come back," Mel pleaded, a little too smoothly, as Alison Byrnes, a fifth grade teacher, quickly exited Mel's office.

Ruth knew Alison only a little. She was friendly enough, and about ten years younger than Ruth. She had never given Alison much thought until right now, and in a flash of memory, remembered overhearing Alison another time as one who was frustrated with Ruth. She could also now picture Alison lowering her eyes as they passed each other in the halls.

"Hey, come on in," Mel encouraged her, clearing off some papers from the small couch she had in her office. "I'm so glad I get to see you two days in a row."

Embarrassed and not really knowing how to start, Ruth searched for her words. "You... were talking about me with her, weren't you?"

"I have never lied to you, Ruth, and I'm not going to start," Mel said to her in her professional voice. "You need to always be able to trust me," she said, patting Ruth's knee. "Do you believe me?"

Believe? This is a word that Ruth only associated with Mr. Gabriello. Ruth hated it when she became confused like this and reached up to massage her temples.

"Ruth?"

"I do," she said slowly, "But were you talking about me?"

"People are curious about your healing and your grief, Ruth. I don't disclose any personal information about you, nor would I disclose any about Alison to you."

Mel patted her own thighs, declaring the subject changed. "Wow, Lydia's wedding was very sweet, wasn't it?"

"It was, and I...I enjoyed myself. I wasn't so sure the night before the wedding, how things would go, you know, going back to St. Francis, but...it was...good."

Mel smiled at her while she was talking, nodding in agreement. Since she was good friends with Ruth and privy to the past year's events, she was able to fill in between the lines as Ruth spoke.

"You're making progress, Ruth, you know. You're able to socialize a little more and feel comfortable about it. I was watching you at the wedding, and you were enjoying yourself. And...I must say...no more phone calls when you get home," she added.

"Home is easier...much easier," Ruth responded, definitely loosening up. "I look forward to going home now. I...I'm starting to remember parts of my past, and... I must admit...well...it's really something, to be able to remember," she responded. "Did I tell you that Bryce and Bev are expecting another baby?" she asked.

"Well, I had heard that from Bev during our morning workout," Mel responded. "Oh, and I know they're just thrilled. Bev's feeling okay, but she's sticking to a land workout from here on out. She gets winded during her pregnancies and doesn't want to risk another water accident."

"Did I...ever tell you, Mel,...that Roger and I lost our first baby?" she asked softly. "A little girl. It was a difficult labor and the cord was compressed for too long, we were told. It's something to think of, you know. If that had happened now, it would have been easier for modern technology to detect," she sighed. "It makes me happy, though, to think that kind of thing can't happen to Bev and Bryce, and...come the new year," she said, more upbeat, "I'll have my hands full with three grandchildren. Life goes on, my friend, doesn't it?"

"It certainly does, my friend," Mel responded, patting Ruth's hand.

CHAPTER FORTY-FOUR

Feeling light hearted about sharing some of her older memories with Mel, Ruth drove the short distance home, eager to see what the night would bring. She often thought about the First Creatures, and hoped they would appear to either show her some of her tucked away past, or just spend some time with her. It was more often than not, that Velo would present herself when Ruth was wishing for company. She enjoyed her matter of fact judgment and knew Velo would keep her thought process on track. Her favorite times spent with Velo included cuddling in her rocking chair, knowing that she wasn't alone. It felt normal for her to have someone to touch and hold. She felt more at peace with herself during this time and yearned for a tomorrow, which she acknowledged to herself, was something she hadn't wanted for some time.

As she pulled into her driveway, she could see a little visitor waiting for her on her porch rocking chair. "Oh, boy, hmmm, ...oh well," she sighed. She made a conscious effort to hold on to the light hearted feeling, and try for a new beginning.

"Hello," she said, smiling, as she reached her porch.

"Hi, Miss Ruth," said the small and shy voice belonging to Hailey. "I brought you some cookies," she said as she motioned to the small brown lunch bag she held in her lap. "I made them for you."

"Well, isn't that nice," she barely got out. She was starting to breathe erratically and feel faint. "Get a hold of yourself!" she thought. "Would...would you like to come in?" she stumbled.

"Okay," Hailey replied softly. "Mommy doesn't know I'm here."

"Well, then, maybe you had better go. Thank you for the cookies," she rushed, thinking this was her out.

"No, I can come inside for a little while. Mommy says you won't talk to me, but maybe you will with some cookies. I...I used to bring you cookies and we'd drink lemonade."

"Oh, okay, would you like some?" she said, taking a deep breath.

"Yes, please."

Ruth poured two glasses of lemonade and set them down on the table. She sat down across from Hailey and tried to calm down her breathing while looking into her little neighbor's anxious eyes. Her head started to pound and she thought for a minute that she heard the same screeching sound that she would hear when traveling back in time with Mr. Gabriello. She squinted her eyes to help block out the pounding and hoped that Hailey would somehow just disappear.

"What's the matter, Miss Ruth?" said her small voice.

"I don't know," she could honestly answer. She really didn't know, but she had a very strong sensation that Roger's death was closely linked to Hailey. "I've just now gotten a very bad headache and...I...I don't feel so good."

"Maybe it would help if you talked about it. That's what Mommy says."

Her words sort of snapped Ruth out of her anxiety and she stared at Hailey. She had the feeling, all of a sudden, that she was once again listening to Father Joe tell her, gently, that she wasn't the only one who experienced a terrible loss.

"Oh...I'm sorry, Hailey," Ruth said, getting emotional, "I get so upset sometimes when I think of whom I'm missing. You miss Mr. Roger, too. I never thought about it from your perspective. Those were very wise words, Hailey." Thinking of how to make more conversation, she added, "How old are you now?"

"I'm seven. I'm in first grade."

Ruth sucked in her breath, frantically calculating her situation.

"I'm not in your class. Is that what you're wondering? Mommy and Daddy say that you can't remember things. I'm not in your class. I'm in Mrs. Adams' class."

Hailey's words were said so sweetly, it made Ruth wonder how she could only be seven. She couldn't believe that Hailey was in Julie's class. "I don't remember Julie mentioning to me that she had Hailey," Ruth thought. "Does she even know that Hailey is my neighbor and that she used to come to my house and play?"

"Can I ask you something?" Hailey interrupted Ruth's thoughts.

Ruth nodded, still pondering.

"What does 'alone since five' mean?"

"I don't understand, what are you saying?" Ruth responded, shaking her head.

"Daddy says that you were alone since five and that's why you're so sad."

Ruth just stared at Hailey, trying to make sense of what she was saying. She was already shaken for not realizing that Hailey was in the first grade for this entire past year, and in Julie's class, and now this, a strange comment, alone since five. She had the strangest sensation that she'd heard this particular description before, but she couldn't pinpoint it.

"I wish I knew what he meant, Hailey, but I don't," Ruth said, sincerely.

"Well, that's all he'll say, and he didn't say it to me. Nobody will talk to me," she said, starting to cry. "Nobody will tell...tell... me anything, and I'm so lonely!"

All of a sudden, Ruth felt such compassion for Hailey. Whatever feelings she had stored up inside her mysterious past seemed to wash away when listening to Hailey cry out in loneliness. This little girl's world was also changed by the same horrible incident which affected Ruth's. No one will explain to Ruth what happened and it sounds as if no one will explain to Hailey either.

"We're both in the black," she thought. I can't remember, and she's too young to be told. "Oh, my gosh, we have kindred connections, and look how I've been treating her," she thought, despairingly.

"I'll tell you what," Ruth began, "I'm just now realizing that I haven't been a very good neighbor to you. I, too, don't understand what's happening all the time, but, I'm learning to move forward. How about we bring these delicious chocolate chip cookies outside along with our lemonade? Maybe we can play, I Spy."

"Really?" was all Hailey could get out.

"Come on."

Together they sat at the patio table enjoying their snack and game, but mostly, they enjoyed each other's company.

CHAPTER FORTY-FIVE

Bev was just returning home from her workout, an early morning run through the city streets of downtown Annapolis. Now that she had confined herself to land-only workouts, she was especially glad on the days she went running versus working out on the ergometer. She was in tune with her body's abilities and checked her pulse regularly to make sure it didn't exceed the maximum rate for pregnancy. She missed the water terribly since the accident, but knew her limitations. Just as with her previous two pregnancies, she became winded easily and knew it was too dangerous to risk being hit like that again by an oar. Mel knew how much Bev missed being on the water, so she invited her family over for the evening to do a little light sculling on Weems Creek. The gentle rowing on the quiet waters mixed with good company was a perfect solution for everyone involved. Bev was so excited, not just to get on the water again, but for a chance to relax with Mel and Pat.

Bryce was already gone on the school run, but she expected him back shortly. He hadn't quite recovered yet from Bev's scare, and found himself checking in with her after her morning workouts before he left for Stonehenge. She thought it was extra sweet of him to be so caring, and knew it would probably wear off a little once her new pregnancy routine was established.

She poured herself a cup of decaf and headed out to the living room with it and a bowl of cereal to ponder her day's schedule. She wasn't due in to work until later, so she enjoyed her alone time in the morning. She was able to tend to her "Chesapeake" in the back yard, and the gardens as well, before heading off to work. But for now, during breakfast, she'd relax with her feet up. Both ends of her couch had reclining backs and foot rests which extended out. She loved this feature about their couch and found it perfect for pregnancy.

She had a good view, from where she sat, of their entire living room. It was decorated in dual companion colors of ocean blues. She and Bryce both liked the nautical theme and found it easy to accessorize when living by the water. They both preferred the silver and pewter accent pieces and had found some good buys of crabs and starfish. She had received some upscale Maryland and Annapolis dish towels as gifts and sewn them into throw pillows. No one knew the better on these cute head cushions. In front of her was a wall display of family pictures combined in a variety of sizes and shapes. In the past she couldn't look at the arrangement without crying, but had received healing through her faith, husband, friends, and like most others in her situation, time. She now used the arrangement as a reminder of how precious life is. She blew a kiss to the gathering of faces and said a quiet prayer.

A short time later, she heard the front door opening. "In here," she called to Bryce. "There's coffee," she added, giggling, because he had made it himself earlier.

"How was your run?" he called from the kitchen.

"Perfect, and I feel great. Oh, and guess what? Mel and Pat invited us for dinner and some light sculling."

"Okay, that sounds good. I haven't seen Pat in a while. It will be good to catch up," he said as he sat down beside her.

"Thank you," she said, tenderly.

He looked over at her, noticed something in her eyes and sensed what she had been remembering.

"No, thank *you*."

140

With that, he leaned over and put his head in her lap, facing her. Gently feeling her abdomen, he spoke. "Hi, little baby. Your grandfather told me that he used to talk to me while I was growing inside of my mother, and he just knew that I could hear him. I'm pretty sure I could...so I...I...talked to your brother and sister while they were growing,...too." His shoulders began to shake and Bev reached for his hands and held him tightly.

After a moment, he asked, "When will it stop?"

"Do you mean, when will you stop remembering? Never, I hope." She gently ran her fingers through his long wavy hair, cherishing life.

"You were asleep last night when I came home from the association meeting, so I didn't tell you that I stopped by my mom's. She didn't answer the door bell so I let myself in to make sure she was okay. I figured she was out back, and she was. I saw her through the sliding glass door, sitting at the table with Hailey. They were having such a good time together and I didn't want to interrupt them, so I just left her a note."

"That's good to hear," Bev said. "Mary told me that Hailey has also been struggling and wanted to spend time with your mom."

"I'm glad they found each other again," Bryce added.

CHAPTER FORTY-SIX

The middle of June brought the end of the school year. And with that came goodbyes to be said to both the first graders and fellow teachers. Though Ruth's classroom had been her saving grace last summer as a chance to reclaim some normalcy, she found herself eager to pack it all away and get home. It had been a little more than a year since Roger died, and she truly thought she could say she was coming to terms with her situation. She was comfortable in her house by herself, she learned to downsize in the amounts of food she prepared, and she didn't find herself talking out loud to him anymore.

At her most recent appointment with Dr. Brooke, she told her upon entering what she was thinking.

"I think I've come a long way in my grief recovery, and I'm wondering if I should, perhaps, stop coming to see you. I mean, I enjoy talking with you and hearing what your Grandma Bailey might have to say on occasion, but, look at me...no tears," Ruth motioned with her hands.

"I'm glad that you're eager to be completely healed, Ruth, as that is our goal for you. The technical term I'll use is that I'd like you to reach a state of psychological equilibrium, and you haven't achieved that yet. The healing process can sometimes take up to two years for some people."

"Two years!" Ruth interjected. "But I can check off so many achievements I've reached this year. While I'm still so very sad about Roger's death, I do think about other things, you know. I haven't had anyone tell me recently that I've forgotten to be somewhere that I should have been, and you know what else, I've been to some social outings just recently."

"Alright…if it's okay with you, I'd like to show it to you in a different way. Say you have surgery to fix a problem. Should you heal without stitches? No…I didn't think you'd agree to that. How about refusing to wear a cast after a bone has been reset? Right. You see, Ruth, by coming to see me and sharing your progress with me, it lets me know if the stitches are ready to come out, or, if the cast can come off. We don't have the ability to take an x-ray of your grief to judge how well you are healing, but I can tell by listening to you, where you are in the process. I may not be that old, but I have helped hundreds through the adaptation to loss," she said with a smile.

Ruth smiled in return and chuckled to herself. Apparently Dr. Brooke could also read minds. Even though Ruth was attentively listening to her counselor, she was admiring Dr. Brooke's young mocha colored skin that was virtually flawless.

"When I first met you, Ruth, I classified you as being in phase one of the mourning process. You were numb to the world, if you will. Your son found you, nearly dead, outside. Do you remember? You desperately wanted the pain to stop, so you did what you had to do and became numb. You erased so much of your life during the two days you spent in the hot sun. Once you were rehydrated in the hospital, though, it was determined that you couldn't speak of what happened, nor could you remember your previous life. You knew who you were, but you couldn't tell me anything, even from the day before. Throughout the course of this year, however, your family and I have witnessed you regaining some of who you were. After you moved through phases two and three, I decided to give you a project to help you with decision making."

"Ahh…grief work," Ruth responded.

"Exactly. To speak of phases implies just sitting passively, waiting to be healed. But, it's the belief of many counselors to prescribe grief work, a physically active approach to healing, and this can be compared to physical therapy. You know, once the cast is off, the healing process is not over. Next comes the physical, strenuous healing. And this, Ruth, is where you are right now."

"She's looking awfully young again," Ruth thought, "even though she's impeccably groomed and dressed, which usually comes with age." But, what choice did Ruth have? She sat in silence for a moment, taking in what Dr. Brooke had said.

"I'm happy with your progress, Ruth, very happy, but I would like you to still come in for regular sessions."

"Alright. I'll continue," Ruth replied, as she stood up to leave. "Dr. Brooke...there is... something I don't understand. I remember you saying something...either to me or to Bryce, and I'm confused. You said if I deny the specifics of loss, then I might suffer from slight distortion to a full-blown delusion. Are you saying that the First Creatures aren't real? Because I can tell you, right now, Dr. Brooke, that I'm not hallucinating. I thought maybe I was at first, but I know now that I'm not."

"I wasn't referring to the First Creatures, Ruth. I know that they are helping you."

CHAPTER FORTY-SEVEN

The First Creatures were safe and sound, with a hand stamped approval from Dr. Brooke. This was important to Ruth because she relied on their friendship, and didn't want to be told by anyone, even her grief counselor, that she should stop associating with them. Truth be told, she didn't know how to stop them from coming to her. She often asked for Velo, who would just appear when called, but the others seemed to come and go at their own liking, and somehow seemed to be involved in the memory with which she was presented. She kept her friendship with them shielded from everyone except Dr. Brooke. She couldn't explain their presence to herself, even though she treasured them, so she didn't want to try explaining to anyone else.

She had just finished picking up two gift certificates for Bryce's birthday that was coming soon. She got him a movie gift pack to a local theatre, and also a gift certificate to The Severn Inn which sat right on the Severn River, overlooking the Naval Academy. It had a beautiful outside deck that made for perfect outdoor dining. The twinkle lights that adorned the deck and shrubbery year round enhanced the atmosphere and created a lovely natural setting. Because she envisioned Bryce and Bev going alone, she also included an offer to babysit the kids. She would leave it up to them where they would like Ruth to babysit, either at her house or theirs. She hadn't offered to babysit in a year, but she believed that this offer was one of the accomplishments she had achieved, and one that she had mentioned to Dr. Brooke.

Rain was predicted for later in the afternoon and Ruth was once again happy that Mother Nature would help her out with her gardening chores. She loved the way the atmosphere changed an hour preceding a storm. The winds picked up, the air temperature dropped, and all of the garden participants swayed to the rhythm of the impending storm song. She'd sit outside and watch the clouds changing colors and stay in her rocking chair until she was forced inside by rain.

She had a while to wait before the rain made its way to her back yard so she took the opportunity to sit with an iced tea at her patio table and watch the coming attraction. Strong breezes from the northwest came in bursts and caused the swaying leaves to rustle back and forth quickly.

"Hello...any friends out here?" she called out to the picturesque grounds. With that, another strong breeze shook all greenery, both high and low. The lowest foliage, which was bejeweled with bright pink miniature petals, continued to shake after the winds died down. Ruth held her breath, hoping for some excitement to explode from the plant, and sure enough, it did. The Temari Verbena appeared to duplicate itself as Ojy danced away from it.

"Ahh, haa, ahh, haa," she giggled as she sashayed toward Ruth. "Did I just hear you call for me?"

"Well, hello, my little friend. Yes, you did. And it's nice to see you on better terms," Ruth said, referring to her unexpected appearance at Lydia's wedding.

"Ahh, haa, yea," she giggled again, rolling her eyes a bit. "I just loveeeee weddings. They're soooo romantic," she cooed, while mimicking the bridal march.

"Well, go ahead now and march to your heart's content," Ruth replied, "because there's no one here to see you."

"Ahh, haa...sorry about that. I just couldn't help myself, though, because I was soooo excited."

146

"So I gather, little one. Um....is there anything you want to show me in the garden? A story, perhaps?" Ruth asked, a bit timidly.

"Ah haaaa...come on...let's go," she said, excitedly, as she sashayed circles around Ruth's feet.

"Um...Ojy...wait for me," called Ruth, as she quickened her pace through the paths. "And remember...I got married the last time you showed me a memory...am I going to see that again?"

"Ahh, haa, ahh...you're funny, Miss Ruth," Ojy laughed in a silly giggle. "You had a lot of fun and exciting times in your life. Ahh, haa, ahh, haa," she said, continuing to giggle.

"Wait a minute...hold on...you're going too fast. And what did you mean about fun times. Who told you that about me?" Ruth said, a little out of breath.

"Mr. Gabriello, silly," Ojy replied, smiling and waiting. "Oooh, I see it!" she said as she took off swirling ahead of Ruth in a mad dash of pink. She leapt in the air while running and caught hold of a higher stone which was pulled way out. "Wheee!" she squealed as she swung back and forth. "Oh, this is so much fun! Come on, Miss Ruth, will you help me?"

"I'd be glad to help," she replied as she easily pulled the stone out all the way. Ruth reached in and easily felt the thick and dampened paper. Noiselessly she opened it, expecting three familiar words. "Hmmm , what does this mean, Ojy? It's just a date on this piece, June 6, 2011. I don't understand. What does it mean?"

Ruth had never seen Ojy stand still before, so it was quite noticeable.

"Ojy?"

"Tch, tch, tch," was the only sound she made while standing perfectly still.

"Ojy! What's wrong? Talk to me, little friend!" she said, sternly, becoming afraid.

"Tch, tch, t...," she went completely quiet.

Ruth quickly reached out to her to hold her, and when she did, the piece of paper fell from her hand. The other side of the paper fell face up when it landed and it contained the three original words Ruth was looking for, "Do you believe?"

"Yes! Yes! Yes! I believe!" she yelled out, still holding Ojy.

All at once, as if on command, Ojy popped back into life.

"Ahh, haa, you scared me, Miss Ruth," she piped, excitedly.

"I scared you? Oh, my goodness, it was the other way around." Ruth replied, sighing in relief.

"Come on, Miss Ruth, let's go find Mr. Gabriello," her bundle of pink petals answered.

Because Ojy had originally led them to a different section of the gardens, they had to cross over to the left side to get to Mr. Gabriello. He was already present by the time they arrived and Ruth quickly joined hands with him, though still shaking about Ojy's shut-down. Because she was still thinking about what had happened to Ojy, she didn't hear the shrieking of time travel or feel the jerk of being pulled in reverse.

When all was calm and quiet within her, she heard some voices somewhere near her. She opened her eyes and discovered that she was once again, still in the garden. She was sitting in some shade and noticed a shovel next to her. She wiped her brow and looked toward the sound of the voices. She saw Hayden coming out of the sliding glass door, carrying a pitcher of fruit drink.

From over to her left she heard Roger calling. "Alright! That looks great. Over here. Where's your mother?"

"She's over there," the small voice replied. "Come on, Mom and Chester!" he called to her and the chocolate lab, which she hadn't noticed sitting to her right.

"Wait a minute," thought Ruth. "Chester? Oh....my goodness. That's not Hayden. It's Bryce and our Chester from long ago." As Ruthie got up to join them, Ruth winced because she remembered what happened next.

Chester ran down in front of her and in front of Bryce without his knowing it. He tripped over the dog and the glass pitcher went flying. The red juice exploded all over Bryce on impact, causing him to look like he was covered in blood. Ruthie and Roger quickly ran to him to assess the damages, only to discover that he was perfectly okay.

The three of them stood perfectly still, surrounded by shards of glass and red juice. When Bryce started to giggle, his parents joined in and soon the three of them were bent over laughing.

Chester was still sitting, at Roger's command, panting with his tongue hanging out, and looking quite pleased with himself.

"Bad dog," Bryce said, pretending to be stern, and they all burst out laughing again.

Ruth could feel her own laughter come from within her as she recalled that silly day. "Please, Mr. Gabriello, let me stay with them a little while longer," she thought.

As she opened her eyes again, she saw little Bryce working alongside of Roger. He was learning how to build the stone walls with his dad. Roger was showing him how to position each stone against the other ones for the best placement, and then how to back fill the soil after each layer was complete. If the stone was of manageable size, Bryce would carry it toward his dad, and with his help, maneuver it so that it wedged itself against its neighbor. They would do this several times before working with the soil. Bryce would bring over a bucket of soil and Roger would dump some of it,

149

pat it, and then move his hand away so Bryce could imitate that movement.

"You got it, fella," Roger would say. "Do you think you can hold out a little while longer?"

"I'm tough like stone, rawrrrr," little Bryce replied, holding up both arms to show his muscles. Roger reached over and tousled his son's black, wavy, and a little-too-long matching hair. "Look at me, Mommy. I'm a stone man."

"You certainly are a tough little boy," she smiled. Ruthie was sitting close by them, lining the edge of the stone walls with liriope. They used it frequently because not only was it a good bargain, but it was great for preventing erosion, even on their steepest hills. They didn't want it to spread too much, so as long as they kept it in the shade, it wouldn't take over. Bryce reached over and ran his little hands over the top soft blades of the plants while he was resting. At one point when Ruthie looked at them, they were both squinting and she realized for maybe the umpteenth time, how identical in looks they were. When they smiled at her, the left sides of their lips went up a little higher than the other. Ruthie noticed that when Roger took a swig of ice water from his canteen, Bryce would do the same. When Roger ran his hands through his dampened hair, little Bryce would follow. Ruthie thought that she could sit and watch the two of them all day long, and sometimes she did, but for now, she had to get back to the liriope.

As the picture faded, Ruth felt no need to move or get up. She basked in the memories of Bryce as a little boy, and smiled when she realized, again, how much Hayden looks like Bryce when he was little. She stayed against Mr. Gabriello for a while longer, remembering some earlier times by herself. She looked down toward her lap when she felt a nudging and was met with a wrinkly nose and a toothy grin. Ruth wrapped her arm around Velo and enjoyed the feeling of warmth it gave. "Hmph, hmph," Velo squeaked, softly, as Ruth closed her eyes in remembrance. As she recalled a few more stories from her past, tears of joy streamed down her face, and little paw-like hands wiped at them with a questioning look.

"It's okay, my friend, they're happy tears," she smiled.

Not too far away, Ojy held up her skinny little leafy arms, showing off her muscles. "Ahh, haa, aah," she announced, happily.

CHAPTER FORTY-EIGHT

A week had passed since Ruth had recalled her memories of when Bryce was a little boy. She found it easier to dwell on the memories after seeing them with the help of Mr. Gabriello. After her visits with him, she could continue the stories at a later time. Usually it helped her to remember them if she were in a quiet place and feeling comfortable. Sometimes, though, it didn't happen just like that. Sometimes, she pushed herself to look back to a period of time that Mr. Gabriello hadn't shown her, and this made her anxious. She didn't feel calm like she did with him, when she tried thinking about new memories on her own. Sometimes, she even threw her hands up to her eyes to block out the memories if they were coming at her too fast because they resembled a kaleidoscope, with hundreds of picture pieces crowding her. She couldn't help but want to remember her life, but she was beginning to feel more frustrated as each day passed.

For example, what significance did June 6, 2011, hold, and why did it stop Ojy in her tracks? Ojy seemed to have an inexhaustible supply of energy and excitement, but she literally froze when Ruth asked her about that date, and Ojy never did answer. And how about the comment made by Hailey's father, Bill. She had given a lot of thought to the words, "alone since five," but she just couldn't place them.

And to top it off, Bryce very politely turned down her offer to babysit the kids. He asked her if she remembered that they had agreed she wouldn't babysit again until she was cleared by Dr. Brooke. She, of course, didn't remember agreeing to this, but knew that Bryce had everyone's best interest in mind. He assured her that they were confident in her sanity, but thought it was best for the time being.

She told all of this and her feelings to Dr. Brooke during her weekly visit, and was, as usual, a bit surprised by her response. How could anyone who looked so young know just what to say? Ruth arrived at her appointment prepared to get some answers, but left as she always did, with another project instead.

"I was wondering," Ruth began, "does the date, June 6, 2011, hold any significance for me?"

"Can you remember that date?" Dr. Brooke responded.

"Well, no, which is why I'm asking."

"Can you remember our agreement, though, Ruth, about my filling in the blanks for you? You have to figure this out piece by piece. I already know your story," Dr. Brooke said, gently, yet professionally.

"Ahhh. Perhaps you have another analogy from your Grandma Bailey that might help," Ruth retorted, smiling.

"Alright, if I must," she responded, also smiling. "I once heard my grandmother tell a young girl in a situation similar to yours to envision her trapped memory as a growing chick inside of an egg. Nobody can crack the egg while the chick is growing because it wouldn't be able to support itself. After a certain amount of time, the chick will slowly, but surely, pick at the shell, until it frees itself from the casing that was protecting it. So you see, Ruth, what your psyche is doing, is protecting you until you are ready."

"Oh, I get it," Ruth responded, nodding her head, "I'm the chick."

"Exactly, Ruth," Dr. Brooke responded, "What happened last May will break away from its protective shell when it's capable of supporting itself."

Ruth sat pondering what Dr. Brooke had just explained and realized that she had a long way to go before her story caught up to the present day.

"I can only remember Bryce as a little boy," she relayed. "Does this mean that it will take years for me to catch up to the present?"

"Oh, no, not necessarily. Just keep chipping away at the egg shell, and you'll get there," she smiled. "And, uh…speaking of chipping at the egg shell. I have another project for you."

"Wait! What about the gardens? I love working in the gardens. You know…that's where I do a lot of my remembering."

"No, no, no. This won't take you away from your gardens. This is different. I haven't asked you this, yet, but it's something I have on your check list. What have you done with Roger's things? Have you gone through them…decided what to keep and what not to?" Dr. Brooke calmly asked.

"Oh, well, I use so many of the things in the shed for gardening so…it wouldn't make sense to give them away," Ruth said.

"No, Ruth, I'm not talking about the outside things. I'm talking about Roger's closet. Have you gone through his clothes? Those that are in nice condition can be given away…Ruth? Are you okay?" Dr. Brooke asked, while leaning forward to reach out to her.

Ruth seemed to be doing exactly what Ojy did the other day. Her mouth fell open a little and her eyes went blank. "I…I…I completely forgot that Roger had a closet," Ruth started. "I haven't opened it since…."

"Since when, Ruth?"

"Since...he died."

"Okay. Are you okay?" Dr. Brooke said kindly, yet with a professional manner. She paused for a minute to give Ruth a chance to collect her thoughts. "So, your grief work this week is to go home and address Roger's closet."

"To whom do I give...his clothes?" Ruth responded, crying a little.

"There are a number of organizations in the area that will pick up your donations, but one that I've found especially helpful is called, "My Angel's Closet." It houses clothes from the deceased which are in good condition. I've heard donors say that they believe that their lost loved one is somehow carrying on by also contributing to the needy.

"Thank you, Dr. Brooke. As always, you've given me some things to think about."

CHAPTER FORTY-NINE

"Hey, I'm home," Pat called out as he walked toward the screened in porch, in search of Mel.

"Back here, Hon," she answered.

"Well, you look wiped. Are you sure you still want to head out?" he said, referring to the water.

"Oh, yeah…it's just what I need. You go get changed, and I'll get us ready outside," she directed.

She was exhausted, that's true. Well, mentally, anyway. Ruth had asked that she accompany her to a donation site so she could drop off some of Roger's clothes. Mel thought it would be better if Ruth made the decisions of what to give away by herself, so she agreed to meet at Ruth's house at eleven, *after* she had finished organizing the clothes. Mel agreed to drive since it would no doubt be an emotional day for Ruth. She had hoped that Ruth would be okay to have lunch out afterwards. She had such a yen to stop at Chick n Ruth's deli on Main Street in the heart of Annapolis. She enjoyed their menu selection, and it was a favorite past time luncheon spot for the two of them. Perhaps they could stroll about the streets of downtown Annapolis afterwards, get some ice cream, and sit on the docks to watch the boats come and go, just like they used to do before last May.

Mel had been in a counseling position her entire career, and was aware of how quickly life can change; but never was it made so real to her as it was this past year, by actually having to experience the change herself through her friendship with Ruth.

She and Ruth had similar lives, and they were intertwined socially, so much so that it seemed to Mel as if they were family. The pain that was affecting Ruth was also felt by Mel, except for one difference; Mel could remember exactly what happened. It both hurt and frustrated Mel that Ruth couldn't yet remember crucial details from her past, especially, the most obvious.

When she arrived at Ruth's house to no answer at her door, she walked around back to see if she could find her because she knew that Ruth spent a lot of time in her gardens. Martha met her at the gate, tail wagging and panting, as if to welcome her to her house.

"Well, hello there, Martha," she exclaimed while patting her. "Where's my buddy? Is she ready for me?"

Martha sat down, clearly happy that someone was paying attention to her. Mel continued to rub her behind her ears while taking in the gardens.

"My goodness! This takes my breath away every time I come here," she said softly to herself. "It's extraordinary what's been done. Roger may have been the mastermind in his planning, but I'm relieved Ruth is carrying on this passion."

Martha left her side and bounded ahead onto a path that began the garden tour. Mel wasn't experienced in gardening and really didn't know the names of the plants, but was always interested in listening when Ruth and Roger explained what they were doing. She learned enough from them to realize that the low lying plants with large leaves, which were called "hostas," were always found in the shady spots. She marveled at the different sizes and colors in which they grew. Some of them were solid dark green and others had white stripes running through them. Further on ahead she saw a beautiful hosta that had an unusual combination of colors. It was both olive green and lime green mixed together. She bent down to get a closer look at it and jumped back instantly. She thought that something had just popped out of the plant, but when she looked around, she didn't see anything.

"Ruth's gardens are alive," she said to herself, smiling. "Ruth!" she called further back. "Are you out here?" She continued walking along paths, stepping onto higher elevated sections by using the stone steps which were so carefully built into the earth. "Honestly, every last detail was thought of back here," she thought as she continued on. "I don't think I've ever been back this far." She reached a sunny spot in this section and noticed that the types of plants were changing. She remembered Ruth telling her that the smaller leaves tolerated more sunshine. She gasped, though, when she rounded a bend and came upon an entire section of low lying bright pink flowers. They were so stunning and looked like a magical carpet for a little girl's room. And they, too, seemed to move with energy as Mel walked by.

"Hello! Ruth, are you out here?" she called again. This time, though, she thought she heard a muffled response. She hurried forward a little and found Ruth against a large tree, curled up on the ground, clutching something in her hand.

"Ruth!" she screamed. "Ruth! Ruth!" She ran to her and knelt down next to her curled up frame.

Ruth was coming to and sobbing, all the while grasping an old t-shirt. "Oh, Mom! He's okay, he's okay, we found him," she cried while pushing herself up to a sitting position.

"Ruth!" Mel said sternly. "I'm not your mother. It's me, Mel. Can you hear me?" she continued rather harshly as she sat down in the dirt in front of her. "Ruth, open your eyes!"

Ruth did as she was told, and as she looked around, she began weeping uncontrollably. After regaining her bearings, she began, "Oh! Mel! I...I...know this doesn't look good, but...I'm okay...really."

"No, you're not! I'm sorry, Ruth, but this isn't good. Please tell me what's going on. I come here at a planned time to help you with the clothes, and find you, way out here, in the middle of nowhere…"

"I'm *not* in the middle of nowhere, these are my gardens!" Ruth interjected.

"You were crying on the ground," Mel ignored her interruption. "And…and…I think you're hallucinating, or..or…or dreaming….because you called me 'Mom.' Now please, Ruth, tell me what's going on!"

Realizing that her friend couldn't possibly understand her unusual way of recalling her past, and not ready to share her treasured new garden friends with anyone but Dr. Brooke, Ruth tried explaining a better way.

"Do you remember when we talked last week, and I said that I enjoyed being home so much more? Well…*this* is how I am remembering who I am and what my life was all about," she shared.

"In your garden?" Mel asked.

"Uh, huh," she replied, nodding her head. "There's something about these gardens that takes me back in time and shows me my life."

"Oh, I see."

"Um…what was I doing when you came here?"

"You were lying on the ground, crying!"

Ruth thought about it for a minute before replying. "Well, in my defense, you'd be crying, too, if you had just relived what I had."

Mel sighed. "Well, then, why don't you tell me."

"Alright…I was going through Roger's clothes, as I was supposed to do, and I kept having flashes of memories when handling his clothes. It's the strangest thing, Mel. Is that normal?" she asked, timidly.

"Absolutely! The body's senses are responsible for so much of what we think and remember. It's not unusual, in fact, it's perfectly expected for someone who's grieving a loved one, to find it difficult to go through his or her belongings. *This* is why I asked you to go through Roger's clothes alone, because I figured that you'd want time to reminisce. I just thought you did your reminiscing inside," she added with a little laugh.

"No, it's out here where it happens. I think Roger and I lived so much of our lives outside that my mind chooses to remember in a place with which it's familiar. How's that for counseling?" she said as she nudged Mel with her elbow.

"Oh, that's pretty good, my friend. So...what was it that you were remembering?"

Ruth sighed and went on to explain, "Well, Roger had a collection of t-shirts from different places we've visited. And...look at this one I found," she said, slowly, as she held up a very old and stained t-shirt. On the front of the shirt was a faded decal reading, "Bryce Mountain National Park."

"We visited the park a couple of times. In fact," she added, blushing, "I believe Bryce's life began there."

"Now, that's a good memory!"

"Anyway, on our second trip out there, Bryce was seven, and we took my mom along. We had told him all about the beautiful stone and rock formations that we had seen on our first trip out there, and he wanted to see it so badly. It had been a great trip, until our next to last day. We had met another family while hiking that day and agreed to picnic with them later at a different location from our cabin. As it was getting dark, we loaded up our car to head back. Roger was going to ride with the other family to show them one more sight that they hadn't seen." Ruth held her hands up to her face when remembering what happened next.

"I called over to him, asking him if he was taking Bryce. He thought I asked him if he had lights."

160

At this, Ruth began crying all over again, while trying to continue.

"W...w...we all drove away and left him, Mel! We all left Bryce!"

"Oh, Ruth! What did you do?" Mel said, shivering.

"Nobody knew! When Roger came back an hour later, we still didn't know that neither of us had Bryce. When we finally realized what had happened, it was horrible! We were all screaming and crying and grabbing car keys. Roger and I tore out of there trying to find our way back to the camp site. It was pitch black outside and we were so upset and we couldn't remember which way was which! We found a ranger station and nearly broke down their door. They were incredibly helpful and made us calm down enough to describe the general direction of where we had been. They were unbelievable, Mel. We went out in two different ranger jeeps and they tried two different locations before we recognized our site.

"Oh, Ruth! Did you find him?" At that point, both Mel and Ruth began laughing because they realized what a funny question it was, since Bryce was alive and well.

"There he was. My sweet little seven year old boy, sitting against a large tree, trying to be so brave... right where we had had our campfire."

"Oh, Ruth," was all Mel could say.

"He knew...he knew we had made a mistake when we drove away without him so he decided to wait for us. He said that Roger had warned him to stop walking and stay put if he was ever lost, and that's just what he did. I tell you, Mel, words can never express the relief I felt when finding him."

"Oh, Ruth," Mel said again. "I'm so sorry that happened. How could you stand that?"

"You know, I don't think Roger and I ever prayed and hoped so hard in our entire lives as we did that night."

"Well, I certainly understand why you were crying today. I would have been as well." Mel said as she patted her friend's knee.

After such an emotional start to the day, the remainder of it was rather calm. Though it was difficult for Ruth to actually hand over Roger's clothing, she knew they were being put to a better use, just as Dr. Brooke had stated. It made Ruth feel warm in knowing that his clothes were helping someone in need. He would have wanted it that way, she was sure.

Because of the delay at the beginning of the day, they ate lunch at Ruth's before leaving. Mel ended up helping Ruth clear out the remainder of Roger's clothes. Ruth insisted on holding on to the vacation t-shirts and Mel didn't have the heart to force her to throw them out. She wasn't even sure she could do the same. It ended up being a long day, and both girls were exhausted after the experience.

Ruth was glad that Mel now knew that her memories were coming to her in the gardens. While she was truthful in telling her about the memory, she had left out how it all began.

CHAPTER FIFTY

Ruth had awakened earlier that morning since she knew Mel was coming at eleven o'clock. After realizing during her appointment with Dr. Brooke, that she had forgotten about Roger's closet, she had gone home and peeked inside it. The memories flooded her with such force that she slammed the door shut. She decided to wait until the morning that Mel was coming before looking again.

After her breakfast with Martha, she was determined to quickly enter into the task, knowing that Mel would be with her in a few hours. It also helped her to remember that Father Joe had overcome a difficult situation, and she hoped she could do the same. She tried to visualize the men who would benefit from some of the clothing she was pulling out of the closet, but as she was flipping through them on their hangers, she was overcome with such a strong presence of Roger that she had to sit down.

"Get a grip, Ruth. You can do this," she told herself, clutching something soft in her hands. She looked down and noticed that she had pulled a t-shirt off the hanger when she had quickly backed away. She instinctively held it to her face and inhaled.

"Oh, how could this still smell like him?" she agonized. As the memories started flooding into her head, she got up and began walking to the only place she felt comfortable in allowing them to come. She stumbled onto the back patio and fell into a rocking

163

chair, all the while pressing his shirt into her face, taking in his aroma. She sat silently in the rocking chair, remained calm, and gave permission to herself to remember.

It was then that she noticed she had left her garden gloves lying on the stone wall in front of her. Was it her hopeful imagination or were the stone and gloves transforming into the particular First Creature, of whom she hadn't seen much lately. To her great satisfaction, the two of them combined mystically in front of her, and it was as she had hoped. She was glad for the company in helping her retrieve her past, and sat up straight to greet him.

"Hi Pheo. I'm glad to see you," she said. "I was hoping someone would come to see me today."

"Yeah, I know," he answered, nonchalantly, as he hopped off the wall and walked effortlessly toward her. She marveled at his chiseled features, taking in the beautiful cut of stone. She wondered what he was going to do since he was coming directly toward her. Oblivious to her staring, he reached up and pulled the shirt out of her hands and laid it on the ground in front of her so the decal showed.

"Oh," she gasped. She had forgotten where Roger had gotten this particular shirt.

"Come on, leth's go get the note," he said, as he bent down and picked up a stick.

Ruth smiled as she grabbed the t-shirt off the ground and began following him. He was unlike the other First Creatures, who were more prone to talking. Perhaps it was a "boy thing," she thought lovingly as she followed him.

As with the first time he'd taken her to Mr. Gabriello, he tapped on periodic stones as he walked, searching for just the right spot in which to find the note. "Got it! Here it ith," he said matter of factly. "Will you help pull on thith?"

Ruth was more anxious than ever to get the note after last time. When Pheo motioned for her to reach inside, she quickly did so. And as with the previous note, this one, too, had writing on the back. This time the writing read, "St. Francis of Assisi with Father Joe Douglass as celebrant."

"Uh oh," Ruth thought. Hayden wrote a note to me while he was at Mass. I wonder how he got away with that with his parents' watchful eyes...and I wonder why he wasn't paying attention...that little rascal. At least I know where this thick paper is coming from," she smiled. And when she flipped it over, the usual question was waiting for her. "I believe," she responded.

CHAPTER FIFTY-ONE

The ringing of the alarm clock at six-thirty in the morning always surprised Ruth, who desperately wanted to turn it off and return to sleep. She knew, though, that after stumbling to the kitchen and starting her coffee, she'd be happy that she chose to get up. She thrived in the summer morning routine she'd created for herself even though she enjoyed the comfort of her bed. Her goal each morning was to get dressed, get her coffee and oatmeal made, grab the paper from out front, and make it to the back patio rocking chair before seven. She felt better about herself when she set small goals, even really small ones such as this. This was one of the things Dr. Brooke had assigned to her some time ago. She had Ruth design a checklist of very small chores each day, no matter how trivial, so that Ruth would gain confidence in herself by completing them. It really did help her, she realized, to look at a list in the evening of what she had accomplished. She hurried out the sliding glass door and dropped into the chair just as the 'show' began. The sounds which the sprinkler system made when turning on were Ruth's timer each morning. If she could get into her chair before those sounds began, she gave herself a pat on the back and a check on the list. She smiled as she looked into the gardens as they began to sparkle with water droplets. She never grew tired of looking into the gardens and found it to be quite mesmerizing to watch them being watered. It made her feel responsible to know that she was nurturing their well being and that she held her duty to them highly. Both she and Roger agreed to invest in the watering system some time ago because it was too time consuming for them to water the gardens in their entirety. They divided the gardens into sections so they could control how much water each section received.

Another small chore for her each day was to read the front page of the newspaper and the front page of the local section. She might not be able to remember what happened in her past, but she was able to discuss today's world and local events, whether she wanted to or not. As the breezes picked up, though, and the newspaper bowed, it became increasingly difficult to maneuver.

"You know," she started, "I'm going to take Hayden's advice and learn to read the news on my smart phone," she said, eying her phone suspiciously while pondering her next move. "Right now, in fact," she added, decisively. She folded the paper and began fiddling with her phone. Though she had owned it for over a year, she used it mainly for communicating. She was pretty efficient at texting Bryce and Mel, but that was about it. Hayden often played with his parents' phones and urged her to become more tech savvy.

"Grammy, you have this cool phone so why don't you use it more?" he had asked her. "Do you want me to download some songs for you? Grammy, I can show you if you want me to."

She could picture his little fingers working her phone while trying to teach her which buttons to push. She couldn't really see what he was doing but she liked watching him try. He'd look at her and smile and her heart would melt. He looked just like his dad when he was little.

"You don't have to push so hard, Grammy. Just touch the buttons," he'd say.

She'd try to follow what he said, but he'd inevitably take her phone from her and start over.

"Ah, ha!" she proclaimed out loud, as she discovered an app on her phone for news. After fiddling with it a little more, she figured out how to enlarge the print to read a couple of articles. "Look at me now," she smiled.

"Um, okay, I'm looking" a little voice squeaked.

"Ahh! Velo, you scared me," Ruth said, jumping, while looking toward the voice. There she was, sitting on the table top, leaning against the umbrella pole. As seemed to be her custom, her little legs were sticking straight out in front of her while tapping her feet together.

Almost as if on command, she cocked her head to one side, pulled up her little paw-like hands, turned her lips inward, yet puffed them out and responded with, "Hmph." She got up and tippy toed toward Ruth, stopping to look in her coffee cup. "Um, did Hayden teach you how to use your phone?"

"Yes, he did, but I just taught myself how to find the news," Ruth responded confidently.

At that, Velo gently hopped off the table and into Ruth's lap, where she snuggled against her to watch Ruth work her phone. They sat together like that while Ruth read the news, periodically looking down into her friend's loving eyes while offering her little pats.

CHAPTER FIFTY-TWO

It was already hot at eleven o'clock in the morning as Julie shielded herself from the sun's powerful rays. She was sitting on a bench at the city docks awaiting her two grade partners for their annual summer luncheon date. She had a sitter lined up weeks in advance to make sure she didn't miss her summer reunion with Ruth and Lydia. Their July outing had become a ritual over the past few years, with the exception of last summer. Ruth didn't join them last summer, and it wasn't the same. Julie and Lydia had tried to make it a joyful event, but they only talked about Ruth's circumstance instead. They didn't think she could possibly come back to teaching in the fall, and were wondering who her replacement would be. They couldn't believe that their once vibrant, full-of-life friend was stuck in a hole so deep, that she couldn't crawl out. Lydia had dubbed it, "the black crater of her mind." They had tried visiting her on numerous occasions, but knew they were dealing with the "elephant in the room syndrome." No one would talk about what had happened, and Ruth would mention things that couldn't possibly be. Julie and Lydia didn't know how to respond to her so they turned to Mel for advice. Mel assured them that Ruth was seeking professional help and needed time…a lot of time. Little did they, or anyone else, know, that a couple of weeks later, the miracle would occur in Ruth's classroom, when she would literally snap out of a large chunk of her depression, and would be able to move forward enough to return to teaching.

Julie looked toward the pedestrians strolling about the docks, looking for either of her grade partners. A few minutes later, she actually heard them, well, one of them, before they came into view.

"You're lucky you didn't take that class with me because there was so much reading," Lydia was saying. "Paul was really surprised because he thought my summer would be completely free. Little did he know that there's a lot to do in the summer, well, not *all* summer. But even though the class ended, I still have to do a project, some kind of a slide presentation, and present it to the lower school. Oh, please don't laugh at me, Ruthie, when I present it. You know how I get," she stopped for a breath and a giggle, but not for long. "Oh! Julie! Julie, here we are," she shouted, waving her arms amongst other pedestrians.

They greeted Julie with hugs, and Julie, in return, gave Ruth an understanding glance since she had already endured a stampede of stories from Lydia during their short walk to the docks.

"I hope you haven't been waiting long, Julie," Ruth said.

"Oh, no, I'm fine. I've only been here since five of," she responded.

"Since five...since five...since five," Ruth heard it echoing in her head. She stopped her greeting and looked down. She shook her head a little and tried to grab hold of a thought. "Those words Julie just said," she thought to herself. "Something...what was it? Was it in a newspaper? No, it couldn't be a newspaper because I read news on my phone now...what am I thinking of? Since five, since five."

"Ruth, are you okay?" Julie asked, reaching out to rub her back.

"I am. I'm sorry. You said something and I was trying to remember what it reminded me of. Oh, well, maybe it will come to me later."

"Okay, if you're sure. Shall we start?"

The trio walked the short distance to the Annapolis Water Taxi port and found a water taxi ready for departure. They asked to be taken only across Spa Creek and dropped off at Carrol's Creek, a waterfront restaurant. They agreed that they were all hungry and wanted to eat first before a longer boat ride for pleasure. They could have easily driven themselves to the restaurant and parked there, but why, when they could be taxied in a boat? That's the beauty of living in water country.

It only took a few minutes to taxi across Spa Creek before arriving at the other side, but the breezes created in those few minutes of boating were a welcome gift to the small group of friends. The captain helped them on to the dock and told them he'd be back at half past any hour, unless they called for a different time.

Though they were hot, they asked to be seated outside on the deck so they could really enjoy the view of the creek. The waitress said to follow her and told them that there was actually a breeze out there by the water.

As they sipped iced tea and shared a crab dip appetizer, they caught up on each others' first month of summer. Ruth shared what she could, stating that her memory was slowly returning in bits and pieces, though she didn't explain the details of how. She kept the knowledge of the First Creatures to only herself and Dr. Brooke, believing that no one would understand her. It was her garden, after all…and her memory.

The view to which the ladies were privy was magnificent. Spa Creek was another one of the Chesapeake's treasures, although it was more urban than the Severn River. Spa Creek housed downtown Annapolis, or maybe it was vice versa. It had become the centralized hub of this water city, and was home to thousands of boaters, both young and old. While motorized crafts passed by them slowly in the no-wake zone, the ladies saw a group of very small children and miniature sail boats just beyond them. They were closer to Ego Alley, where the girls had picked up their taxi.

"Aren't they adorable?" their waitress asked while refreshing their tea. "That's Annapolis Yacht Club over there, and those little sailors are called 'Creek Critters.' They're only five and six years old. There's another program for the seven and eight year olds called 'Sea Squirts.' My daughter is learning to sail with them in the afternoon. She loves it."

"Oh, that's wonderful," Julie commented. "Do you sail, as well?"

"Well, not yet, exactly. My husband's job brought us to Annapolis. It was one of my requests, since I was leaving my family, that we all learn to sail. My daughter started her class already, and my husband and I will start next week. We're actually very psyched!" she said as she turned around to get their meals off the tray.

"That's great. Maybe I'll check into classes for my boys," Julie responded. "They love the water!"

"I'll tell you what, Julie," Ruth joined in. "If you're thinking about having your boys take sailing lessons, then I'll speak with Bryce about Hayden and Heather. They would love that as well."

"Here you are," said the waitress, placing the first plate down. All three of them had ordered the crab cake sandwich, accompanied by coleslaw and fries; a standard summer feast in Annapolis. Crab cakes, and other crab related meals, such as crab imperial, stuffed flounder, and steamed crabs for picking, were on practically every restaurant's menu near the water, which promoted the well-known quote, "Maryland is for crabs!" The Chesapeake Bay blue crab is one of the most recognized symbols for Maryland, and said by many to be the best tasting crab meat in the world.

As Ruth looked out to the water while eating, she enjoyed watching the children take part in their classes. While listening to them squeal and splash in the water, she visualized the waitress's daughter and quickly thought of Hailey.

"That's it!" she blurted out, causing the others to quickly stop eating. "It's Hailey, and something she said to me. That's what I couldn't remember before. She told me that her father said I was alone since five. I have no idea what that means," she said, laying down her napkin. "Please, girls," she said quietly, as if not to allow the guests next to them to hear, "Do any of you know what 'alone since five' means?"

"Oh my goodness, Ruthie! What did you say?" Lydia gasped, returning her gaze to the table from the water.

"Alone since five. Do you know what that means?" Ruth replied directly to Lydia.

"Oh, I'm sorry, Sweetie. I...I thought you said something else."

"Please, Lydia. What is it?" Ruth begged.

"Oh, I...I...could never say in public," she covered herself, giggling. "I'm sorry, I wasn't listening too well."

Ruth nodded and looked out to the water once again just as Lydia caught a glance from Julie, who shrugged her shoulders, not understanding what Lydia did.

The conversation remained pleasant through the remainder of their meal, but when the Creek Critters from across the way called it quits, the girls paid their bill, gathered their belongings, and headed for the dock.

CHAPTER FIFTY-THREE

Ruth had just finished making coffee after dinner. On most nights, she served herself leftovers. She usually made one large meal a week and ate off of it for days. This, too, had become a more comfortable routine over time, and she found it easy to follow. She ate most of her meals either in the back room or on the back patio. But tonight she ate in a small room that was actually part of the kitchen, in a rocking chair near the fireplace. She and Roger had sectioned off an indented small part of the kitchen, next to the large table, as a small sitting room. The room had only three walls, with the missing fourth wall as the opening into the kitchen. It wasn't very big, and might have acted as a mud room at one time to the previous owners. It had a door to the garage off of it, and a wall of built-in cubbies and hooks that they had designed some time ago. They kept many of their shoes in the cubbies and hung their coats there during the colder months; it just seemed easier than the closet farther away. They had also added a smaller sized fireplace and raised it about two feet off the ground. It had a unique look all its own, and they had received many compliments on it through the years. But Ruth realized tonight that she had ignored this room for quite some time. It had room enough for only two rocker recliners, so it seemed only natural that it be inhabited by two, not one.

It just sort of popped into her view, though, while she was heating dinner, as if it had never been there.

"It's okay, Ruth," she said to herself. "You can sit in there. You used to love it in there."

She carried her plate of chicken salad, fresh sliced tomatoes, and corn, already cut off the cob, along with a glass of iced tea to the little room and hovered in front of one of the chairs, not so sure she wanted to stay.

"Hee, hee, hee, hee, ahh, haa," a giggling sound met Ruth and shocked her into making a decision. "Ahh, haa, ahh, this is fun!" shrieked a flowery mess of bright pink from one of the chairs.

Ruth quickly looked to her left and couldn't miss the bright display of an outdoor plant sitting in one of the rocker recliners. The little face amongst the petals was clearly enjoying herself. The green leafy stems which made up her arms and legs were pushing and pulling while working the chair into a rocking motion.

"Ahh, haa...you have to try this. Come on, sit down!" she excitedly invited Ruth.

Ruth began laughing at the sight and promptly sat down in the chair beside her. "You're right, Ojy. I had forgotten just how nice these chairs are."

"Who sat in them?" Ojy responded, still working on the motion.

"Everybody, I think," Ruth answered. "But they were always used in pairs."

"I'll sit with you while you eat," Ojy answered her, petals swaying in the rocking motion.

They sat in comfortable silence while Ruth ate her dinner. Thought-like puzzle pieces seemed to be floating just beyond her grasp while she quietly rocked with her eyes closed, and she had the suspicion that memories were trying to reach her.

"Ojy, do you think we could find a note from Hayden so I could visit Mr. Gabriello?" Ruth asked.

175

"Yeeaaa, ahh, haa, ahh, haa," she laughed. "I love showing you things."

At that, the two of them headed toward the sliding glass door. Ojy sashayed circles around Ruth's feet as she walked. Her excitement was always difficult for her to contain, and Ruth enjoyed witnessing it. Ojy ran on ahead of her, as was customary, and Ruth found her swinging and laughing on a protruding rock. Ruth had no trouble retrieving the note, and had decided to look at the back of the note quietly. She remembered what happened last time to Ojy, and didn't want her to freeze again. Ruth nonchalantly looked at the flip side of the note, and gasped in surprise. She wasn't expecting to see Roger's name. There was more writing below his name, but it was smeared too much and she couldn't read it.

Ojy heard the gasp and looked up at her. Ruth just nodded her head to let her know that she was okay.

"What was Roger doing with Father Joe?" she wondered to herself. "Maybe this was a different function not held at the church, but it's the same paper, I can tell by the texture. And what is this writing below his name? I wish I could read it."

"Ahh, haa, ahh, haa, come on!" Ojy sang out as she danced ahead of Ruth.

When Ruth got to the oak tree, she stepped right up in front of it. She felt the rough exterior of the tree and wondered how a creature could possibly come from it. This tree was as normal as any other. She shook her head and stepped back, stating confidently and out loud, "I believe."

There was no explaining the transformation that took place before her eyes. For out of a tree as normal as any other, a figure, her size, evolved. His appearance didn't frighten her anymore, and she thought she was also detecting something new; confusion, perhaps? Allowing herself to be taken with him, she raised her right hand to meet his left. Upon joining him, she flew backward in time, holding her breath until the screeching blare stopped. Knowing that she had arrived at a planned destination, she opened her eyes and found herself seated at the kitchen table. Across from her sat Bryce, and to her left, at the head of the table, sat Roger. He was only slightly graying at the temples, which allowed Ruth to know that this was some time ago, but Bryce didn't look much different.

"Where was Bev?" she wondered.

"It's good to have you boys back home," she heard herself saying. "Because now there's someone to help with the dishes," she added, laughing.

"Ah, Mom. Thanks for the dinner. This was great," Bryce responded. "Yea, there's only so many seaside meals I can endure," he added, laughing, referring to the trip he and his father had just taken to a learning center in the coral reefs in the Florida Keys.

"Oh, Bryce!" she said, playfully swatting him with her napkin.

"I'm just kidding, Mom, this is great. And...um...I was wondering. Would it be okay if I brought someone here for dinner next week?"

"What? Oh, my goodness. Who? Where did you meet her? Why didn't you tell me?" she got out, all in one breath.

"Heh, heh," Roger chimed in. "I knew it."

"Knew what? You knew and didn't tell me?" she responded, now swatting at Roger.

"Well...there's been this cute girl coming around my office at school, and I got the distinct feeling she wasn't there to talk with me. You should have seen her on the trip. Her eyes lit up every time *this* guy came around," he said, clapping Bryce lovingly on the shoulder.

"Hey, for your information," Bryce interrupted, looking directly at his father, "We had already had a date before the trip. And...I like her," he added, turning toward his mother.

Roger leaned toward Bryce and added with a wink, "She's a keeper, like your mother."

Ruth exhaled, allowing the dream state to linger a little, but she could remember all of this as if it were yesterday. She thought of the first time she met Bev. She was so sweet and a little shy at first, but she warmed up quickly. What Ruth remembered most about first meeting her was her vivacious laugh. When she and Bryce would joke about something, they'd start laughing, but hers was contagious and filled the room with joy. She was tall, slender, and had freckles that sprinkled across her nose and cheeks, probably from the sun, Ruth imagined.

"Hmm...she still looks like that," Ruth thought, smiling, "Except her hair is shorter."

Bev's hometown was a few hours away, so she enjoyed being able to accompany Bryce to his parents' home for Sunday dinners. Bryce was two years older than Bev, so while she was finishing her schooling, he was busy establishing a small plant nursery with the comfort of living at home with his parents. They were eager for him to get his business off the ground, and happy to help him.

Ruth smiled when she fondly remembered the beginning days of Stonehenge Gardens. Bryce may have been living at home, but they didn't see a lot of him. He used all of his savings, and then some, to get the business growing. It wasn't easy working such long hours, which included a lot of back breaking duties, but Ruth and Roger rarely heard him complain. He'd come home late, drop into bed and sleep for a few hours, and be out the door again. They also knew that part of the reason they didn't see him was because of Bev. She was everything they could hope for in a daughter-in-law, and were ecstatic when they became officially engaged.

Ruth paused here and remembered the daughter that she and Roger had lost. She'd be older than Bryce. Perhaps she'd be married, or maybe have children. Ruth and Roger didn't have any other children after Bryce. They believed in fate and accepted the plan that was laid out for them. They loved their only child immensely, worked at their careers and gardens, and enjoyed a fun, faith-filled life. They were happy; *that* she remembered.

It did seem, though, that they were gaining a daughter when the wedding plans began. Bev knew that Annapolis was now her home, and wanted to be married in the church with which she was now affiliated. She loved St. Francis of Assisi, and held it dear to her heart because this was the church that she and Bryce attended from the very beginning. Her parents understood, and still helped plan the wedding as much as they could, from where they lived. The fact that they were a distance away, though, enabled Ruth to help. She did her best to give Bev the space she needed, but to her delight, Bev frequently took her along for decision making. Ruth often thought that perhaps Bev allowed her to help because Bryce was her only child. Whatever the reason, though, they planned a beautiful winter wedding that included bits and pieces of all their likings.

Bev and Bryce knew immediately upon becoming engaged that they would be married in the winter. It was the only slow season for Bryce's business, and the most opportune time for him to get away.

Ruth sighed peacefully at the pictures she was remembering in her mind. When she became more coherent, she looked around and realized that she was sitting on the ground against Mr. Gabriello's tree. It was so peaceful right here against his tree, and she could feel the contentment all about her. She smiled when she remembered Bev telling her recently that her gardens were never quiet. She was right. Even now at dusk, she could hear some of the birds tucking themselves in for the night, and she could always hear the frogs talking once darkness came. She wanted to remember more of that time period, but thought she'd better get inside for now, as it was getting darker.

Martha met her at the patio, tail wagging, glad to see some company.

"Oh, Martha, Ole' Girl, so glad to see you," she said, patting her gently on her head. Martha would run up the paths through the gardens when Ruth made her way out there, but she never stayed. She wasn't allowed in the gardens, and the paths just weren't interesting enough for a dog.

Ruth knew exactly where she was going to sit upon entering the house. She headed straight for the sitting room with two chairs, and much to her amusement, they were already taken! The same bright pink flower bunch from earlier was having a party all by herself in one of the chairs, laughing, squealing and working the chair into a rocking motion. In the other sat the Frances Williams look-alike, who tugged at Ruth's heart strings.

This time it was Ruth who didn't have much to say. "Hmph," was all she could utter through her smile.

"I'll move over and you can sit with me," the olive and lime green striped figure responded.

And so she did. Ruth realized that this was one of her favorite things now-a-days; to sit with Velo snuggled in her lap, while remembering her past.

Her dream continued here, without the help of Mr. Gabriello, and she could remember loving this room and whoever was sitting with her. She enjoyed many occasions in this spot with Roger, Bryce, Bev, and later, Hayden and Heather. A lot of planning and reminiscing happened in here because there were only two chairs and a fireplace. There was no television to cause distraction and the room's purpose, to offer togetherness, was accomplished.

Ruth went on to remember the wedding. She wasn't dreaming about it, though, because her eyes were open. She was definitely using her memory, and she couldn't wait to share this exciting news with Dr. Brooke.

Bev and Bryce were married during the Advent season. Even though it was particularly helpful to be married during the slow season of Bryce's business, they found it to be very special to be married in a season that stood for new beginnings; the dawn of their lives together. Ruth remembered their wedding day as if it had happened just last week. It doesn't snow a lot in the Annapolis region, and if it does, rarely until January and February. But that year a beautiful light and fluffy snow fell, covering the grounds with a few inches of the powdery gift. It made for a breathtaking background in pictures, yet didn't cause any troubles for the travelers. The girls wore midnight blue floor-length gowns and carried white roses surrounded by baby's breath. The men were in black tuxedos and each wore a single white rose. The church was adorned in white roses, and the warmth that radiated from the walls of St. Francis was displayed in the glowing faces of the young couple in love. When the wedding day came to an end, Bev came to Ruth and hugged her tightly. They laughed as they realized they were both crying, but knew that they were shedding tears of joy. Bev asked Ruth what she would like for her to call her.

"I know you have a mother," Ruth said out loud in remembrance, "But would you like to call me, Mom?"

"Okay, Mom," Bev smiled, and hugged her again. And with that, Ruth regained a daughter.

When they first married, they lived in a tiny historic apartment on Prince George Street in downtown Annapolis. It was perfect for just the two of them, and they often referred to it as "the closet." They were on the third floor of a row house, and from their back kitchen window, they could see the Naval Academy Chapel dome. From out their front door was the St. Johns College campus. They knew that they could stay here as long as it was just the two of them, and that was fine with them. The rent wasn't high, which was unheard of in downtown Annapolis, but after all, they were renting "a closet," and they were able to save for their first "real" house, which didn't come for a few years.

It was here in their first house that Bev discovered there was a rowing club within walking distance of her home. She traded her swimming arms for rowing arms, and never looked back. She made some really good friends on the rowing team, including Mel.

Ruth smiled as she drifted off to sleep, peacefully remembering the love that was shared in this room and in these chairs. But just before she fell asleep, she could hear Dr. Brooke calling this day, "a day of progress."

CHAPTER FIFTY-FOUR

The days continued to bring a lot of hot weather, which usually resulted in late afternoon or evening thunderstorms. Even in August, the temperatures were well above ninety degrees, and Ruth knew not to expect any relief for a few more weeks. She'd be starting back to school the third week in August, and shortly after that, people and gardens alike would find some relief in the temperature.

She was sitting on the back patio in the shade, kind of biding her time for a little bit. She was venturing out to dinner at Hailey's house for the first time since last year. Hailey had once again become a standard fixture in Ruth's backyard when she could. Ruth would be on her hands and knees, pulling some weeds, when she'd hear a small voice behind her, offering to help. Hailey would have on her little gardening gloves and be carrying a bucket in which to put the weeds. How could she refuse her?

It was always Ruth's first instinct, upon seeing Hailey, to tense up. She had learned since their first reunion that she had to remind herself that Hailey was just a little girl who was also hurting and confused. One day last week when the two of them were weeding, Mary came over, checking on them. She had sensed that Ruth was loosening up, and took a chance on inviting her for dinner once again. Ruth accepted, knowing that she had to make a conscious effort to regain as much normalcy as she could.

She had a feeling that she and Roger had spent a lot of time with this young couple, yet she couldn't quite remember the circumstances. Hailey would often ask her if she remembered certain get-togethers, but Ruth's answer was always the same. It did, though, give her something to think about and perhaps Mr. Gabriello would help shed some light on the circumstances. A quick glance at her watch let her know that it was time to go. When she stood, she automatically headed further back in her yard, but toward the side fence. She stopped herself, shaking her head, wondering why she was walking in that direction. After a second thought, she continued, curious as to why she instinctively walked towards that area.

She had found herself recently doing things like that without consciously thinking about it. Her body movement would take her a certain direction because maybe that's the way she had always done it before...before Roger died. For instance, when she picked up her mail each day, she usually walked it to the kitchen and sat down at her desk to look through it. Lately, though, she'd walk to the office and put it on Roger's desk. Why was she all of a sudden moving on instinct? And, another thing that she'd recently been thinking about...where were her bills? She knew she wasn't paying them, so who was? She must ask Bryce about this.

She continued to walk toward the back side of her fence, but stopped when she heard a fluttering noise. She looked around and saw a mourning dove fluffing its feathers in the dirt near the back of the shed. She stood still, waiting to see if this might be who she was hoping to see.

"Ceepa, is it you?" Ruth asked quietly.

Once again, the mourning dove began its graceful transformation into the soft-spoken First Creature who had shown Ruth the memory of losing her first baby.

"Hi," Ceepa said gently. "Follow me. I want to show you something," she said as she fluttered ahead of Ruth on her very skinny knock-kneed legs. Feathers flew out of her dirty blond hair as she scurried ahead of Ruth; the long tail feathers of her coat, Ruth noticed, resembled a dove's long wing span.

Ceepa's arms fluttered like that of a dove's wings to show her excitement at what she had to show Ruth. There was plenty of room behind the shed to enter, so she did. Once behind there, Ruth saw a short gate that was only about four and a half feet tall. With a powerful flash of remembrance, she could all of a sudden remember this gate and how it came to be here. Hayden and Heather loved playing with Hailey so much when they visited their grandparents that they asked Roger if he would build them a secret gate that only the kids could use to go back and forth between Hailey's house and theirs. Ruth paused and smiled when she remembered that the adults used the secret gate just as much. It was faster, after all, than using their front entrances. They really had to bend over, though, to get through it, and after some time of getting used to the unusual height, they didn't even slow down at all when passing through. Now that Ruth thought about it, the secret door's location explained how Hailey had been showing up in her yard without coming through the main gate. Now that's something she should have wondered about, she thought. She needed to make a more conscious effort to be aware of her surroundings and to understand all she could if she were to continue on a path of progress.

She smiled as she remembered Roger working on the secret gate and wondering if they would be able to fit through it. He was so good with the grandchildren, just as he had been with Bryce when he was little. She hadn't known, though, how he would react when they asked him to cut a hole in the fence he had built. But Roger thought it was a great idea, and told them that he wished he had thought of it himself. He'd assembled all the tools that were needed for the project, and had Hayden, who was the tallest, stand against the fence. He made the cut only a couple of inches higher than Hayden, and the kids squealed in delight that their grandpa was so cool.

"Oh, Roger, I miss you so much," Ruth said out loud while standing next to the shortened gate and feeling the construction of it. "You were the best grandpa in the world…why did you have to go?" She patted the gate fondly, happy to have been shown yet a bit more of her yesterdays.

Ceepa waited for Ruth to open the gate and then scurried through ahead of her, beckoning her with her call to follow, "Oo-wah-hooo, hoo-hoo." Ruth had the sensation that Ceepa was clearing the path for a renewed friendship; in a sense, opening the door for a new start.

She knew there was no way she could go through gracefully since it had been so long, so she bent over carefully and followed. Once through, she stood up straight and entered into a world she used to know. She drew in her breath quickly and smiled. She had forgotten just how cute the Davis' back yard was. She remembered thinking that their house resembled a beach cottage with the white on white décor. The outside walls were made of cedar shingles that had been stained white and the windows were sheltered with white hurricane shutters on the outside and white plantation shutters on the inside. She enjoyed the 3-D depth which the void-of-color layers created.

She looked around, trying to find Ceepa, but she was gone. She looked toward the house again, and quickly felt a rush of emotions upon seeing mother and daughter preparing the table. She had forgotten how gentle Mary's touch was with everyone with whom she came into contact, and smiled while watching Mary teach Hailey where to place the silverware.

"Miss Ruth, Miss Ruth, you're here!" Hailey beamed as she ran toward her.

Mary also stopped what she was doing and walked toward her. "Oh, Ruth, it's good to see you. Thank you for coming," she said while giving Ruth a pat on the back. "Bill is so anxious to say hello."

After a warm reception, they sat down to dinner on the back patio next to a small pond with a gentle waterfall. The stone that created their pond walls was stacked high enough to be used as a seat, and there perched on one of the stones, sat a mourning dove, seemingly unafraid of its human company. Ruth smiled, but drew no attention to it for fear it would leave. The evening went on smoothly while they caught up on as much news as they could. Bill even approached the subject of her progress, much to Mary's resistance. He had promised his wife that he wouldn't probe too deeply, but he wanted to let Ruth know that it was okay to talk about her situation with them.

Ruth thanked Bill for asking and told him that most people wouldn't broach the subject. She thought it was okay to share with them that her memory was coming back to her in bits and pieces and that she was anxious for a full recovery. When Mary and Hailey went inside to get dessert, Ruth remembered her new promise to herself to understand as much as she could, so she asked Bill the question to which she wanted an answer so badly.

"While we're on the subject of....me, I'm wondering if you can clarify something that you said to Hailey about me. You said that I was alone since five. I...I just don't know what that means, Bill, and I...I...I really am trying to understand."

"Alone since five?" he repeated a couple of times. "Ruth, I'm sorry. I would tell you if I knew what that meant. You know, perhaps she misunderstood me," he said, shaking his head.

"Please don't ask her in front of me, Bill. She seems to be as confused about my predicament as I am. We're just now friendly again, and I...I...I don't even know why I put up such a wall."

"Ahh, Ruth. I...I want to talk about it more in depth, but Bryce says that your grief counselor has advised against it for now.

"Yes," she said nodding. "I'm to remember in my own time to better fill in the gaps. It is coming, Bill. One day, and I hope soon, I'll be able to remember all the details of my past and put it behind me."

"Okay, Ruth. It's a deal. We're right here, though, if you need us...right through the..."

"Triple H gate," she finished for him, smiling. "You see," she said, clapping her hands together, "I just remembered what we called that little gate."

CHAPTER FIFTY-FIVE

With just a week left before having to report back to school, Ruth decided to shop for her necessary classroom items that had to be replenished. She liked to refresh her bulletin boards, stock up on seasonal name tags, and replenish her colored chalk supply. It didn't take her long inside the store because there were three clerks working the registers in anticipation of returning teachers. She was feeling rather hungry afterwards, and wanted to get a bite to eat, but didn't feel comfortable eating by herself out in public. She was told that this, too, will get better in time, but she didn't think so. She'd never enjoyed eating alone in public before Roger died, so this was nothing new.

"Oh, Stonehenge is right around the corner from here," she thought out loud. "Maybe I'll get some takers there."

The heat of August didn't bring out the gardeners, so Stonehenge was calm and quiet.

"Another good reason for a lunch break," she smiled to herself.

Most of the personnel working the floors knew her and greeted her warmly.

"Hi, Ruth. He's back in his office if you're looking for Bryce," volunteered a woman about Ruth's age. She looked awfully familiar to Ruth, but she couldn't remember her name.

Ruth continued back until she reached Bryce's office, and knocked on the open door.

"Excuse me, Sir, are you accepting applications for volunteers at the fall festival?"

"Mom, how's it going?" he replied, getting up to give her a kiss. "Really? Would you like to work the festival again this year? How about a paycheck this time?"

"I wouldn't miss it, Honey, and no, I just like helping out," she smiled.

"So what brings you around? Did you bump into Bev? She was just finishing a class."

"Well, I was in the area, and feeling rather hungry. I was wondering if anyone was available to go for lunch."

"You know, I think that just might..."

"Grammy!" Heather squealed as she ran into the office. "Miss Carolyn said you were here."

"Carolyn...that's it!" Ruth replied, now remembering the employee's name while holding out her arms for Heather.

"Bryce, can you report to pickup when you get the chance?" they all heard over Bryce's walkie talkie.

"I'll be right back, and I'll go find Bev as well," he said as he walked out of his office.

"What are you doing here, Grammy?" Heather asked as she pulled her miniature garden gloves off. "I like your shirt. It's pretty," she said as she felt Ruth's new periwinkle blue tee.

"Oh, thank you, Sweetie. Well, I was shopping close by and I wanted to know if anybody wanted to go to lunch. Would you like that? How about Hayden? Does he want to go?"

"Grammy...J Camp, remember?" Heather replied while also checking out Ruth's purse. "I like this, too," she added, referring to the purse.

"J Camp?" Ruth asked, looking perplexed.

"You know, Jesus Camp," she corrected herself while getting a paper cone of water from the five gallon cooler dispenser.

"Oh, well, we called it bible school in my day, but okay. Don't you also want to go?" she asked Heather.

"No, Grammy. I don't want to go," she answered rather assertively. "I'm staying here and helping Mommy."

"Okay," Ruth nodded, surprised that Heather chose to stay at home.

"Mom, hi, how are you?" Bev asked as she came into the office.

"I'm doing great and oh, look at you," she said, smiling, referring to the just visible showing of Bev's pregnancy. "I should be asking how you are. Are you feeling okay?"

"Never better," she smiled, "But hungry, definitely hungry, so getting some lunch is a great idea. Let's go."

CHAPTER FIFTY-SIX

When Ruth returned home late in the afternoon, she was feeling a little agitated with herself. She was glad she had made the decision to be more assertive in her progress, yet she kept bumping into roadblocks. Not only had she asked Bill last week about the saying, "alone since five," without any answers, but she was able to talk with Bryce today about things which she had been wondering, only to still be left feeling lost and frustrated.

They'd had lunch on the outside deck of Mike's Crab House, located in Riva, which borders Annapolis just to the southwest. They enjoyed eating at Mike's because of its casual waterfront appeal. The restaurant is seated directly on the banks of the beautiful South River, yet another gift of the Chesapeake. Constant boaters are coming and going during meal time, with plenty of docking provided. As with most of the restaurants in the Chesapeake region, crab is the main attraction.

While Bryce's group didn't choose to pick crabs for a quick lunch, they all ate it in some form. As an appetizer, both Ruth and Bev ordered cream of crab soup, and Heather and Bryce each ordered Maryland crab soup, a spicy tomato and vegetable based soup. And it was crab cakes for all of them for their main course. It has been insinuated that Marylanders are born with the crab gene. No worries, though, for the newly transplanted residents, as the locals are happy to teach others how to pick. It was at Mike's that

Bryce taught Bev how to pick steamed crabs, and then later, taught his children there as well.

During lunch Ruth had the opportunity to speak with Bryce about questions that were popping up in her mind.

"You know, Bryce," she began softly, so as not to interrupt Bev and Heather's conversation, "I realize that I've been through quite a year of adjustment, but it just occurred to me that I have not been paying any bills. I'm hoping that you're going to tell me that you've taken care of this, or I may be getting kicked out of my house," she finished with a nervous giggle.

"You're okay, Mom, and you're right," he said, patting her hand. "I am doing it. I wasn't at first, but Ted, at work, suggested that I move your accounts to my address to relieve that burden from you."

"Oh, Bryce, you should have just told me…I…I could have learned."

"Really, Mom, it's okay. Most of your accounts were already on automatic payment, so it's not that bad. I have to ask you, though. Do you remember my saying anything at all about the bills, because…I did talk to you about them."

Ruth shook her head slowly and lowered her eyes. "Sometimes I think I'm making such progress, and then…this," she said quietly.

"Hey…don't…Mom….you've come a long way…and you're getting there. In the beginning, you couldn't remember anything we'd tell you… about…Dad… and…that…that time. So…don't beat yourself up. You're fifty times better than you were last summer."

"Thank you, Son," she said, nodding her head and looking at him lovingly. "Did I tell you that I went through Dad's clothes and gave most of them to an organization that will distribute them to the needy? Mel helped me…um…it was kind of hard."

"Uh...I...I...I know.   Yes, it is," he said, nodding. "I...um...gathered some of Dad's personal belongings last summer, like his wallet...license...keys...and put them in a box, and put them in the office. Have you gone through that?" he asked, almost irritated.

She shook her head again. "I bet you already told me about that some time ago, huh?"

Heather, who had just returned from the restroom with her mother, picked up on what they were saying and added, "I bet you didn't forget that we're having a baby, huh, Grammy?"

"Now that, I'm holding on to tightly," she responded, smiling.

CHAPTER FIFTY-SEVEN

When the alarm clock began its usual ringing at six-thirty on Saturday morning, something told Ruth that she wasn't going to make the 'show' by seven o'clock in the back yard. It had been her ritual all summer to get out of bed quickly, get her breakfast ready and sit out back before the sprinklers turned on.

This morning, though, she was feeling rather low. From an outsider's point of view, she had had a good week. She had gone back to school for a week of preparation along with the other teachers. She enjoyed seeing the staff and hearing about everyone's summer, or so she thought. After a week of being asked by too many co-workers how her summer had gone, she was tired of the charade in which she was participating. It wasn't 'good,' and she was tired of saying that it was. She just wished people would stop asking her in passing, because she knew they only wanted to hear the word, 'good.' And it wasn't good. Do they really want to hear that she's still struggling with her memory, and still missing Roger terribly? Do they want her to spill all that out as they pass each other in the hallway? She didn't think so.

And to top it off, she bumped into Alison Byrnes twice in the hallway this week, and almost felt like calling her out on it. "I'm the one who lost my husband!" she felt like saying to her. "How about you just look me in the eyes and say something instead of running away from me?"

She continued to lie in her bed and mull over these feelings.

195

"Go ahead and pity yourself, Ruth, and see where it gets you," she said out loud to herself. "Did anyone tell you that this was going to be an easy process? Are you the only person in the world who is hurting? Stop being a ninny, and get out of bed!"

And with that, she stood and headed for the bathroom. After looking in the mirror for a while and continuing her pep talk, she decided to add something fun to her 'to do' list today, and decided to think about it over coffee. She returned to her bedroom to make her bed, but when she pulled on the covers, she heard a definite squeaky voice.

"Um, I'm under the covers, okay?"

Ruth sucked in her breath by surprise and pulled back the blankets she had just moved. And there she was, looking happy as a clam, leaning back on her paw-like hands, with her little ballet slippers tapping together. She tilted her head to one side, turned her lips in, yet puffed them out, and shrugged.

As frustrated as Ruth had just been feeling, she could only shake her head and smile.

"How do you always know when to show up?" she asked, sitting down next to her. The toothy grin that Ruth received in response erased so much of her heavy heart, that she couldn't help but laugh and scoop up her dearest friend. Together they made their way to the kitchen to start the day.

She didn't make the 'show' on time, but she was now working on her new perspective for the day. As she finished her toast, she smiled at Velo, who was tippy toeing on the patio table, being careful not to slip through the iron pattern of the table top.

"Um, what did you like best this summer?" Velo squeaked.

"Hmm," Ruth thought out loud. "I feel bad saying this, Velo, but there were actually a lot of things I liked about this summer. I'm sorry I was being such a baby before," she added, tearing up.

Velo effortlessly hopped off the table top and into Ruth's lap, which is where she spent a lot of time.

"My past is weighing heavily on me, and I think the part that feels so heavy, is…is…the part that I really don't want to know. Someday I'm going to be ready to know everything, but maybe not yet."

"Um, are you having a baby?" Velo squeaked.

"Yes! We're having a baby," Ruth smiled, while closing her eyes. She tried to envision the new baby coming in January, but she couldn't because other picture pieces were crowding her thoughts. She squinted her eyes tightly closed to help the picture focus in her mind, but she couldn't quite catch it.

"Velo!" was all she had to say. In response, her olive and lime green striped companion knew what she wanted and pulled on her hand to get her to stand and start walking toward her answers. She walked through the rain of the sprinkler system, but she didn't care. She knew her gardens well enough and was able to walk with her eyes mostly closed to keep out the water. She finally stopped when she felt Velo pushing on her legs.

"Take this," Velo instructed as she handed Ruth a piece of paper.

"I believe," she said, the second she had the paper in her hands. Velo pulled on her pant leg for her to meet Mr. Gabriello, and she didn't bother to read the other side before handing it over to him, claiming what was rightfully hers, yet stuck in nowhere land.

What a strange noise she heard this time. It was different. It sounded like a see saw going back and forth. Was she rocking? She didn't know. When the confusion stopped and her excitement steadied, she discovered that she *was* rocking, and looking down into the most beautiful face she had ever seen: Hayden's. Hayden as a newborn. Ruth found herself sitting in Bev's hospital room, so full of emotion, that she thought her heart would explode. She was holding her grandson, her very first grandchild, and there were no words to describe this feeling. Oh, it wasn't to say that she loved her grandchild more than her own son, but at this moment, in this very exact place in time, it was the same as if she had just given birth to him without the work. The emotions and the memories gushed at this point. They were coming at her so fast and she wanted to drown in them; she actually would volunteer to *drown* in them because she loved him that much. When he started to become a bit agitated, she stood to walk with him.

"Um, stop! Stop walking," Velo tugged at her leg. Ruth thought she was being ripped away from Hayden.

"No! Let me stay!" she answered, severely.

"No!" Velo squeaked as loudly as she could. "Stop! Stop!"

All of a sudden Ruth tripped over a root and went sprawling.

"No!" she screamed. "I dropped the baby!" She began crawling on the ground through the dirt, frantically searching for Hayden. "Hayden! Hayden! Where are you? I'm so sorry. Where are you?"

"Mr. Gabriello. Please help!" squeaked Velo.

At that moment, the piece of paper that Ruth had traded over to Mr. Gabriello for a memory, fluttered from his hand to the ground. The dream ended and Ruth stopped in her tracks. It was silent except for her panting. She was on her hands and knees, covered in dirt, and still dripping wet from the sprinkler. She was coherent, but dazed. She pulled herself into a sitting position and looked around. There was Velo in front of her, but standing safely at a distance.

Ruth looked at her, continuing to pant, until Velo broke the silence.

"I said, stop."

CHAPTER FIFTY-EIGHT

Ruth had certainly learned a lesson, and was severely chastised by Velo, which she didn't think was possible. When she took a step back later on, though, and thought about it, it was necessary for her to learn. She had never given it much thought as to what she did when she traveled in time with Mr. Gabriello. Velo explained in her most stern, yet squeaky voice, the importance of staying still when traveling with Mr. Gabriello. Ruth wasn't sure how to stop it from happening again, but assured her that she would certainly try.

After making her way back to the house, she was aghast to see her reflection, and headed straight for the shower. She cleaned up quickly because she had every intention of reclaiming the memories of Hayden's birth all by herself.

She chose to sit in the little room off the kitchen with Velo nestled in her lap comfortably. Her intentions were achieved, and she spent the better part of Saturday remembering Hayden's early years. She remembered begging Bev not to ever get angry with her for being around too much, and had promised to control her longings, which she could for the most part.

"Blame it on love," she'd say to Bryce and Bev as she'd invite herself over time and time again. To her delight, both parents had to work in the summer while Ruth did not, and this was her time, Ruth claimed, to let the love soak in. She was privy to Hayden's first steps and words, and to so many other firsts. Bev and

Bryce were more than generous in sharing their bundle of joy with his grandmother.

If it weren't bad enough longing for babysitting time with him, Ruth also had to compete for time against his adoring grandfather. She and Roger would laugh and kid with each other to see who'd get to hold Hayden first, and the stories at the dinner table almost always centered on him.

With both grandparents being teachers, they had just enough sense to know where to draw the line between loving and spoiling him. In following Hayden's parents' wishes, as he grew up, he had rules to follow, with consequences to pay if he failed to obey.

"Within limits, of course," Ruth giggled to herself.

Ruth and Roger learned all the do's and don'ts as grandparents with Hayden and were able to apply them later when their little neighbor, Hailey, was born, and then again when Heather was born. They learned a magic phrase that worked well in not being held accountable for the kids' tears.

"Let's check with your parents first," Ruth said out loud, laughing. "I wonder how many times I've had to say *that*?" She learned the hard way by saying 'yes' to Hayden, only to find out that the answer should have been 'no.' By using this phrase, it released her from any guilt in causing tears, if there were any.

"Being a grandmother is a gift. I have found no other joy that can top it, I think," she admitted. "Parenting Bryce was my dream, but sometimes I was tired…or, the cause of the tears. There's a little more guilt in parenting," she added, nodding.

Ruth remained in the chair for so long, but was still able to scratch off 'doing something fun' on her list. She had thoroughly enjoyed reminiscing about becoming a grandmother, and was already looking forward to remembering more.

"I'm only so sorry, Roger, that you're not here with me anymore. Nobody loved being a grandfather more than you."

Ruth felt a slight tugging on her pant leg and looked to see Velo rappelling down her leg.

"You taught me more than one lesson today, my little friend. To think of how filled with pity I was this morning. You've helped me to see, once again, how much I already have, and to look forward to in the future. We have a new baby coming in January. Look out, because here I come!"

By now, Velo had plopped down at the base of the fireplace. With compliments swirling all about her, she returned them with her best shrug and a good, "Hmph."

CHAPTER FIFTY-NINE

Ruth was relieved to finish the first few weeks of school. By now the students were familiar with the classroom rules associated with first grade, which allowed the school day to flow smoothly. She loved teaching this age group, and never grew tired of the students' endless energy and openness. They were just old enough to practice their manners, yet not quite old enough to hold it all together when something went wrong. She didn't have to pry too deeply to find out the truth when seeing one of her students upset. Often times when consoling one of them, she could almost grab hold of one of her own memories that seemed to be dancing so close to her grasp. Perhaps she was consoling someone in this memory, or maybe someone was consoling her.

"I really want to be able to remember my past anytime I want," she said softly to herself during her break. "Mr. Gabriello, can you hear me? Please show me a sign that I'm ready." She sat down, closed her eyes, and rested her head gently on the back of her chair. "Please show me a sign."

"Miss Ruth?" she heard softly while feeling a tug on her sleeve.

"Oh," she gasped. "Hailey, I'm sorry. I didn't hear you come in."

"Were you sleeping?"

"Oh, I was just resting my eyes. How are you?" she smiled at her little neighbor.

"I brought you a cookie. Mommy said I could," Hailey responded while placing a cookie in the shape of a sailboat on Ruth's desk.

"Why, this is beautiful, Hailey. Did you make it?"

"I helped my mommy," Hailey said while walking away. "I have to go now."

Ruth picked up the cookie and smiled. "I wish I had been friends with Hailey last year while she was in the first grade," she said out loud, putting the cookie aside for later. "That's just another example, Mr. Gabriello. I have never figured out why I distanced myself from that sweet little girl. Please, oh, please, show me a sign."

She sat back and closed her eyes again, intending to rest for the remainder of her break. As quiet as her first intruder had been entering her classroom, though, the following trespasser gave loads of warning.

"Ruthieee," she heard coming from down the hallway.

"Really, Mr. Gabriello? Is this my sign?" she said, smiling, as Lydia swirled into her classroom.

"Hi, Sweetie. I picked up your mail for you. Not much here except for this little ole' paycheck," she got in, smiling, while placing it on Ruth's desk. "I just passed Hailey coming out of your room. She said that she brought you a cookie and that she's your neighbor. Now, how come I never knew that? Oh, well," she said, giggling. "I'm excited for tonight. Did I tell you that Paul and I are going to see that new movie tonight with that guy, what's his name? You know, the really funny guy with a dry sense of humor? And then, that lady that's in so many movies. She's so good. Do you know who I'm talking about? Oh, it will come to me later," she exhaled loudly. "It was nice chatting, Honey, but I've got to run to the restroom before the kids come back from recess," she squeezed in, turning to walk out the door.

"Lydia... There's something I wanted to ask you, but...I can't remember," replied Ruth as the bell rang.

"Gotta go, Sweetie," Lydia sang out as she dashed out the door, thankful that Ruth couldn't remember the particular question that Lydia hoped to never have to answer. Lydia heard it as plain as day when Ruth asked her the meaning of 'alone since five' during their summer luncheon get together. Ruth had asked her one more time at the beginning of the school year, but Lydia said she couldn't remember what she had thought it meant.

"Oh! I know she's going to ask me again," Lydia said to herself as she hurried down the hall.

As Ruth watched her scurry down the hallway, she noticed Alison Byrnes do an about face when approaching her, and go the other way.

CHAPTER SIXTY

"You can come in now, Ruth," the sweet natured, young receptionist said as she held the door for Ruth.

"Hello, Ruth," Dr. Brooke said as Ruth entered her office.

Grace Brooke sat down across from Ruth and crossed her legs. She was wearing brown slacks, a teal colored blouse with a scarf draped across her shoulders that pulled in all the colors of the changing leaves outside. She was the picture of outdoor elegance combined with stylish confidence. With one graceful sweep of her hand she pushed her long silky black hair behind her and gave a smile toward Ruth, who was staring at her a bit stupefied.

"Ruth?" Dr. Brooke started.

"I...I...I'm sorry," she responded, giggling. "Are you sure that you're a doctor and not a beautiful super model. I mean, look at you...your hair...it's beautiful. It's different. I mean...your curls were beautiful as well, but...this is stunning."

"Thank you," she answered genuinely. "I thought I'd go for a bit of a *change*."

"Change is good," Ruth heard herself saying and then smiled. "Now how did she just get me to admit that?" she wondered to herself. "She's good."

"How are the first graders? Everyone continuing to fall into routine?" Dr. Brooke started off the session.

"It's a good crop again," Ruth answered her, smiling. "We'll keep them," she added, chuckling to herself.

"And how's your crop at home?"

"My crop at home?" Ruth wondered out loud. "Do you mean Bryce and Bev, or…do you mean m…m…my friends at home?" she asked timidly, referring to The First Creatures.

"Both," Dr. Brooke responded, nodding her head.

"Well…," Ruth began, tapping her fingers on the comfortable leather chair in which she was enveloped. "Bryce is upset with me. You know, I have kept my garden friends, if you will, between you and me. I…I…didn't want to tell anyone about them because they're so private and special to me, but…I slipped in referring to them while talking with Bryce. He's….more cautious than ever in speaking with me, I can tell. A…a…and…he has been since his father died and….he won't let me babysit the kids until I'm…'healed.' And now I've blown it, I'm afraid," she blurted out, getting agitated.

"And how is your progress with your recovery coming along?" Dr. Brooke asked.

"I tell you that my son is upset with me after finding out about the First Creatures and all you want to know is how I'm doing?" she questioned.

"I'm interested in *your* recovery, Ruth, not your son's reaction to how you're healing," she added.

Ruth exhaled, gathered her arms close to her chest and held her hand up to her mouth, weary of her next question.

"Am….I crazy?" she barely got out, starting to cry.

Shaking her head and giving Ruth a compassionate smile, she began, "You're a remarkable woman, Ruth," Dr. Brooke replied, shocking Ruth. "You've taken your pain and your inability to remember your past and you've created a way to remember where

206

you've been. You are unique, as are all individuals. You are *not* crazy."

"I...I...I'm okay?" Ruth stumbled.

"You're more than okay. You've been coming to me for more than a year and you bring reports of progress each time we talk."

"M...m...my friends are okay?"

"Your friends are helping you remember. Yes, your friends are okay," she smiled at Ruth.

CHAPTER SIXTY-ONE

Martha's constantly wagging tail was the only proof that Ruth needed in wondering if her trusted companion still enjoyed their walks. Ruth didn't care to walk in the heat of the summer so Martha was left to wander the yard for exercise, but fall…fall was another story. Ruth loved the change of seasons and always looked forward to whichever one was coming next, but she finally agreed that the coming of fall was close to her favorite. The picturesque view that met her eyes was endless, and the leaves that decorated the path of her walk were of every shade of red, orange, yellow, purple and just a hint of brown. The sky was bright blue, the air was crisp, and she was wearing her first sweater of the season. It made her smile when she thought of Dr. Brooke's new look and the beautiful scarf that had been draped across her shoulders. Everything about her subtly demonstrated that change was a natural progression in life.

"A natural progression," Ruth said out loud to Martha. "I'm changing, too, Ole' Girl. I'm ready, Mr. Gabriello. Can you hear me?" she added as they carried on briskly down the lane.

As she approached her driveway, she could see a little hand waving to her outside of a car window. She realized that Mary was just pulling up into her own driveway and that Hailey was desperately trying to get in a wave. She stopped and gave them both a big wave, and Martha did as well, by offering them a bark.

"What a sweet little family," she thought out loud to herself as she walked toward her door. And as she was about to enter her home, she noticed the same small silver car driving away. "I've got to ask Mary about that car. Maybe she knows something."

After reheating a serving of tuna cheese casserole for herself, she headed out back to enjoy her meal in Mother Nature's parade. The gardens were glorious, but at the end of the season, Ruth was exhausted from the constant care and attention she gave to them. She'd have her lawn care company come in a month or so to clean out the fallen leaves once the change was complete.

As she finished her meal, she was just beginning to wonder why she was sitting alone. She usually had some form of company surrounding her by this point. To her satisfaction, though, she didn't have to wonder for long as the Frances Williams' leaves began to rustle. She enjoyed it when Velo appeared to her in this fashion. A little star rose from inside of the hosta and floated toward Ruth. It popped directly in front of Ruth's eyes, and from the star landed Velo, who fell directly into Ruth's lap.

"Um, you were thinking about us, weren't you?" she squeaked as she climbed from Ruth's lap onto the patio table. She carefully tippy toed toward the empty luncheon plate and examined it.

"Yes, I was," Ruth smiled at her dearest companion. I was also thinking about Hailey's family, and wondering how long they've been in my life. I'm trying, Velo. I keep telling Mr. Gabriello that I'm…Velo! Watch out!"

Ruth instinctively jumped out of her chair and caught Velo in midair, who had tripped in the iron pattern of the table, and went flying off.

"Oh, you scared me! Are you okay?" she asked Velo while cradling her.

"Um, you're squishing me," she squeaked through a toothy grin. "Come on, let's go get Ojy, and we'll show you something."

Ruth set Velo down gently, and she tippy toed ahead of Ruth through the gardens. Velo stopped and looked at a couple of verbenas which were beginning to exhibit the ragged look of the end of the summer, and then continued walking. While heading back a little further, Ruth heard the distinctive giggling that could belong to only one.

"Ahh, haa, ahh, haa. Here I am. I fooled you," she sang out to them, jumping out of a cluster of verbena around the bend.

"But why are you…?" began Ruth.

"Just because. Come on. Follow us," she sang out once more as she sashayed circles around Ruth's feet and then dashed ahead, all the while spinning and giggling.

Ruth was close to the back of the garden when she found her friends waiting for her. They were both pulling on a rock that was flush with the rest of its row.

"But it's not out of line," she said to them.

"Ahh, haa, but Velo says it's here," Ojy replied. "Will you help?"

It took Ruth a few minutes to rock the stone back and forth just to get it to budge.

"Shall I?" Ruth motioned to them, referring to the note inside.

As Ruth pulled out the note, Velo took Ojy by the shoulders and turned her around, away from Ruth. Ruth didn't understand what was happening, but looked at the note as she flipped it to the back side. She saw the name of St. Francis of Assisi Church, and more writing below it that read:

"We thank you for your prayers and condolences during this difficult time.

~Ruth, Bryce, Bev…"

The rest of the writing was smeared just as the other note had been.

"Oh!" Ruth sucked in her breath, kneeling down with tears falling quietly. She held the note close to help herself calm down. "I...I'm holding the obituary article," she said quietly. A few moments passed when she added, "No, it can't be because of this type of paper."

"Oh!" she sucked in her breath again. "I'm...holding...the funeral program," she whispered.

She looked toward Velo who met her gaze with compassion. They continued to look at each other while Ruth slowly digested what she had just found. After a moment, Velo reached toward the paper and pushed on it to show that there was more. Ruth slowly opened it and read the last section. It was a poem that read:

Crossing Over

Oh, please don't feel guilty

It was just my time to go.

I see you are still feeling sad.

And the tears just seem to flow.

We all come to earth for our lifetime,

And for some it's not many years

I don't want you to keep crying

You are shedding so many tears.

I haven't really left you

Even though it may seem so.

I have just gone to my heavenly home.

And I'm closer to you than you know.

Just *Believe* that when you say my name,

I'm standing next to you,

I know you long to see me,

But there's nothing I can do.

But I'll still send you messages

And I hope you understand,

That when your time comes to

"cross over," I'll be there

To take your hand.

-Author Unknown

Ruth sat and wept quietly while Velo leaned against her legs, facing her.

"You stayed…you stayed with me…and why did you turn Ojy around? Why won't she look at me?" Ruth asked, tearily.

"Um, she can't," she squeaked softly, while tippy toeing closer to Ruth, who was now sitting on the ground, to hold her hand.

"So this is why Hayden was allowed to write notes during Mass," Ruth whispered. "Because it was his grandfather's funeral. His own father was too upset to notice."

Ruth looked toward her truest friend and tried to offer a brave smile. "Am I going to see the funeral?" Ruth asked cautiously.

Velo shook her head. "Um, you don't have to see that. You'll like this one. Let's go," she responded, pulling on Ruth's hand. She turned Ojy around to face Ruth again, and Ojy immediately began talking.

"Ahh, haa, ahh, haa. I was holding my breath for so long. Come on, I'll help," she said, also pulling on Ruth's hands to get up.

Ruth followed them a little bit further until they reached the familiar oak tree. Mr. Gabriello was waiting for her with his left hand raised. Into his other, she exchanged the program note and her promise to believe for a little more of who she was. She was mentally exhausted from what had just transpired and hoped to see only a part of her past that would bring cheer to her heart. The travel time down memory lane was quicker than other times and she immediately heard laughing and felt something soft in her hands. She knew that feeling, but what was it? Oh, yeah, she remembered just before the picture came into focus. It was a feeling she treasured. It was a little hand in hers. It was Hayden's hand, and he wasn't more than two years old. As the image became clearer, she found herself walking hand in hand in Mary's backyard. There were friendly faces mingling with one another and then she saw Bev and Mary stepping out of the house.

"Look, Hayden, look who it is," Ruth said, pointing toward Bev.

"Mommy," he replied with a raspy bit of sleep still in his voice. Letting go of Ruth's hand he eagerly made his way toward Bev with wobbly two year-old sleepy legs.

"Ah, there's my little man," Bev said as she scooped him up. "Did you just wake up from a nap at Grammy's?" she asked, wiping his wavy brown hair off his dampened forehead.

Hayden nodded and nestled his head on Bev's shoulder.

Mary approached them and patted Hayden's back. "Well, I'm glad you woke up in time for my baby shower," she said.

Hayden reached his hand down and patted Bev's protruding abdomen.

"Mommy's baby," he said groggily.

"Yes, that's mommy's baby. We're both having babies," Mary said, giving him another pat.

"That's right, Little Man, but Miss Mary's baby will be here *very* soon and we still have to wait a while for our baby," Bev said, giving him a kiss on the top of his head.

Ruth opened her eyes at this point and basked in the memory of that time. Each time she closed her eyes she was able to put herself right back into her past. She remembered Hailey being born a few weeks after the shower. She was so small compared to Hayden's two year old frame, and looked like a little angel. Ruth and Roger were so excited with the news of her birth, that they rushed to the hospital and treated her like a second grandchild. And it wasn't too long after that, when Heather was born. Ruth's memory seemed to bounce down the birthday trail at this point, and she remembered pink ballerina cakes, chocolate cowboy cakes, cakes with trucks and dirt, and cakes with flowers and fish. She got the feeling that their families enjoyed celebrating together, and did so often.

As Ruth came to, she shivered and realized that she had been sitting in the garden for some time. She rubbed her hands up and down her arms over her sweater to get warm as she looked around to get her bearings. When she looked at Velo, she noticed that she, also, was rubbing her paw-like hand up and down on her dingy, butter-colored jacket. Ruth raised her eyebrows lovingly toward her with a questioning look, and was met with a good, "hmph."

CHAPTER SIXTY-TWO

Fall was truly upon the Annapolis area, and the days were glorious. The skies were vivid blue, the leaves were of every imaginable array of autumnal bliss, and the air felt crisp and clean. The mornings were quite chilly, and jackets were a must for the school children. Though they often stood shivering in the early morning hours, waiting to say the Pledge, the autumn sun worked its magic, and by lunch recess, the coats were discarded in exchange for squeals of warm delight.

Ruth loved recess duty, and she especially loved it during the fall. Not only did she know the children better by this point than she did in September, but it was just plain, old fashioned fun during the fall. If there was a pile of fallen leaves anywhere on the playground, gathered together by a recent breeze, there would definitely be little feet skipping through it soon thereafter. Fallen leaves were just as much fun for children to play with, as they were for the adults who admired their changing beauty while still on the trees.

When Ruth stepped outside of her classroom door for recess duty, she could hear the fun before she could see it. The sounds of laughter, chanting, and games being played met her ears as she rounded the corner toward the playground. As she passed through different groups of children playing basketball, dodge ball, and soccer, she was greeted by many of her former students.

"Hi, Ms. Lily, look at me, Ms. Lily, look how fast I can run, Ms. Lily."

She reached out her hands to touch their passing outstretched fingers as a way of greeting those who couldn't slow down enough to talk, but didn't want to miss the opportunity to greet her.

She always had a smile for them and was known to be very approachable should one of them need comforting. At one time she thought it was her nature to be so compassionate with the students because she was a grandparent, but then realized that she had always been that way.

"Does it get any better than this?" she wondered for the thousandth time. "Where else can one get a job where hugs and smiles are abundantly offered?"

At that very moment, two little arms wrapped around her from behind without ever losing step with her. Knowing exactly whose arms they were, she knew whose face she'd see upon turning around. And there it was; a beautiful smile chiseled into a young boy's face. He was quick to whip out some cartoon cards from his pocket to share with her. And while he was talking, another voice joined in.

"Hi, Ms. Lily," added the small, but vibrantly spoken voice. "Ah, ha, I really like your jacket today. Oh, it's so pretty," she said, feeling the print on the outside of Ruth's jacket. It was difficult for this little girl to contain her happiness and she twirled about Ruth as they visited.

As was customary, two other little girls ran up toward Ruth, joined the group, and greeted her affectionately. One of them was soft spoken and was quick to offer Ruth a shy smile. She had a gentle way about her and she seemed to flutter close by. The last little girl was the one who had the strongest impact on Ruth. She never missed an opportunity to make Ruth laugh and feel special. She had an animated way about her, and often times acted like her favorite stuffed animal, which she kept close to her. She'd share stories with Ruth about her stuffed animals and the adventures they encountered.

In the mix of supervising the playground, attending to scraped knees and a few tears, it was always these four children who consistently visited with Ruth. They weren't first grade students anymore, but they had remained close to her and they enjoyed each other's company. Ruth didn't understand why these particular students remained close to her, but she was so very happy that they did. They reminded her of Hayden an awful lot, and the closeness she shared with him, and it made her wish that he attended her school.

"I want to visit with my grandchildren," she thought, angrily. "Why can't I remember everything and be done with it? Bryce isn't going to allow me time alone with them until I'm healed. Is this healing ever going to be complete?"

"Um, excuse me, but you're standing in our leaf pile," a small and squeaky voice uttered.

"Huh!" exclaimed Ruth. She whipped around to look for Velo near the ground, but only saw life size feet and legs. When she looked up, she found herself looking at Elizabeth, the little animated student. "What?" Ruth barely got out, feeling as if she were having a déjà vu moment. She could swear she had just heard Velo speaking to her, but only Elizabeth was standing there.

"You're standing in our leaf pile, Ms. Lily," Elizabeth repeated.

"I...I...I'm so sorry...I....I...I was th...th...thinking about something else."

All at once the leaves about her feet were being scooped up by the children and being thrown into the air. They were laughing, squealing and calling at each other. The motions were repetitive and seemed to repeat over and over. Their voices began to overlap with each other and become slurred. They seemed to be more distant than they actually were and Ruth thought that either she or the children were disappearing. She tried to remain calm, but thought she was having trouble breathing. She saw flashes before her eyes and puzzle pieces seemed to be swarming about her…or was that the leaves? She didn't know. She needed it to stop. She couldn't breathe. They were laughing. The leaves were circling her in the air. She heard her name. Ruth….no, Ms. Lily…no, Grammy. Hayden was throwing something in the air. Hayden? Was it leaves? No, it sparkled. Sparkled? They were laughing…

"St…st…STOP!" she remembered screaming before falling to the ground and covering her eyes to stop the flashing and the puzzle pieces. She saw flashes again and heard screeching. And then… all was silent.

"Ruth…Ruth…back away…give her some room," another teacher was yelling.

"Ms. Lily…what's wrong, Ms. Lily?" the children were saying in the distance.

Ruth kept her eyes closed, or was she unconscious? She couldn't tell the difference. She remembered gasping for air. She remembered the nurse helping her into a wheel chair and being brought inside. When Ruth became more fully aware of her surroundings, she realized that she was sitting in the nurse's office being offered an inhaler.

"Breathe this in, Ruth. You'll feel much better," the nurse was saying. "The ragweed and dry leaves are terrible at this time. You were having a hard time breathing out there, and it's no wonder with the high count. I've just pulled your health chart and I see that you have fall allergies. I also see that this is your inhaler. It's okay to be outside during this time, Ruth, but you shouldn't be playing in the leaves, or throwing them, for that matter."

Ruth nodded her head in agreement, just wanting the nurse to stop talking. How could anyone understand what just happened? Ruth couldn't.

"Would you like to lie down for a bit? We've got your class covered."

She nodded again and headed for the cot. Once she was lying down, she rolled over to face the wall because she needed some privacy.

"What just happened out there?" she thought. "There is no way I'm telling the nurse that I was that confused. Sure, I'm allergic to leaves, but something else happened. How could I be so confused that I thought Elizabeth was Velo? But come to think of it, she does remind me of her. But what else? Why did I think Hayden was there throwing leaves around? Is it because I was just thinking about him? I've *got* to push forward and get myself healed or I'll never be able to be normal again. I don't know why, but I think I'm very close to remembering what happened to me."

CHAPTER SIXTY-THREE

Ruth used that time in the nurse's office to make mental notes of the steps she needed to take in order to reclaim her memory. At first she thought about telling Dr. Brooke what had happened, but she could just see Dr. Brooke smiling at her and telling her that she was making progress.

"I know I'm making progress, but come on!" she thought. "Be proactive."

She thought about Bryce and some of the things he had asked her. He had asked about a box that he had left at her house some time ago, and if she had looked through it. She hadn't looked in it and thought she had subconsciously pushed it aside. She couldn't exactly remember doing that, but at the same time, she was aware of its presence in her home office.

"That's one thing I'm going to look for," she thought.

And she *knew* that there was something Lydia understood but didn't want to talk about with Ruth.

"Imagine that," Ruth chuckled to herself. "There's something Lydia *doesn't* want to talk about. She talks *all* the time. Why not this? I definitely need to corner her."

She thought that this was a good start to being hands-on in her quest to finalize her healing process.

She went home from school early after her incident that day. She stopped by to see the second graders before leaving, though. She knew they had to be frightened about what had happened. She explained to them that she was very allergic to dry leaves and because she had been standing in the middle of the leaf throwing, she had had an asthma attack. It turns out that their teacher had already explained the same thing to them, so Ruth felt relieved. She wasn't about to talk about her confusion, or her healing process, with them.

Her principal had stopped by the health room as well. Ruth could hear the relief in his expression when the nurse explained that Ruth had an asthma attack. She had an underlying suspicion, though, that he was always watching her to make sure of her stability around children. She was glad of that, and would want the same thing from any principal.

She made herself a cup of coffee and sat down in a rocker recliner in the very small room next to the kitchen. She got up and grabbed a blanket to wrap around herself because the cold air was moving in. When she was snuggled once again comfortably in her chair, she looked down at the photo on the small table between the chairs. The frame held one of her favorite photos of Roger and her. It was taken a couple of years ago during the fall in their back yard. Roger had just finished carving a pumpkin and had told Ruth that he modeled it after her. She had tried making the same expression that was on the pumpkin's face, but determined that it was a better fit for Roger's face. They were both trying to match its expression when someone snapped a picture of them. They received the framed picture as a gift, and Ruth had treasured it since.

While she was admiring the picture, she began thinking the same thought she usually did for the past year and a half: "*Why* did you die?" But what came out of her mouth was decidedly different.

"*How* did you die?" she asked out loud.

The words startled her and she froze in her tracks. She stopped the rocking motion and stared at the picture.

221

"*How* did you die, Roger? *How* did you die?" she asked, repeatedly.

She knew she was ready for some real answers, so she stood and robotically walked toward the office. The box for which she was looking was sitting in the open as if it had magically appeared. She knew, though, that before now, she wasn't ready to notice it, even though it was sitting on Roger's desk.

She sat down, took a deep breath, and exhaled slowly. Was she about to learn some answers about which she had been wondering for so long?

She pulled off the rubber band slowly and lifted the top. She closed her eyes in anticipation of a shock, so she had to force herself to slowly reopen them, preparing for the worst. To an outsider, the contents of the box looked harmless. There was a wallet, a set of keys, and an identification card. Ruth continued to breathe slowly while fingering through them. When she picked up the wallet, she rather expected to feel more emotional, like she did when she went through his clothing. She dared herself to smell the wallet, but it only smelled of leather, not of Roger. She then picked up his keys and felt the grooves of each one. She recognized their house keys, her car keys, and some of his keys for work, but she also saw another car key. It was an oversized one, which she instantly remembered as being his. Without warning, there were puzzle pieces flashing in front of her eyes and she heard a deafening screech that she associated with traveling back in time with Mr. Gabriello. The key instantly felt like hot iron on her fingers and she dropped it, shaking her hands and then quickly covering her ears to block out the noise. After a moment when the noise subsided, she lowered her hands to gather her bearings. Through shallow breaths she allowed herself to picture Roger's truck in her mind. It wasn't a great big truck like Bryce's, but a smaller version of it. It was dark gray and rather old. She smiled when she remembered Roger referring to it as, 'Old Faithful.' He could have easily afforded a new truck, but was very satisfied with Old Faithful.

Remembering what she had set out to do, Ruth whispered, "*How* did you die, Roger? And *where* is Old Faithful?"

She could have sat for a lot longer to reminisce about Roger and his truck while using her memory, but she had to finish this part of her quest.

She pushed aside the keys and began sifting through more of the contents. She picked up a folded newspaper and read the title: *Memorial Day Parade Brings Patriotic Rhythm to Annapolis*. She looked at the colorful photos from the parade, but there was nothing important that jumped out at her.

"Why did Bryce put this paper in here?" she wondered out loud. As she continued to look at the pictures, Martha walked into the office and nudged Ruth's knee.

"Huh!" Ruth gasped and dropped the newspaper, not aware that Martha had quietly trod into the office. "Hey, Ole' Girl, do you want to go outside?"

When the newspaper fell, it flipped to the other side and as Ruth bent down to pick it up, she froze at the words she read: *Local College Professor Killed in Memorial Day Accident*.

She fell to the floor and held her gaze on the title. She half expected herself to spin into a memory, but nothing happened. She looked at Roger's picture below the title and reached out to touch his face. As she stared at his picture, the tears began to come, but not before she saw the words: *beloved professor, award winning gardener, especially tragic because...* She pulled the newspaper close to her heart and rocked.

"Oh, Roger. I'm so sorry," she sobbed. "I c...c...couldn't remember how you died...I'm s...s...sorry, Roger...I love you...I love you...I...I'm s...so sorry you died!" She continued to sit and rock back and forth on the floor until her sobs subsided.

Ruth looked about the room from her sitting position as if to see something different. Perhaps this room or life as she saw it would look different now that she 'knew.'

"I found out," she said out loud. "I found out...now I know...but I...I...I can't remember it...does this count, Bryce? I know your dad died in a car accident, but I just can't remember it. How much longer must I wait to be considered healed? What else can I do?" She sat quietly for another few moments, willing her memory to come to her, but nothing...nothing happened.

"Well, I answered the first question I needed to know," she told herself. With an intense, yet desperate presence about her, she added, "I need to talk with Lydia...she knows."

CHAPTER SIXTY-FOUR

Ruth had a restless night's sleep and was glad when her alarm clock finally buzzed, allowing her to end her agonizing dreams. She had actually dreamed of Roger all night long, and had replayed different versions of car accidents that resulted in his death. First she envisioned a multi car accident pile-up on Route 50 as he came home from work. Then in another version, he actually got hit by a car while stopping to help someone on the side of the highway. The version that caused her to wake up screaming, though, was of Roger being bumped over the side of the Severn River Bridge by the small silver car she kept seeing out front. He loved that bridge and took it daily to and from work; never growing tired of the scenic commute. The thought of the bridge taking his life made her angry as well as hysterical. And who is driving the small silver car? She had asked Mary, and she didn't know either. In all of the dreams, though, the accident occurred at five o'clock. After all, she'd been alone since five; at least that's what Hailey had heard her father say.

"This is crazy!" she uttered while climbing out of bed. "I've got to speak with Bryce. I've completed my share of proactive detective work, and I'm done! I need to speak with him, Dr. Brooke, and with Lydia as well! I want some answers, I deserve some answers, and I want them now!"

Feeling empowered by this newest decision, she marched into the kitchen to make her coffee and write out a plan. But there on her kitchen counter was a flyer that advertized the on-going fall

225

festival at Stonehenge. She had left it there to remind her that she was scheduled to volunteer at the customer service desk on Sunday, which was tomorrow.

"There's no way I can demand some answers from Bryce during his busiest season. What was I thinking?" she thought out loud. "And my appointment with Dr. Brooke isn't until Monday, so that's two strikes against my action plan, and I've only had it for five minutes. Some detective you are. You can't even start an action without coming to road blocks. That leaves only one person: Lydia."

Ruth knew that if she called Lydia at home, then she would somehow manage to evade her. "I've got to go directly to her house and ask her. It's the only way," she decided out loud.

Knowing that she had a tentative plan for cornering Lydia today, Ruth set about making some breakfast. As usual, she enjoyed planning her food around the seasons and the current temperature. It was cold outside; not freezing, but cold, so hot oatmeal was a definite this morning. It only took a few minutes to prepare, and after adding a spoonful of brown sugar, she headed for the small room, her new favorite. She paused, though, when standing in the entrance of the room, and instead, walked into the back room. It had been a while since she had sat back there and she knew the room was calling her name.

She didn't have a fire going in the back room so it was rather chilly. She grabbed a large bear blanket and wrapped it around herself before sitting down.

"This is a perfect Saturday morning," she thought out loud. "I've got a plan to get more answers today, and I know that change is in the air. Hmm…," she continued to talk with herself. "Just as with Dr. Brooke, I can accept change. I'm ready…and it's time to move forward," she smiled. "And look at it outside. Most of the leaves have fallen, and most of the colorful flowers are spent."

Ruth stopped talking and thought for a second. "Wait a minute," she said hesitantly. "The flowers are spent? Wait...wait...wait a minute. Wait!" she shouted, jumping up and running to the sliding glass door that led to the gardens. She practically ran into the door, grasped the glass, and peered out.

"Where are you? Where are you? Wait, wait, wait, wait," she said, stumbling back to her chair, feeling full of panic. Falling backward into her chair, she screamed when landing on a small lump in the chair and jumped back up.

"Oh! Velo, what are you doing here? You scared me! And where have you been?" she cried, falling to her knees. She scooped up her dearest friend and cradled her close. "Please don't leave me like that. I...I....I don't want to be alone."

"Um...I wasn't gone...and, um....you're squishing me," she squeaked.

"But...but...but I haven't seen you recently. Where have you been?"

"Well, um, I *was* just sitting in the chair and you sat on me," she offered in reply, cocking her head to one side while looking at Ruth, nonchalantly.

"But...but...," Ruth began to cry and could hardly speak. "Y...you're my b...b...best friend. Y...you're a hosta plant, I mean y...you come out of a hosta plant, and I just realized th...that they're d...d...dying and I don't want you to die, too," she sobbed.

Velo pulled back a little from Ruth so she could see her better. She patted Ruth's arm with her paw-like hands and made little 'hmph' noises.

"Um, I'm not leaving you," she squeaked while once more cocking her head to the side and patting Ruth.

"Who...are...you...really?" Ruth asked slowly. "I mean, really, who are you?

"I'm a First Creature, like the others."

"Yes, I know, you've told me that before," Ruth replied, "But…*what* are you? I don't really understand, Velo."

Velo had climbed out of Ruth's grasp and began walking on her tippy toes in a circle in front of Ruth while trying to explain.

"Mr. Gabriello will let you know when you're ready," Velo answered.

"I know you said you were here first, but I don't know what that means. And I seem to have more and more questions all the time. I see flashes so often before me like puzzle pieces floating in the air, and sometimes I hear a screeching sound like when I travel back in time with Mr. Gabriello. And who is Mr. Gabriello anyway? And I keep seeing this silver car. Who is that? And how do you get here, my little friend? Can Mr. Gabriello show me?"

"A little bit," Velo answered. "Um, you have to ask Lydia something, don't you?"

"Yes, but let's go out back and visit Mr. Gabriello first."

Ruth grabbed a light jacket and together, she and Velo walked through the gardens.

As Ruth walked along, Velo tippy toed ahead of her. Ruth noticed considerable changes in the garden that worried her. A light frost had fallen already and the plants were all showing signs of natural decomposing. When they neared the back, Ruth stopped and knelt down.

"Velo, I'm scared," she said tentatively. "Where are the others? The garden is preparing itself for winter. Will you still be here? Please don't leave me."

When Ruth knelt down, Velo began walking in circles again. "They're still here," she squeaked. "And we won't leave you."

"Okay," Ruth nodded. "I believe you….I believe *in* you, my friend. And I believe in you, too, Mr. Gabriello. I…I…I don't have a note, but please show me more. "

She stood and looked toward Mr. Gabriello's tree. Just as she had wished, the tree widened and once again, a crudely formed figure evolved. She studied him before walking toward him and held his gaze. What was it about his eyes, she wondered. They looked familiar to her. She had visited him so frequently during the last few months that she felt comfortable around him. She paused for a moment when thinking back to the first time she saw him from a distance. It seemed so long ago. And then she thought of the first time when she met him face to face. She was so afraid. He never said anything…but he had answers to her past and he showed them to her. She smiled at him and met his steady gaze.

"I'm ready, Mr. Gabriello. I'm ready to see more. Please show me," she said as she raised her hand to his.

Ruth felt the usual sensation of falling as she went back in time with him. She was prepared to hear the screeching sound she so often heard lately, but she heard more of a whirring sound instead. As her view came into focus, she found herself looking out of her kitchen window. She had just started the dishwasher and that was the cause of the whirring sound. Right at that moment, the screen door burst open and three little figures came flying in.

"Grammy, let's go. You said after dinner. Come on, we're waiting for you," their voices said in unison.

Hayden, Heather and Hailey were dancing around her, holding small packets in their hands.\

"I'm finishing up and then I'll be right out, I promise," she said, smiling at them.

She pulled out a dry towel, laid it over the counter of the sink, and then joined them outside.

"Now let's see. Let's read the directions again, shall we," she said as she pulled Heather close to her, taking her packet. "Oh, yes, I think the conditions are perfect, just as you all thought, because the grounds are dry."

A chorus of squeals met her ears as they delighted in her approval.

"Okay, how about I open the packets for you so the contents won't spill?" she suggested.

"Grammy, do you really think this will work? Do you think we're really going to *grow* fairies? Heather asked excitedly.

"Oh, no," Ruth answered dramatically, but in a hushed tone, smiling. "This is fairy dust. This is *food* for the fairies. You're just to sprinkle it throughout the garden so they have a little something extra on which to snack, like a treat."

"Oh," Heather replied with awe. "Do you mean that there are already fairies living in the garden, Grammy?"

Ruth continued to draw on Heather's wonderment and nodded. "Oh, yes, I've seen them before, just once or twice. The first time was early in the morning. I saw something glittering right in the middle of some vinca vines. When I walked a little closer to see, I saw a tiny little figure flying through the garden, but it was using the vines to help it swing from plant to plant."

"Whoa, Grammy! You never told me that before," Heather replied with pure astonishment.

"And another time after dinner it happened again," Ruth continued, smiling. "Grampy and I had just finished having dinner outside. He brought in the dishes and left me outside to check on some potted plants. I thought I heard some music that sounded like a fiddle, but I couldn't tell from where it was coming, except that it was down low. I pushed aside some hosta leaves and I saw them, but just for an instant. It looked like a tiny little hoedown inside that big ceramic pot over there," she added, pointing to the other side of the patio.

"No way!" Hailey chimed in. "Did that really happen, Miss Ruth?"

"It certainly did. I only saw them for the briefest of moments, and then they were gone. They're quick and they move with lightening speed. And I do think that I had recently sprinkled fairy dust throughout the garden just prior to that happening, so this ought to do the trick."

"Look," Hayden began, adding to Ruth's chronicle and pointing to his packet. "It says right on here that fairy sightings are rare, but possible, *but* can only happen if the holder believes. "I believe, Grammy, I believe," he said.

"So do I, Hayden," she said, turning to offer him a loving glance. Right at that moment she was met with one of his smiles that caused him to look exactly like his father and grandfather. She gasped at the resemblance and then began fading out of the dream. Just before arriving back to reality, she saw the children sprinkling, shaking, and tossing the fairy dust around the garden. As the magical fairy dust settled among the plants, it added a new vibrancy to each leaf and petal it lay on as it caught the remainder of evening's breath.

CHAPTER SIXTY-FIVE

Ruth really didn't have a plan on how to speak with Lydia. She was just jumping in full force to collect answers and put herself back together again. She treasured her last memory, crediting herself by asking Mr. Gabriello to show her more. She remembered the fairy dust now as if it had happened only yesterday. She remembered more of the story by herself later on. The fairy dust had been a big seller at Stonehenge, and Bryce's staff had a hard time keeping it on the shelves. The content of the packets was harmless sparkles and filler, but the children didn't know that. There was something definitely mystical about fairies that brought out the inner creativity in the dullest of souls. Ruth was pleased for being able to draw out more from that scenario, but why couldn't she remember these things on her own, she wondered. It's as if Mr. Gabriello triggers the memories, or allows them to surface.

"One day I'll be in control of my own memory and I'll have myself put back together again," she thought out loud, turning her car onto Lydia's driveway. Fearing an uncomfortable confrontation with Lydia, or worse, another denial on her behalf, Ruth chose to sit in her car for a few more minutes while trying to create a plan.

A soft rapping on the driver's side window surprised Ruth and snapped her out of a trance.

"Oh, Paul, you scared me. I must have been daydreaming," Ruth started.

"Hi there, Ruth. I saw you from inside and thought I'd come out and talk with you before Lydia sees you."

"Then you know why I'm here?"

"To tell you the truth, I expected you a long time ago. Way back in the summer when you had lunch with Lydia," Paul added. "She told me what happened and I figured you'd be questioning her."

"I did ask her once, but she denied knowing anything."

"Look, Ruth. I'm not aware of how much you remember, but Bryce has asked Lydia to not talk about your incident."

"I understand that, Paul, but I have made a lot of progress in my healing. I know about the accident...Roger's accident, that is. I read about it, but I still can't remember it," Ruth added, quietly. "I'm just trying to piece together parts of my life that don't make sense."

"You're a brave woman, Ruth," Paul replied, nodding. "Lydia's inside."

Not intending to go inside right away, Ruth was feeling at a loss for words while knocking on her door.

The look on Lydia's face when she answered let Ruth know that she had truly surprised her by showing up at her house.

"Why, Ruthie, sweetie, w..w..what are you doing here? I mean, come in, honey," she tripped over her words. I...I...wasn't expecting you. I..I mean, Paul has some friends stopping by and I thought maybe they were here. It...it's okay that you stopped by. Paul! Paul, look who's here. Ruthie's here, Paul. Come on back here, Ruthie, and sit down. I...I...I'll be right back. I just want to tell Paul to listen for the door."

"He's outside, Lydia. He knows I'm here. Lydia, I...I...I don't want to make you uncomfortable, it's just that I was in the area...and I wanted to stop by and see..."

233

"No…I know why you're here," she replied, softly, shaking her head. "I've been waiting for this day to come for a long time."

Ruth didn't think she had ever heard Lydia speak so softly and felt terrible for the stress she was causing her.

"I'm trying so hard, Lydia, to allow myself to heal. I think perhaps I wasn't ready to acknowledge Roger's accident…"

"Huh!" Lydia gasped.

"Yes, Lydia. I know that my Roger died in an accident. I know it. I just can't remember it yet. But I…I…I think you know something that will help me. Please…please…tell me what alone since five means."

Lydia sat silent with her head bowed and her hands folded together. She appeared to be praying, but Ruth knew that she was fighting against her will or the instructions from Bryce to not talk about it.

"Lydia, please."

Very quietly and without looking up, Lydia whispered, "The little girl's father didn't say that you were alone since five. He said…he said…you were the lone survivor."

Ruth sat very still trying to comprehend what Lydia had finally released. And then squinting her eyes because the all too familiar screeching sound was beginning, she finally understood.

"I was in the car?" she barely got out.

Lydia's silent sobs were the confirmation that Ruth needed to continue putting her puzzled life back together.

Ruth's silent escape went unnoticed by Lydia, who was now consumed by her breach of trust.

CHAPTER SIXTY-SIX

Ruth couldn't remember saying anything else to Lydia. She wasn't sure if Lydia saw her leave, or if Paul did either, for that matter, but she knew that she probably shouldn't be behind the wheel. She was weaving her way in and out of traffic, but where was she going? She didn't know. She kept rehashing in her mind what Lydia had said. *She was the lone survivor.* Nothing about being alone since five. She was in the accident with Roger. She was *with him.* And she couldn't remember that! She felt so many emotions right now, but more than any other, she felt angry. How could she have not known that she was with Roger when he died? Didn't she owe that much to him to remember that he wasn't alone when he died? Did she ever wonder if she had been with him? She didn't know. Did she ever imagine him at the end? She didn't know that either. What did she know? Why didn't Bryce tell her that? Or anyone of her friends for that matter. And why not Dr. Brooke? Of all people, why not her. She'd been struggling with this for a year and a half. She faithfully attended counseling sessions; trying to regain her memory, and no one told her this? She was angry!

All at once there were horns blaring and Ruth had the sensation that she was doing something terribly wrong. All cars were facing her in the driving lanes, and the horns were honking. She was beginning to feel the same way she did at recess the other day. The noise was intense. Horns sounding, flashing lights, pieces of puzzles just within her grasp.

Ruth realized that she had stopped driving when she heard a soft knock on her window. An old woman with a friendly smile stood at her side.

"You look like you could use some help," the friendly face offered. "Do you think you have the ability to pull over into this lot?" she asked, pointing to the next driveway.

"Oh, my goodness," Ruth responded. "Oh, I'm so sorry. I got turned around. Thank you for being so kind."

"Oh, sweetheart, at my age, I know that all it takes is a kind word to get me back on track. Now I'm going to stop these cars, and how about you pull into the lot and get yourself turned around."

Ruth did as she was directed and waved at the friendly face as she pulled into the lot. Instead of turning around, though, she pulled all the way into the lot and turned off her ignition. She needed another moment to regain her bearings.

She knew it was dangerous to be driving when she was this upset, and wished she hadn't have put so many people in danger. She closed her eyes to rest for a moment and to make sure that she was okay to drive. Still feeling angry about what she had just learned, she tried to imagine why Bryce and the others in her life wouldn't have told her something as important as the fact that she had been with Roger when he died.

A couple of squirrels chasing each other in front of her car brought her attention to where she was. She was surprised to see that she had pulled into St. Francis of Assisi's parking lot.

"Father Joe," she said out loud to no one. "I wish I could talk with you. You were angry once, too. Your family lost a son and your parents stopped attending mass. They stopped…believing," she said with a quiet realization as to where this was heading. "I haven't stopped," she said out loud. At this precise moment, all alone in her car, with no one watching, and no fanfare, Ruth came back to God. "I haven't stopped believing in you!" she cried out. "Please help me," she continued to cry.

When her sobs subsided and all was quiet, she felt herself remembering. Not the falling backward in time like with Mr. Gabriello, but just quietly thinking back. She remembered being in a hospital, and remembered Bryce's body wracked with sobs; his head leaning forward onto the bed on which she lay.

"You did tell me, didn't you?" she said out loud, quietly. Somehow she knew she had been told, but she surely couldn't remember. She could also picture herself talking with Dr. Brooke. Perhaps that was the first time they met, she didn't know. Come to think of it, she couldn't remember meeting her.

Ruth knew her clogged mind was beginning to focus. She couldn't pin point a particular feeling she was experiencing, but it was as if she were ready to wake up from a dream from long ago.

"I need to get home," she said out loud again. "I need Mr. Gabriello's help." As she turned on the car's ignition and pulled out of her space, she stopped next to the front of the church. "Thank you....I do still believe," she said, nodding.

CHAPTER SIXTY-SEVEN

Bryce was rounding the corner of the fall annuals section, pushing a large rolling cart full of yellow mums. Though not always working the floor of Stonehenge Gardens, he was quick to lend a helping hand when necessary.

"I got it from here, Mr. Lily," a soft spoken teenage boy volunteered.

"Anytime," he answered, smiling. He paused for a moment to take in the sight before him. The parking lot was full and swarms of happy customers were circulating throughout the grounds of Stonehenge Gardens' Fall Festival. The crowds seemed to grow every year which was credit to the hard working team that Bryce had created.

As he began making his way toward his office, he heard his name being paged over his walkie talkie.

"Bryce, come back," it blared loudly over the crowd.

"This is Bryce, go ahead."

"We just got a call from one of your mother's friends who seemed rather upset and wanted to speak with you. I told her I'd let you know. Let me know when you're ready for her number."

Assuming it was Mel, he wondered why she didn't call him on his cell.

238

"Alright, I know who it is. I'll give her a call later on," he responded.

"Oh, and Bryce, we just got a call from the boys working with the stone. It seems as if they have accidentally knocked a couple of pallets over with the riding forklift, and..."

"Ahh! Any injuries," he cut her off.

"No, Bryce...but they're pretty scared because I told them I was notifying you."

"Well, good! I hope they weren't playing around because someone could get hurt; or worse. I'm heading there now," he replied, starting to jog in that direction.

CHAPTER SIXTY-EIGHT

Ruth pulled into her own driveway, so relieved to be home after a crazy day.

"Progress," she said out loud, getting out of her car. "If this is progress, then who needs it? I just about killed myself and others! I can certainly see the importance of complete concentration when driving."

She gathered her purse and headed inside.

"Martha, Ole' Girl, how are you?" she asked her furry friend who met her with plenty of wags. "Go on, it's okay. I'll be out with you in a minute."

Ruth dropped her purse and headed back outside to join her closest companion. Like clockwork, Martha did her business and then proceeded to a clean spot to roll over on her back and wiggle. She routinely finished her time outside by scratching her back. She was a pretty predictable dog who seemed to enjoy her routines as much as Ruth.

Ruth shivered while watching Martha roll over on the cold ground.

"I don't know about you, Ole' Girl, but it's getting too cold to be lounging out here. Come on, let's go," she called as they both headed toward the front.

Just then she noticed the same, small silver car pulling away from the curb. "Wait!" she yelled, running toward the curb. It slowed down, stopped, and the driver's door opened. As the figure stood, Ruth let out a gasp.

"I...I...I've been wanting to talk to you for so long. I...I'm so sorry," cried a sobbing Alison. "I'm not allowed to say anything to you...but, I'm so, so sorry!" and with that, she sped away.

Ruth stood speechless on her driveway. What had just happened? "Alison must have been involved in the accident," she said out loud. "But, what? I simply can't remember. Please, God, please help me. There's so much coming together and I just can't grab a hold of it!" She went inside, more eager than ever to concentrate on everything she had experienced today.

"I think I need some coffee to get warmed," she added toward Martha. "How about you and I get that prepared and then we'll try to find my little friends? I'm almost there, Martha. I think I'm so close to figuring out my past." Ruth was feeling almost giddy at what had taken place earlier in the church parking lot, but it was being smothered by what Alison had just said.

"Oh, Lydia, you held the missing key," Ruth said to herself. "I have got to call you later and thank you. I just ran out of your house and who knows what you're thinking. But, because of you, Lydia, I think I'm finding myself again. And, I believe, Lydia, I still believe," she said, now laughing. "I can't explain it," she continued, now looking at Martha. "I feel different...more alive...it's okay...yeah, I'm going to be okay," she said to a wagging tail.

Ruth got up to pour her coffee. "I have a good feeling about today, Ole' Girl. With a little help from Mr. Gabriello, I think I'll have it...my life back, that is. Just think, Martha," she said, nodding toward her dog. "Once I've completed this journey, then it's smooth sailing from here on out."

Ruth sat down in a rocking chair in the back room and gazed outside. She didn't know what to expect so she sat quietly, waiting, and sipping her coffee. She pictured her future, full of family once again; and trust. No more whispering behind her back, wondering if she was okay. She'd come so far, and she *was* okay.

She continued to sit for some time, periodically looking around the room and even around her chair, looking for a sign of the First Creatures.

"Where is everyone, Martha?" Ruth asked, looking at her companion. "They should be here," she added, beginning to feel nervous. "I mean, I just saw Velo earlier. Where is she?"

Martha looked at Ruth and wagged her tail as if to help, but Ruth couldn't help but notice the complete stillness that surrounded them. The room was so quiet and yet she wanted to plug her ears from the deafening silence...or the sound of screeching...she couldn't tell the difference. Maybe she was forgetting something...a particular way to call them. She didn't know that either. She stood and nervously started looking in the back room.

"Velo...Velo, are you here? I don't understand. You said you wouldn't leave me," she continued, now pacing the kitchen and small room.

Peering out the back sliding glass door, she fervently scanned the gardens looking for any sign of movement.

"No! You said you wouldn't leave me! Where are you?" she cried out loud.

Looking at Martha, who was also beginning to act nervous because of Ruth's behavior, she said, "Stay here. I've got to find them. They promised. They promised they wouldn't leave me, and look at the gardens. Just look at them! They're dying!"

Leaving Martha in the house, she ran into the back yard, calling their names.

"Velo! Ojy! Where are you? Ceepa! Pheo! I'm ready. Can anyone hear me?" she cried, maneuvering the paths toward the back of the property. As she continued, she took in the shabby appearance of a once vibrant garden, now going to sleep. She winced at its appearance and wondered why she hadn't noticed just *how* far along this phase had progressed. It was much further along than she noticed this morning. The verbena plants were no longer colorful, no longer pink. Ruth thought that they resembled straw as she continued further toward the back. She refused to stop, trudging forward until she reached a certain point, the location where it all began.

There, at the very back of the property, in a darkened spot near a solitary oak tree, sat a lone and ragged Frances Williams Hosta. Its limp and colorless leaves hung to the ground; no apparent life remaining in them.

"No, no, no, no, no!" Ruth cried, falling to her knees. "No, please, no," she sobbed. She reached out to gather the leaves of her favorite plant, but they detached into her hands, crumbling…withered life.

"Ah!....No!......," she fell over the plant, hugging the ground. "Please come back…please come back, No…Velo….please…I miss you…I…I…I love you," she quietly whispered.

As quiet, heart wrenching sobs muted into silence, a soft and gentle breeze picked up its pace bringing a swirl of fallen leaves circulating about Ruth, who remained hovered over the lifeless plant. The mood changed slowly in the garden and Ruth heard movement near her. Her head was so heavy, but through tear stricken eyes and her mourning heart, she slowly made out a mirage of color mingled in with the dead plant.

"Huh?" she gasped as she pulled herself into a sitting position. "Is it you? Is it really you? I was looking for you for so long."

And there she was, the tiny little creature who resembled a rabbit, a lop-eared rabbit. She stood in front of Ruth in all her glory. She stood on her back legs; well, actually on her toes. Her little brown tattered ballet slippers seemed more ragged than ever, and her outfit brought even more tears to Ruth. The olive green and lime striped tutu had seen its better days, and the butter colored linen jacket hung on her tiny shoulders. Her barely peach colored fur covered her hands, neck and head, but not her face. There was always a bit of straight brown hair falling in her face, mixed in with her lop ears. As Ruth had come to expect, her paw-like hands were held at her chest when not in use. She cocked her head to one side, turned her lips inward, yet puffed them out, and gave Ruth a small little 'hmph,' almost as if a question. This is what Ruth craved. This is what she wanted to see every day, and this is how she wanted to feel. She wanted to *love*. She wanted to *love* again.

Velo tippy toed toward Ruth and paced a few circles in front of her.

"Um, you're not looking in the right place anymore," she squeaked.

"What do you mean," sniffed Ruth, wiping away her tears with soil covered fingers.

"You're different now. Mr. Gabriello says that you're ready to remember. Come with me. We're back here, waiting for you."

She *was* different, she knew that. She had been healing for a long time. If her own son wouldn't let her babysit his children, then it had to be serious. She had been having more glimpses of her past…of her original stay in the hospital, following the accident. She *knew* Bryce had told her about the accident; she knew it. She just couldn't grab hold of that memory. Or perhaps…she *wouldn't* grab hold of it. So many times in the last few months, she had the sensation that a broken picture was just out of her reach. Sometimes it seemed like shattered pieces; puzzle pieces. And often times there were noises associated with this feeling. Like when it was quiet, just before, in her back room. It was so quiet, yet she wanted to plug her ears to block out the noise. What was that noise?

Ruth followed Velo just steps away toward Mr. Gabriello's tree.

"I need a minute to collect my thoughts," she stammered before falling down at the base of the tree. "I have the strangest sensation that I'm walking into my past. Velo, what's wrong with me? I don't feel so good."

"It's okay," squeaked Velo. "You're starting to remember, but it's ok. We're here with you."

"I don't see anybody yet," she cried softly.

And then, slowly, but surely, she saw rustling from behind Mr. Gabriello's tree and out came the trio of miniature creatures to complete the set.

She should have been relieved by their sight, but she couldn't speak. Had she ever really seen them all together before? This was like a meeting. Was she in charge? She didn't know. Should she speak? If she did, she knew she would start the ball rolling...rolling backward into her memory. They, too, remained quiet, looking at her...waiting.

"Who...are...you?" she finally asked so softly, close to exhaustion.

Pheo, the one who came to life through her teal colored garden gloves and stone wall, was the first to speak. She hadn't seen him too often, but was once again, mesmerized by his finely cut appearance. His face was chiseled from finely cut stone, which resembled strength, yet he moved effortlessly in oversized black boots that were shuffling on his skinny knock kneed legs.

"We're the Firths Creatures," he said strongly, yet through a lisp. We were here firth."

"I know. I know, but I don't understand," Ruth replied.

"We're parts of you, Miss Ruth, that don't work," replied a soft spoken bird like creature. Ruth turned and looked at the appearance of this creature. What gentle eyes she had. There were feathers interspersed throughout her dirty blond hair, and her arms flapped like that of a bird's as she walked toward Ruth.

245

"We were here before the accident. Can you remember?" she asked softly. "Can you remember sitting here in the garden, against that tree, after the funeral?"

As Ceepa spoke, she painted a picture in Ruth's mind that slowly began to take focus. It was almost as if some of the puzzle pieces were joining together to form a more complete depiction from that time.

"You came out here to the garden a few days after the funeral; after everyone was gone," Ceepa continued gently. "Your purpose in life was gone, you thought. You sat against that tree and read the funeral program over and over. You used it to cry into for hours. You came out here to the gardens where you and Roger created your life together, in hopes of finding some comfort. You had put all of yourself and your future out here in the gardens. But when a large part of your future died, you died with it. Your body remained, but we were cast away. At one time you found all of us out here, but you pushed us away that day. You didn't believe in yourself or any of us anymore."

Through silent tears Ruth nodded toward Ceepa.

"But I.." she tried.

Ceepa scratched out the spelling of her name in the dirt with her foot. As a breeze blew softly, the letters rearranged themselves to spell the word, *peace*, before blowing away directly before Ruth's eyes.

"Your peace was lost that day, and you couldn't get it back," Ceepa said softly. "It blew away into the wings of a mourning dove that was living in your garden. You said, 'No,' but it understood."

Ceepa paused for a moment, allowing Ruth to take in what she had just said.

"I have protected it for you all this time. I am your peace."

Ruth sucked in her breath at the remembrance of Ceepa leading her toward a renewed friendship with little Hailey next door.

She remembered Ceepa sitting on the pond's edge while she dined with Hailey and her parents. She allowed Ruth to experience peace once again where only anger and solitude lived. Ruth was perfectly content, or so she thought, to stay wrapped up in her lonely world, unwilling to understand.

"You're a part of me? You…you helped me," she cried softly, reaching out to touch her feathered friend. "Thank you."

Ceepa bowed her head gently, indicating the acknowledgement.

Ruth turned her attention back toward the stone figure.

"Who…who…are?" she tried asking.

"Your thun stopped shining that day and your world became dark," replied the chiseled creature. "You couldn't thee tomorrow. You didn't want any more tomorrows," he continued.

He bent down and retrieved a stick very much like the one he used to tap the garden walls in search of notes. He used it to scratch his name into a stone.

It, too, rearranged its spelling in front of Ruth. This time the word, *hope*, appeared briefly before turning dark and crumbling before her eyes.

"Huh," she gasped.

"Your ability to look ahead ended that day and your hope was shattered. It crumbled into the ground and found thtrength in the stone walls."

"Oh, Pheo, I…I…don't…is it gone?"

"I have been holding onto your hope for you tho that I could keep it safe and give it back to you when you were ready," he said with a mighty voice.

Ruth looked at him with her eyes wide open, not believing what she was hearing. Another creature had just explained a little bit more of her puzzled existence, and she sat in awe.

"My hope and my tomorrows," she smiled at him. "Thank you, Pheo, for helping the sun to shine again."

At that, he breathed in deeply causing his little teal colored jacket to swell.

"Ah, ha, ah, ha. It's my turn, isn't it?" sang out the undeniable chipper voice of Ojy.

Ruth couldn't help but smile when she looked at Ojy who was never short of energy. Thoughts of dancing, fun and silliness came to mind when looking at the bright pink flowery ensemble.

"Your life was full of so much happiness. You found me everywhere you went. Ah, ha, ah…I was your laugh and I was part of your spirit. Everyone could see me inside of you."

Ojy then turned around and wouldn't face Ruth when further describing her purpose. Ruth was shocked at Ojy's tone because she had never heard her speak with such solemnity.

"But, you lost me that day," she said somberly, "Actually…you threw me away. You didn't want me anymore. When your tears poured into the earth, I was safely buried there; waiting. I came back when you were ready," she added, her pace quickening again. "Your buried tears were used to create me, your new enthusiasm."

She turned to face Ruth and shook her limbs. An abundance of bright pink petals fell to the ground and spelled out her name. And just as with the others, the petals lifted and rearranged themselves to spell the word, *joy*. Ruth smiled, shaking her head at this new realization, but as she did, the petals turned to liquid and were swallowed once again by the earth.

"Oh, Ojy, I...I'm so sorry. You're right, you were my joy. I was so happy; all the time. What has happened to me?" Ruth pleaded, reaching out to her.

"Ah, ha, ah. Don't worry. You wanted me back in your life...you asked for me...and I'm a part of you again."

Ruth smiled at Ojy, glad that her joy was depicted as such a colorful flower. She looked at the three of them, taking it all in. How lucky she was to have her life described to her in such a way. She took a big breath, knowing that she was about to hear the final describing characteristic of herself.

She turned to face the little rabbit upon whom she had grown so dependent, to carry on with her everyday life. She was met, of course, with paws drawn upward, head cocked to the side, lips turned in, yet puffed out, so she could give Ruth a couple of 'hmphs.'

"I know you...I know you...I know you," Ruth cried, barely able to speak. "You're *love*," she sobbed. "You're *love*...you're *love*...you're *love*."

Velo tippy toed toward Ruth, paced in a few circles before rubbing against her arm and crawling into her lap.

"I don't know how I couldn't recognize you," Ruth cried softly to her dearest friend. She cradled her in her arms and held her safely, rocking back and forth. Velo managed to squeak out a few, 'hmphs,' when Ruth realized that there were often times no words for love. Words were simply not necessary so much of the time. Ruth thought of the love she shared with Roger. They didn't express their love out loud every day. It was understood. It was lived. It was heard in their conversation and their laughter. It was found in their friends and in their grandchildren, and it was definitely found in this garden. Ruth smiled at Velo when she realized that her abandoned love was rescued by a lop-eared rabbit.

She sat quietly for a few minutes, feeling more complete than she had in a long time, when suddenly she froze.

She looked over to the oak tree and asked, "Who's he?"

The First Creatures looked among themselves, wondering who would speak first.

Velo climbed out of Ruth's lap and paced in a few circles on her tip toes.

"The four of us escaped that day and we were rescued in the garden," she began. "But you stopped believing," Velo squeaked. "You told God that you didn't believe in life anymore. You stopped trying. Do you remember?"

Ruth squinted her eyes closed to picture what Velo had just said. She *did* remember. She *did*. She remembered leaning against this old oak tree and ripping the funeral program to shreds; throwing it in the air. She remembered lying down without any intention of ever getting up again.

Ruth's earliest memory before losing consciousness was from a time when she was only four. She had loved her father dearly and remembered a game they used to play. He'd ask Ruth to state her name, but always interrupted her, causing an eruption of giggles from Ruth. She'd tried to say, Miss Ruth Gabrielle, and he'd interrupt with, hello. In repeating it over and over, it became intertwined and was finally declared as, Mr. Gabriello. Her earliest memory played repeatedly in her mind with the name, *Mr. Gabriello*, over and over, embedding itself into her final conscious thought while the sun pounded upon her, drawing her closer to her final breath.

The hours that followed were very quiet, and almost successful in taking Ruth's life. She remembered, now, being told that she was found in the garden, so very close to death from heat exposure and dehydration. She remembered, also, being told that she had been found after having spent two days in the hot sun. She could picture Bryce, again, half lying on her hospital bed, crying. He had said *something*...something to her that caused her so much distress that she shut down. She remembered not being able to speak. What had he said? She felt sure that he had told her more than once. What was it? She couldn't remember!

"Velo, I can't remember what Bryce told me," Ruth whispered. "Something is still missing. Please help me to remember," she pleaded as she looked deeply into Velo's hazel eyes. She saw nothing but love, and knew that *love alone* would help her through what she needed to know.

Velo looked up toward the oak tree with questioning eyes.

"Will he help me? Just this one more time," Ruth begged, pulling herself up to meet the tree.

"I believe," she said through pleading sobs. "Please help me remember, Mr. Gabriello."

When the figure evolved from the tree, Ruth was horrified at his appearance. She had become used to his form, but knowing what she knew now, knowing that all of her pain, disbelief, agony, and horror made her shudder.

"Is...is...this me? A...a...are you me?" she asked looking at the saddest eyes she had ever seen. She saw his pain and knew exactly how it felt. She saw his loneliness and heartache and knew that she exhibited both of them as well.

He never spoke; never said a word. His encompassment of her ache was all too real and close to Ruth.

"I...I've come so far, Mr. Gabriello. I...I...I just need a little more. I can't remember what he said. I can't remember what Bryce said! I believe in life, and in God, and in living. I just want my life back. Please...please help me this one more time," she begged.

She never stood, but remained kneeling, to look directly into his eyes. She never lost his gaze while meeting his hand. She fully expected to fall back in time with him, but nothing happened. She remained in the present, hand in hand with the creature who held the very rest of her.

She continued to hold his stare because she was not going to stop until she remembered.

"Please…please…," she uttered.

Slowly, finally, as she looked into his eyes, she, herself, forced a picture, a memory, into forming.

CHAPTER SIXTY-NINE

The sun was beginning to lower itself into the far western horizon, inching its way closer to the golden tree tops of Stonehenge Garden's property line. The temperature was dropping and Bryce's shoulders shook a bit as he rounded the corner going toward his office in search of a sweatshirt. The sun had done its job throughout the day in keeping the air warm enough for him to be without it, but he was getting uncomfortable. It had been a typical fall day in Maryland; cold start, warm but brisk afternoon, and a cold evening.

As he walked back out of his office, he walked directly into Mel and Pat who were in search of him.

"Ah, there he is," Pat smiled as he extended his hand toward Bryce. "We've been enjoying ourselves, as usual," he said with a cinnamon donut still in hand. "You've done yourself well, Bryce. Quite a successful business you've got."

"Oh, honey," Mel added. "I never questioned Bryce's intentions to start his own business," she said, patting her husband's back. "And I can still remember when you brought up the idea with your parents," she said, turning her attention toward Bryce. "I'm so glad it's doing this well. Really, look at this crowd, and it's almost closing time."

"Well, I guess I'll have to kick them out," Bryce added, laughing. "I hope there's a few more donuts because that looks pretty good," he said, acknowledging Pat's.

"Oh, we bumped into Bev," Mel added. "She looks great."

"Oh, yea, thanks. Just a couple of more months and the baby will be here," he smiled. "Hey, it was great seeing you, but I had better help close up shop."

They said their goodbyes, and as they were making their way through the crowds toward the parking lot, Mel heard Bryce calling after them again.

"Hey, sorry guys, I forgot. Was there something you wanted earlier when you called, Mel?"

"I didn't call you, Bryce," Mel said shaking her head.

"Oh," he said, perplexed. "The girls up front said earlier that one of my mother's friends called, and I thought it was you. I'll check it out at the front desk."

CHAPTER SEVENTY

As the picture continued to form in Ruth's mind, she released her grip from Mr. Gabriello and sank to the ground. She continued to will herself to hold the memory that was forming. There were sounds of laughter and crowds as the picture became clear. Red, white, and blue streamers were blowing gently in the breeze as the sound of a motorcade passed slowly in front of the crowds. Children waving small flags lined the wall of the parade, bending down to pick up pieces of candy being tossed from the cars. Mostly older gentlemen, some in their uniforms from years past, were inside the first number of cars, slowly waving out to the crowds. As the parade progressed, Ruth noticed the age of the participants was younger. The uniforms changed as well and she recognized the sandy colored camouflage pattern worn in Desert Storm.

"Wow, look at all this candy," Hayden said as he held up his hands. "Do you want some, Grampy?"

"Sure, how about this Tootsie Roll?" Roger said as he unwrapped it, popping it in his mouth.

"I'll trade you a red lollipop for the blue one," Heather piped in toward Hayden.

"No, I was going to eat that. Do you want this orange one?" he replied.

"You all sound hungry to me," Ruth said. "I think your parents are probably ready for us back at the house. Shall we go?"

Ruth relaxed as the dream faded somewhat and she remembered taking Hayden and Heather to the Memorial Day Parade. The kids weren't as interested in the history of why the parade was taking place as they were in seeing how much candy they could collect. She and Roger had agreed to take the kids to get them out of the house for a while so Bev could prepare for a BBQ. Bryce had to work, of course, but was able to meet them later.

Ruth quickly tensed as she remembered that she might be shown a memory, one that should help her reclaim her past. When she forced herself to relax, her thoughts started, once again.

As Ruth walked down the back patio steps of Bev and Bryce's home, she could hear Bev explaining her work of art to Mary, whose family was also invited to the BBQ.

"I've named this whole pond system, The Chesapeake," Bev said, smiling toward Mary.

"It's incredible, really. You've added so much since I was last here," Mary said. "I love the miniature houses along the edge! How do you think up all of this?"

"Well, you see, a long time ago I had this professor," Bev began, giggling. "He, uh, well, he was so passionate about The Chesapeake Bay and I learned so much from him."

"Hmm, that's not how I remember it going down," Bryce laughed, rounding the corner of the house.

"Daddy, you're home!" Heather yelled as she ran toward him and was scooped up in his arms.

"As I recall," Bryce added, continuing to laugh. "You signed up for Professor Lily's water ecology class because he had a very handsome son."

"What! I didn't know that when I signed up," Bev laughed, turning red.

"Hold on," Roger chimed in laughing. "Do you mean to say that the young ladies only signed up for my classes because of you? All along I thought my classes were full because I was the coolest teacher on campus."

"Oh, my goodness, Roger, don't listen to him," Bev said, patting her father-in-law on the back. "You *were* and *still are* the coolest teacher on campus. I know because I get the scoop from the college girls at the shop."

"What? Whose side are you on," Bryce retorted, laughing.

"Hi, honey," she said, giving Bryce a kiss. "I'm on nobody's side. I'm glad you're home, the burgers are ready to start grilling and we're all hungry."

"Hey, Dad, can I help grill? You said you would teach me, remember?" Hayden asked.

"I do. Come on. Let's get started," Bryce replied. "And go get Grampy. He can help."

As the afternoon progressed, and her 'three men' were busy barbecuing, Ruth had a chance to sit on the patio with a glass of iced tea and take in the sight before her. Bev and Bryce truly had the most picturesque backyard. Though still a little early for the perennials to be in bloom, they made sure they had adequate annuals to bring out early color. 'The Chesapeake,' which Bev had created, was a marvelous sight to behold. Bill was at the water's edge helping Hailey and Heather sail miniature six inch sailboats through the water. When they navigated them out too far in the middle, he was able to scoop them back with a long handled net so they could see them better from the side.

'Life is good,' Ruth remembered thinking, as she rested her head back on the rocking chair.

"Mom, could you bring us a platter?" Bryce called up to her.

"I'll get it, Ruthie," Roger called back. "Three cooks are too many," he chuckled as he passed her to go in the kitchen. Coming back out he added, "Hayden has really got the hang of…"

Roger's foot suddenly slipped off the bottom step and he yelped as he fell.

"Roger! Dad! Grampy!" everyone yelled at once.

Roger pulled himself into a sitting position and laughed. "I'm okay…really. Let me just get up here and see." As he pulled himself up backwards on one step he was able to use the railing as a crutch. "See there, I think I'm okay," he said as he tried to take a step, stumbling. "Phew, okay, ladies, now's your chance," he said, laughing. "Could I beg a couple of shoulders to help me to a chair? And maybe some ice?"

Bryce leaned down and effortlessly pulled up his father, helping to get his right arm around him and hop a few steps to a chair.

"Now who's the coolest one?" Bryce winked at him, clapping him on his shoulder.

Ruth began to fidget as she came to. She remembered Roger falling and spraining his ankle. He kept his foot elevated during dinner with a bag of ice on it, but to no avail. As bruising began to form, they decided he needed an x-ray. Ruth couldn't remember if his ankle was broken or not. She couldn't remember him getting an x-ray.

"Velo, what happened?" she pleaded. "Please, Love, tell me what happened."

She slipped back in the memory, just as one would fall back asleep.

Bryce was helping his dad into the passenger side of his truck.

"I can take you, Dad, it's no problem," Bryce was saying.

"No, it's not necessary," Roger replied. "Your mom will get me a wheelchair once we get there. We'll keep you posted."

"I'm sorry, Dad," Bryce said. "But hey, I'll sign 'coolest professor' on your cast," he added.

Ruth began to fidget again and come out of the memory. "I don't remember a cast. I don't remember a cast," she cried, quietly.

"Go back. It's okay," Velo comforted her.

Ruth closed her eyes and saw the faces of those she loved around the car, waving goodbye.

"Bye Grammy. Bye Grampy," called Hayden, who then turned to hear what Hailey was saying.

"That's a good idea, Hailey. Hey, Grampy, can I come along? Grammy's going to need some help tonight after you get back home. Please?" he asked with a begging look.

Ruth became very agitated and pulled out of the memory again. "Say goodbye, Hayden. Say goodbye!" she cried. "I'm the lone survivor! I'm the only one who survives this. You won't see your grandfather again," she sobbed, falling back down into the dirt, willing herself to stop the memory. She felt something warm rub against her arm and opened her eyes. Through her tears and confusion, she could still see Velo, who was right there in front of her.

"Hmph...it's okay," she squeaked.

"No...no...no...no...I don't think I can," she whimpered.

"It's time," she said again, patting Ruth's arm.

Believing her, she relaxed and the memory returned.

"I think you're right, Hayden. You can stay with me when Grammy gets the wheelchair. I think you'd be a big help," Roger agreed.

"Oh, yes!" Hayden yelled, as his little body climbed into the truck. "This is cool. Thanks, Hailey," he called out the window.

"Fasten your seatbelt, Hayden. What a sweet little man you are. You'll be a great help to me," Ruth smiled back at him, reaching back to squeeze his little hand.

Ruth slammed her hand on the dirt floor. "Nooo....!" she wailed.

CHAPTER SEVENTY-ONE

Unbeknownst to the Lily family, another grandfather was leaving his family for the last time. Al Green, Alison Byrnes' father, had spent the day with his daughter's family, and had enjoyed viewing his grandson's wedding pictures and hearing about the tales of Ireland from his honeymoon. But he begged out of dessert, not feeling like himself. He wasn't one to usually turn down any kind of sweet, but his indigestion had kicked in, and all he wanted to do was take something for it and rest at home. He was suffering more and more from heartburn, and figured it was time to tell his doctor.

Alison had the sneaking suspicion that her father was suffering from more than heartburn because his complaints were the same as last year just prior to having a heart attack. His departure went unnoticed, though, because she was busy entertaining her son and his new wife.

Al knew immediately after starting the car's ignition that there was something different about this pain. He thought about turning off the engine, but the thought of explaining the ache to his daughter seemed too much for him. He just wanted to go home. The throbbing that was now traveling into his jaw reaffirmed his decision to keep quiet. He pulled out of her driveway.

He didn't make it very far on the two lane highway before he lost consciousness. His life ended before reaching the four-way intersection, before blazing through a red light, striking another vehicle, and taking two lives with him.

CHAPTER SEVENTY-TWO

Ruth had never been part of such an explosion as this. She had never heard such noise, screeching, and shattering as this. It took just a couple of seconds for her to realize that she was involved in this horrible chaos and that she was holding on to something so tightly just to stay in place. Was this the safety bar on a rollercoaster? She didn't know. She was still spinning when she opened her eyes. There were puzzle pieces floating in the air, raining down upon her ride. They were shimmering, dropping and continuing to shatter all around her. What kind of ride was this?

One look to her right brought her to reality. She tried screaming. She opened her mouth wide to scream, but there was no sound. She tried grabbing for Roger; screaming his name, but no sound escaped her mouth, and no fingers reached his lifeless form.

"Get me out…get me out of here…Roger!" she panicked, desperately tugging at her seatbelt to release. Once freed, she tried opening her door, but the mangled metal was twisted and bent, deeming it useless. She turned a little more to the right to reach Roger, but in doing so, she caught sight of Hayden in the back seat. His still, limp, and beautiful body, like that of the door, was twisted in such a way that Ruth knew he was gone. She couldn't breathe and remembered getting sick. As hard as she tried to crawl over the console to reach him, she couldn't. With one final stretch she was able to make contact with his hand, grabbing hold of it. She desperately didn't want him to be alone.

"Grammy's with you, Hayden, Grammy's with you," she silently cried, holding onto her most treasured gift.

"This can't be happening, this can't be happening," she silently screamed. "Please, God, make this stop!"

"Stop!" Ruth now screamed in the present as loud as she could in her backyard. "Stop! Stop! Make it stop! Get me out of here! Get me out of this car!" she screamed as she jumped up. Thinking it was still Hayden's hand, she let go of Velo and began running blindly through the garden. "Make it stop!"

"No! Stop run..." Velo tried to intercept her.

It only took a second of sightless running for Ruth to fall. But all of her pent up agony fed her speed, causing her to fly when her foot caught hold of a root. She went over the ledge head first, striking the side of her head on the stone wall. Her pain and confusion ended; her tears halting. All of her memories which she had buried so deeply within her were released for just a short time before once again being laid to rest. Her beaten and broken spirit lay motionless amidst the stone walls that she so dearly loved.

CHAPTER SEVENTY-THREE

All held still in the Lily garden, waiting for a decision to be made from a greater source. The creature who was granted permission to move first was the greatest of all; the greatest found in all of mankind. She quietly looked at what lay before her. With paws drawn inward, on her tippiest of toes, she started toward Ruth. She circled her motionless body twice, rubbed against her shoulders, and nestled down inside the crook of her neck. She looked back at the others, acknowledging them to come forward.

Ceepa followed next, quietly joining Ruth. She ruffled her feathers and wedged herself under Ruth's head, pillowing it against the cold, hard earth. She breathed out gently, allowing the tension to subside from Ruth's taut frame and to lessen the creases that were carved into her forehead.

Pheo was next to stand. He stood proud and strong like that of the stone. He went to Ruth and repositioned her arms to lie in a more natural position. He brushed away the dirt and leaves that were embedded in her hair from the fall. When seeing that he had somehow helped her, he took his place, also near her head, and sat to watch guard, waiting for more decisions to be made.

It was difficult for Ojy to join the others, for her nature was happiness. Not knowing what the future held, she slowly approached, walking backward. She reached her leafy arm out toward Ruth's chest, trying to lay a hand on her heart. She wanted

Ruth to know of the joy that she still held for her, wanting to somehow heal her with this contribution.

Together they sat quietly for a few moments, unsure of the next step. It was Velo, who after a moment, looked toward the tree.

"She's broken," she squeaked. "She needs you...she needs you now."

The others, too, looked toward Mr. Gabriello, waiting.

"Please," Velo uttered softly.

Slowly, and without a change in his expression, Mr. Gabriello moved. He quietly took a step away from the tree, and then another, toward Ruth. His footsteps couldn't be heard on the earth's floor as he cautiously made his way toward them. He very slowly knelt down and looked at Ruth and the others. He reached underneath his sheath and pulled out a stack of neatly folded notes that Ruth had been handing him in exchange for memories. He gently placed the stack in one of her hands and persuaded her fingers around it. Tenderly, without a sound, he very slowly crawled on top of her. He lay flat on her back; his arms spread out over hers, and his legs doing the same, as far as they could reach.

Once he was in position, he dissolved into her and disappeared. Ruth let out a gasp and then breathed out peacefully.

CHAPTER SEVENTY-FOUR

Bev hung up the phone and paced about the living room a couple of times. She saw Bryce pull into the driveway and braced herself for his reaction. They had both seen Ruth making such progress and knew that sooner, more so than later, she would come to the realization of what she had been blocking since the accident.

"Hi, Honey," she said, giving him a quick kiss.

"How are you feeling? Baby okay?" he responded.

"Yep, yep, I'm okay, but…I just got off the phone with Lydia," she said cautiously. "She said she called you today."

"Oh, that's who called. I thought it was Mel."

"Honey….she knows. Your mom knows about the accident. She cornered Lydia about that crazy saying, and she told her. Lydia was crying, Bryce. She was so upset to have told her, but she didn't know what else to do. She said your mom came to her house and asked her directly."

"Ahh, it's not her fault," Bryce started, shaking his head. "It was bound to happen and…hopefully she's ready this time. She's got to move on," he said, pacing. "Has anyone heard from her?"

"That's just it, Honey. Lydia's tried calling her all day since she left, but she won't pick up her cell."

"You know, I tried calling her earlier as well, but she didn't answer," Bryce said. "I was calling to see if she would work the information desk tomorrow. Let's try her again, and if we can't reach her, then I'll go and check on her, myself. I just don't want this to start all over again."

CHAPTER SEVENTY-FIVE

Bryce made his way to Ruth's house after unsuccessfully reaching her by phone. He was relieved to see her car in the driveway, but his relief was short lived when he couldn't find her inside.

"Hey, Martha, how's it going, Old Girl?" he said, stopping to scratch his mother's beloved companion behind the ears. "Where's Mom? Huh? Where is she? Do you want to go out?" he asked and was met with an excited bark.

Bryce let her out the sliding glass door, and she sniffed around a bit before doing her business. She ran directly back to the house, wanting to go in.

"I know, it's cold, Old Girl. In you go," he said opening the door once again. Needing to check more thoroughly for his mother, he stayed outside.

"Mom! It's Bryce! Are you out here?" he yelled into the gardens. "Mom!" he tried one more time, shivering. He walked up the path, toward the back of the property, calling her name. He used the flashlight on his cell phone to see where he was walking because it was now completely dark in the garden. Knowing it was senseless to be checking out here at this time of evening, he turned around and headed back. He gave the back yard a final glance, checking around the side of the house, not really sure what he was looking for.

He gave the outside wall of the house a pat as he entered, almost as if beckoning it to come alive and speak. He turned and looked once more into the garden, admiring the quiet and peaceful tranquility that it depicted.

"Where are you, Mom?" he said out loud, shaking his head.

He pulled out his cell phone and tried her number once again. When he heard it ringing quite close to him, he spun around in surprise. There lay her purse on the kitchen table with her phone ringing inside of it.

Feeling a little more alarmed now since Ruth's purse was still at home, he walked next door to Mary and Bill's to see if his mother was there. Reaching another roadblock when she wasn't, he tried the police. Just as he feared, he was told that they couldn't help him at this time. His mother hadn't been missing for twenty-four hours, and possibly, she might not be missing at all.

He sat in the back room facing the sliding glass door, frustrated once again with his mother. "Where are you?" he said angrily, pulling out his cell phone to call Bev. He stopped, mid-dialing, when he remembered that last time he had asked that question of himself, one and a half years earlier. Looking out into the darkness, he pleaded silently, "Please, Mom, please don't do this again." He opened the door and ran, once again, through the paths with the help of his cell phone flashlight, toward the same location he found her last year. When reaching the same tree in the back of the garden, he called her name numerous times, only to be answered with complete silence. Hearing only the panting of his own breath, he wandered in circles, calling out to her. Relieved to not be repeating history, he convinced himself that she could be anywhere...and not necessarily in danger.

He walked back slowly toward the house, wanting to get home to Bev and talk about this with her. She was always a good sounding board.

CHAPTER SEVENTY-SIX

An hour later, a frustrated and nervous Bryce pulled into his own driveway. What should have been a ten-minute drive from Ruth's house to his seemed to take forever. There was so much road work going on and the use of the highway was brought down to only one lane. He had time to mull over what was happening as he inched his way home, and he had a gnawing fear that he was forgetting something. He even went so far as to place an emergency call to Dr. Brooke, and was told by an answering service that she would return his call shortly.

Bev informed him upon his return that she had tried both Mel and Julie, but neither of them had heard from her. They had both agreed with Bev that Ruth had been making progress and seemed much happier, almost like old times.

As Bryce's cell began to ring, he motioned that it was Dr. Brooke, put her on speaker phone, and began pacing the room while telling her of the events.

"I disagree with your plan not to tell my mom what happened," he said angrily. "She's been walking around in a fog…she's got friends who live in her garden…come on! She's crazy! And now…she's missing!"

"We've talked about this, Bryce," Dr. Brooke replied calmly. "Your mother is not crazy. She created her own way to deal with the grief that was too much for her to bear. I call that, survival. And I suspect this isn't the first time your mother has had imaginary friends," Dr. Brooke continued. "She was an only child who was hurt and lonely after her father died."

"I'm an only child and I didn't have imaginary friends!"

"There's no one particular reason that one has imaginary friends and another doesn't. It's just the way *your* mother handled her grief. Each and every person's psyche handles grief in its own personal way. Some are proactive during grief, wanting to shout out the memory of their loved one. Others, like yourself, need to organize and take care of all essential matters. Not your mother, though. She couldn't face it all at once, not all of it anyway. She needed more time to process the deaths, as I've told you before. Most people accept death and don't require a prolonged period of time. And we, who are accustomed to dealing with grief, recognize this. This is just your mother's personal way she's created, whether you believe me or not. She's healing...in her own time and by her own methods.

"But she's different," he continued. "I'm afraid for her...she's not strong...the strong one died...she's...she's...all about love...she doesn't have other traits to help hold her head above water," he said, struggling to put his thoughts into words. "Her family is all she has...we're it...and part of us is gone...she's not the strong one," he said emotionally.

"I think you've got it wrong about your mother," Dr. Brooke shot right back. "She *is* strong...stronger than you know. Yes, she was crushed and broken when your father and son died. Victims of this type of accident often times feel tremendous guilt in surviving, though no fault of their own. The most important people in her life, those whom she loved more than herself, were gone in an instant, without warning, but she was left behind. She suffers from full denial of reality. You know that. Each time we talked about the accident, she shut down. So I thought, *and I still do*, that it would be best to let her come to grips with reality in her own time. I've seen your mother change so much during the past year. She was an empty shell when I first met her. Slowly, in her own time as she healed, she invited parts of herself, if you will, back into her life. It's okay for her to use her love as her strength. You're absolutely right, Bryce. She is all about love and joy. It has slowly crept back into her everyday life and she's able to express it again. Her imaginary friends are just who she created so she could survive and continue to love. She had to *give* herself permission to allow love back into her life, and she did so through the creation of her garden friends. And now, she's using her love to continue living. She found life in her gardens, Bryce. Trust me on this. Your mother is not a danger to herself. She's been putting her past back together piece-meal with her creative strengths. She's expressed…"

"Garden…her garden was quiet," Bryce interrupted. "Her gardens are never quiet! Oh, my God…wait a minute…She's there! I know she's there! I didn't look well enough. I couldn't see. I needed more light. Just like last time. I gotta go!" he said, hanging up abruptly.

"Bev," he said turning toward her, panicking. "I should have looked better…I couldn't see. I know she's there!"

"Alright, go," she responded. "But, Bryce, Honey, I agree with Dr. Brooke. Your mom is not who she was back then. She doesn't want to hurt herself; she wants to live, Honey."

"I believe that now, but something's wrong," he said, giving her a hug. "Oh, wait a minute. I can't get back there…the traffic."

"Oh, try Jerry. I saw him earlier driving his rig over that way by your mom's. Maybe he's still on duty. Have him bring lights."

CHAPTER SEVENTY-SEVEN

The sound of quietly beeping electronic monitors soothed Bryce's anxiety like that of an old-fashioned alarm clock helping a new puppy remain calm. Once again he found himself in a hospital room, next to his mother's side, waiting. But for what, he didn't know. He was correct in his assumption that his mother would be found in the very rear section of her garden. His buddy, Jerry, a paramedic out of a firehouse close to Ruth's home, was on duty last night. With Bryce's exact directions and more lighting, Ruth was found unconscious, suffering from slight hypothermia and a large contusion on the right side of her head.

After an examination and a multitude of tests, Ruth's prognosis was good. The medical staff was simply waiting for her to awaken. Bryce was only somewhat fearful they were heading down the same road as a year and a half ago. Dr. Brooke's words rang through his thoughts, and he really did agree with her. What his mother was doing in the garden at night, he didn't know. She couldn't have knocked herself out on purpose, but what was happening? He laid his head down at the side of her bed and sighed heavily.

After drifting in and out of sleep for a while, he felt someone softly touching his hand. Quickly remembering where he was, he jerked up his head. "Mom."

"I'm sorry," she whispered, closing her eyes. "I'm so, so sorry," she cried. "I...I...I know," she started, reaching out her hand toward him, "I know that H...H...Hayden's gone.

He shook his head, tears falling in agreement. "Yes, he's gone."

"I miss him," she said quietly with her shoulders beginning to shake. "I miss him so much."

"I know, Mom. I do, too," Bryce said, tears streaming down his face.

"Oh, Bryce. He's your son. I'm so sorry, Honey. I wasn't there for you!"

"I've been missing him for a long time, Mom," he said. "It's just good we can talk now." The quiet embrace that followed spoke more than words, and they continued to hold on to each other until their sobs subsided.

Unsure of how to ask, Ruth spoke ever so softly, bracing for his answer. "D...Did I do anything wrong?"

"No, Mom," he said, holding her shoulders and shaking his head. "An older gentleman, Mr. Greene, had a heart attack while he was driving."

"Mr. Greene?"

"Oh, yeah," he said cautiously. "There's a teacher at your school. Um...Alison Byrnes. It's...her father. She's been real upset this year, but Mel wouldn't let her talk with you."

"What? Alison's dad? Oh, now I know what she meant. It all makes sense."

"He never knew what happened. He didn't make it either; you were..."

"The lone survivor," she whispered.

"Lydia?"

274

Ruth nodded in agreement. "How are Bev and Heather?"

"They're good, Mom. They can't wait to see you."

A quiet knock on the door interrupted them.

"W...w...well, h..hello. I...I was t...t..told that I...I could find you here."

"Father Joe...hi...come on in," Bryce said, standing and extending his hand.

"Is...is....is everyone alright?"

"We are, Father. We are. Mom took a big fall and got pretty banged up, but...she's going to be okay," Bryce said, nodding toward his mother and holding her hand. "I'm going to go call Bev and let her know that you're awake. Excuse me Father."

"I've been able to remember the events from the accident, Father," Ruth said quietly. "A..a...all of them. I couldn't remember anything from that day," she said, quietly crying. "I couldn't remember that my sweet Hayden died in a car accident. And...and I couldn't remember that I was with him!"

"Acc...accidents are tragic and un...unexpected. I...I...I can o..only i...imagine th..that it would be d...d..difficult to p...process when b..being d..directly involved."

"I loved them, Father! And...and...I miss them so much," she wept.

"M...may I p...pray with you?" he asked, reaching for her hands. Ruth's sobs slowly subsided as he held her hands and prayed comforting words of eternal life in a place where pain didn't exist.

"They're together, Father? Roger and Hayden?" she asked.

"In a..a..a better world," he smiled.

"I don't remember a funeral though I have proof it existed," Ruth said as she remembered tearing up the program.

"W…would y…y…you be in…interested in a memorial service for R…Roger and Hayden?"

"Oh, Father, thank you!" she replied, her eyes brimming once again. "That would be so nice."

Another knock on the door announced Bryce coming back followed by another.

"Hey, Mom, look who's here. Do you remember Jerry?" Bryce asked.

"Oh, sure. Hi, Jerry. It's been a while."

"You're looking good, Mrs. Lily," he responded.

"Mom, Jerry was the one who found you last night in the garden after I called him. The highway was shut down and I couldn't get to you."

"My unit was right around the corner from your house when Bryce called. You're looking a whole lot better than you did last night. You took quite a tumble, huh?" he said, smiling at her.

"I guess I did," she responded, sighing.

"Your gardens are really something, even at night. But, hey, the reason I'm stopping back is because I forgot to bring in your blanket with you last night. It fell off of you in the rig and I didn't notice it until we got back to the firehouse. I brought it home with me and my wife really liked it. She said you'd be missing it, though, so I wanted to get it back to you."

As Jerry handed Ruth the bag, Father Joe excused himself, needing to visit a few more patients.

"I've never seen this blanket before, Mom," Bryce said as Ruth pulled it from the bag.

"It's hers," Jerry responded, "Because it was wrapped around her when I got to her. And it's a good thing, too, because it was only forty-five degrees out there last night and her body temperature wasn't as low as it could have been. So, your blanket saved you, Mrs. Lily," he added, smiling toward her. "I assumed that you tripped over it, though, and luckily, it went down with you. There was even a part of it tucked under your head, protecting you from the ground. Go figure," he added. "But anyway, I just wanted to get it back to you. My wife loved it. She wanted to know where you bought it."

Ruth lay mesmerized in her bed, looking at the blanket. "It...it was a gift," she said quietly. "I don't know where it was bought."

"Mom, I'll walk Jerry out and let you get some rest," he said, bending down to give her a kiss. "I'll be back later with Bev and Heather."

When all was quiet, Ruth looked down to what she was holding. She knew that she had never before seen this blanket. But she also knew, with every fiber of her being, that she was holding a miracle in her hands. The blanket, indeed, was very unusual in appearance. The outer layer was a blend of browns; different shades streaked with a touch of mossy green. It was wrinkled and resembled the bark of a tree. The inside layer of the blanket was pale in comparison, soft, and very warm to the touch.

The edge of the blanket was decorated with tassels of fringe in an explosion of color. Some of the tassels were a combination of teal, black and grey. Ruth smiled when she thought of Pheo and how he formed himself out of her garden gloves and stone wall. He presented her with the gift of hope and helped her see a clearer tomorrow. His image made her think of little boys, endless hours of playing, and imagination. The memory of Hayden playing in her garden was forever etched in her heart. She knew she would miss him forever, but was so thankful she could remember him and the beautiful memories they had made together.

Her fingers moved to the tassel that reminded her of Ceepa. Different shades of tan, blond and brown ran through the tufts of décor that represented peace and forgiveness. She could hear the cooing of Ceepa's call when feeling the tassel. She gasped when realizing that she had subconsciously blamed Hailey for suggesting that Hayden tag along with Ruth and Roger on that fateful day. She shook her head and cried, knowing that it wasn't Hailey's fault. She had no doubt that she, herself, would have asked Hayden to come along if Hailey hadn't mentioned it first.

The next colored tassel, which Ruth examined, was bright and lively. She couldn't help but smile when holding onto an assortment of pinks, so vivid with life that they nearly giggled. Ruth sighed and shook her head when remembering the situations that Ojy had gotten into. In Ruth's mourning and confusion, she had given up on happiness. The bright pink verbena, which came to life, forced Ruth to acknowledge joy once again. She laughed out loud when thinking of her, closed her eyes, and imagined her future, being happy again.

The final tassel, which Ruth examined last, was nestled in between every other one. It created a warmth that spread throughout all of Ruth's body when she touched it. Through her tears she could see the olive and lime green strings that created the tassel of love. There were also soft yellow threads interspersed that created an image so strong of the lop-eared rabbit who was Ruth's greatest comfort. Ruth knew without a doubt that Velo was a part of her now. She was a First Creature. She lived and thrived in Ruth first, before the accident. Ruth's love was rescued by a lop-eared rabbit when she had traded her life for death. Velo was the part of herself who Ruth loved more than any other part. Ruth was healed; she knew that now. The First Creatures were back where they belonged, tucked safely inside of her; ready for what life might hold.

"How lucky I am to have known you," she cried, hugging the blanket close to her. "We've been on quite a journey, you and I. You healed me with love, joy, peace, and hope, and you never left me, just like you said."

EPILOGUE

As Ruth stood on her back patio, she took in the morning sunshine, peeking its way through the branches, which were bearing the first hint of spring. She closed her eyes and let the sunshine soak into her skin. The view of the Lily Gardens in Ruth's back yard consisted of mostly tans and browns throughout the winter, with the exception of the evergreens and red berries. She loved the change of seasons, but her favorite, she now knew, was the coming of spring. And as was customary, with a smile and nod of approval, she acted as president of the welcoming committee and greeted the new growth in her gardens, which was creating a slight hue of lime green throughout the air on every twig and branch.

The arrival of spring had always been exciting for Ruth, probably because of her passion for gardening, which she had shared with Roger. Though clear and bright this particular Saturday morning in April, it was not yet warm. Maryland tended to side with the northern states in spring temperatures, and took its time warming up. She pulled her beloved blanket, which she had named, Velo's Blanket, tightly around her as she walked through the gardens, greeting each new growth. Martha ran ahead of her, also enjoying the first of many days to be spent together in the gardens.

When she arrived at the rear of her property, she stopped to pay respect to a lone unambiguous oak tree. It stood tall and strong against the test of time, and its width was proof of its age and loyalty to its home. When standing directly in front of it, she reached out and caressed the outline of a silhouette. Though unnoticed by others who strolled through her gardens, or thought to be a fluke of nature, Ruth held close to her heart the symbolic significance of the form permanently impressed into the tree.

"Mr. Gabriello was a mirrored image of myself; the part I threw away," she thought out loud to Martha. "Coated with pain, suffering, guilt, shame, and without God. He took what I was unable to process and held it for me. I am eternally grateful," she said, nodding. She smiled as she breathed in deeply and looked around the area where so much life, and almost death, occurred. "I'm back, fully," she said to the garden. "All the parts of me that I discarded, I have reclaimed! Yes, I still have pain…but the pain just shows me that I am alive. I remember those I loved….still love…always will love," she added quietly. "I have love all around me…still…I have joy in my friends and family….I have hope in tomorrow…and peace in my heart…but mostly…mostly…I have love."

While walking through her gardens wrapped in a blanket of love, she declared out loud, "I know that it's the colors of life that decorate who I am. This rough outer layer," she said, embracing the outside layer of the blanket, "is in remembrance that I am real. My life has ups and downs; it's interesting and joyful, but it also includes pain. I am real…and I am alive!"

As she made her way back down through the gardens toward her house she heard laughter and her name being called out loud.

"Grammy, we're here!" Heather's voice rang out as she ran toward Ruth, toting something behind her. "Look, Grammy. Mommy bought me a new suitcase for sleepovers. Do you like it?"

"Oh, wow. It's so cute. I love the flowers on it," Ruth answered her, examining the new case.

"Mommy said you would," she smiled. "Do you think we can make cookies tonight, just like we used to, Grammy?"

"I think we can as soon as we get Holly to bed," she smiled.

As they made their way inside, Bryce was still bringing in a couple of bags of clothing and a diaper bag.

"This is it, Bev. How could one little baby have so many bags?" he asked, nuzzling his infant daughter's face. "Alright, girls, we're off. I have no doubt that you will have a great girls' weekend."

After saying their goodbyes, Ruth snuggled into one of the rocker recliners in the small room off the kitchen and read some books out loud to her granddaughters. It was one of her favorite past times to do with them, and she had added a small bookshelf that fit perfectly into the tiny room.

After listening to a few stories, Heather asked to go next door and see if Hailey was ready. She, too, was joining them for the sleepover.

When the door closed and all was quiet, Ruth looked down into the eyes of Holly and her heart melted once again. Holly had made her debut into the world a couple of weeks early, just before Christmas. In keeping true to the origin of the 'Triple H Gate,' she was given the name, Holly.

At three and one-half months old, she was forming a cheerful personality all of her own. She was a relaxed baby, and just seemed to go with the flow. And sometimes when Ruth would coo at her, Holly would smile with one side of her lip turned up, just the way someone else used to do. And Ruth wasn't sure if she imagined this or not, but she thought she heard Holly make noises that sounded an awful lot like, "hmph."

-The End-

About the Author

Tami Liberati is a first grade teacher and host to a widely vivid imagination. Her dreams of writing a novel were ignited in her classroom when four of her students brought to life the characters found within, *First Creatures A Journey Through Grief.* Thoroughly enjoying the second half of life, as she likes to say, now being over the age of fifty, she lives in Bowie, Maryland with her husband and two children. When she's not busy spending time with her extended family, teaching, and volunteering at her church, she enjoys writing short stories about life viewed from the other side of fifty, which can be found on her website, www.thesilversideoflife.com

41064404R00164

Made in the USA
Lexington, KY
01 May 2015